Coming Clean

Jen Trinh

Published by Jen Trinh, 2023.

This is a work of fiction. Similarities to real people, places, or events are entirely coincidental.

COMING CLEAN

First edition. May 1, 2023.

Copyright © 2023 Jen Trinh.

Written by Jen Trinh.

To Becca, for the inspiration and endless support

Chapter 1

Di

Manifesting: is it still a thing? Is it kind of like crossing fingers and toes, or is it more like meditating, but instead of clearing your mind, you fill it with stuff you want?

I don't know if manifesting works when the decision email's already in your inbox, but I take a deep breath, sucking in all my hopes and dreams and clenching every hole before opening the email on my phone.

Dear Diana Ho,

Thank you for your interest in the RWB Emerging Designers Fund. We regret to inform you—

My hopes and dreams come rushing out, already suffocated, and I stop reading. I know the rest.

The gist of this email, like all the other ones? *Thanks for wanting our free money, but we think you're a bad investment. Maybe check out the closest pawn shop or California Lottery ticket stall? Toodles, and good luck on your fashion design career! You'll need it.*

I put my phone away and doom-gape at the sky, a vibrant haze of melted Starburst candies where *someone* up there doesn't like cherry flavor. I'm allegedly taking a break from work this weekend, hanging out in the Hollywood Hills, pet sitting my best friend's lionhead rabbit, but I don't really think that it counts as a break. Time isn't stopping, I'm not aging any less, and the bills haven't stopped growing, so I guess this feels more like giving up for a weekend?

One doesn't just *take* a break. And as for *getting* a break, especially a big break? At this rate, the only way I'll get one of those is from a novelty Kit Kat bar.

Even my friend's bunny, Attila, is working me. Chewing through my laptop charger, scratching my hands when I save her life, and pooping up a grassy hailstorm in protest. I know, right? She's the best.

After making sure that Attila is still okay—not trying to electrocute herself? Cool—I gather my stash of snacks and goodies and drag one of Mischa's balcony lounge chairs into a spot in the last rays of afternoon sun, looking out over the silver, shimmery city to the south. I lie down and plug my bluetooth earbuds into my ears to kick off an hour of forced relaxation, pressing play on the only album that's right for this moment: *Disintegration* by The Cure. And I'm not getting up until my ass and this lounge chair are ready for a divorce.

Dear Diana Ho, Thank you for your interest in the RWB Emerging Designers Fund. We regret to inform you—

Usually, a weekend for myself is all I need to recover, but with the end of my lease approaching, this feels less like a power cycle and more like the reset button is stuck and the virus is replicating non-stop.

The only thing left to do is Force Quit.

Sighing, I focus on the music, letting The Cure's dreamy, nostalgic sound wash over me. But it's only when I reach the song "Closedown," the third track of *Disintegration,* that the lyrics hit me. It's Robert Smith's song about approaching the age of 30, having not yet accomplished enough, of feeling washed up before you'd really had a chance.

Try being *over* 30 and having nothing, Robert.

If only I could fill my heart with love, he laments.

If only *I* had started earlier.

If only I had more time, money, skill, help...

Or even a little push, a little luck. That could go a long way.

Most of all, I need *a sign*, something to show me that this is the right path. That every ounce of effort from this past year—the long hours, side jobs, fights with my mom, and so on—has meant *something*.

So if the Universe is listening...or Satan, Grandma's ghost, my fairy godmother, or maybe even Rumpelstiltskin, because gold thread sounds pretty sweet right now...*please*.

Show me.

Send me a sign.

But nothing moves, nothing changes.

Nothing.

Of course there's nothing. My destiny is in my own hands.

And yet, *we regret to inform you,* my hands aren't enough.

Oh well. Whatever. The world's going to end in fifty years anyway.

I nestle into the lounge cushion, waiting for time and vodka to work their magic. The next song comes on, "Lovesong," and I begin to drift into that place that—

"Hey!"

My eyes snap open, lasers set to kill, but they bounce off the shiny pecs of the hottest, beefiest Asian guy I've ever laid eyes on—abs for days, strong, clean-shaven jaw, and dark, piercing eyes. His chest and arms are thick, and he doesn't seem to skip leg day, either, or neck day, or finger day, or any day at all. Standing on the neighboring balcony, he's glistening wet and almost naked, dressed in only a pair of black swim trunks, the same color as his slicked back hair. With cheekbones and angles that could cut glass, he's got the kind of sleek, sultry look that dares you to buy stuff, which is why I half expect a camera crew to be shooting an advertisement behind him. But as far as I can tell, it's just the two of us out here.

Weird. Creepy old men, I understand. Guys like *him* don't talk to me except to ask for Mischa's number, and she's not around. I may as well be invisible to his kind. Still, that doesn't stop the sudden one-two punch of scorching lust and dampening bitterness, and it only sharpens my curiosity.

I pull out an earbud. "What?"

He gives me one of those slow, head-tilted smiles, like I'm a cute girl who's asked for his number instead of a cranky woman who's flung a flat *What* pie into his face.

And then he says the strangest thing.

"Hey there. Could I have some of your shrimp chips?"

I stare at him, assessing every possible intent behind his words.

I'm not sure what kind of sign I was looking for, but it wasn't this.

Chapter 2

Darien

Though faithful to the original source material, the fine, intricate mysteries of The Agents of Icarus are overshadowed by the great, whopping mystery of why Lee was cast in the starring role.

My fingers curl around my phone, and it takes everything I have not to throw it out the window. Instead, I torture myself and keep reading, skipping ahead to the worst parts.

The bedroom scene is a masterclass in awkwardness, which comes as no surprise after a decade of starring in teen love stories and romantic comedies where sex is only implied. Sans de Santis to buoy him, Prince Charming inspires as much passion as a dry bowl of cornflakes—which you might recall were used in anti-masturbation campaigns.

Worst of all: *He's best known for his role as Prince Charming, but he's still Victor "The Loser" Lu at heart.*

Dozens of rom-coms, dramas, action films, and I still can't shake the nerd association. This time, it's not even fair. Things had sizzled between me and my costar, Oriana Pendle, during the chemistry read, but after I didn't fall into bed with her like she'd suggested, I may as well have flirted with the Cocaine Bear. Where is the criticism of *her* role? Why is it my fault that we had no chemistry?

Tam watches me from the rearview mirror, impassive. "It's not that bad, Darien."

"They called me 'hot, but wooden, except where it counts.'"

She tries to hide a wince, but fails. "That's not so—"

"And 'James Bond, but shaken *and* stirred until there's only a watered-down mess,'" I read, before locking my phone and shoving it into my pocket.

"You know how these things go. Reviewers love hyperbole." She turns right, and the car grumbles up the steep incline. "Why do you even read that site? It's complete shit. The other reviews aren't that bad."

Right, they aren't that bad. They're worse. They're serious editorials with actual clout, and they hate the movie, too.

Boring.

Clichéd.

As fun as a midnight filibuster.

"Don't take it personally. The movie's doing fine. It's not your best, but it's—"

"It's my worst." The box office numbers are great. Chalk that up to all the other A-listers attached to the project. But it feels like for every pat on the back from a critic, there are two slaps to the face.

"Your worst is behind you, okay? Trust me, this isn't that bad." Tam slows as she scans the houses for address numbers. "Are you sure you want to be alone this weekend? There's that party that Don is throwing. Could be good to—"

"No, thanks. I need this." And *schmoozing* in this state of mind sounds like wading into a piranha tank. All I want is time away from everyone, Tam, Eliza, my friends and family. Time away from myself and being Darien Fucking Lee. After two months of non-stop travel and endless interviews to promote *Icarus*, I'm ready to tear him off, toss him in the corner, and breathe.

Tam pulls up to a door that I assume leads to the rental her assistant has booked for me. As I gather my things, she turns around to face me. "Sammy says you haven't gotten back to him about the most recent set of scripts yet."

Not this again. Every conversation I have with my agent starts with, *You won't believe this project, it's going to blow your mind.* Sammy's enthusiasm was infectious at first, but after pinning my hopes on each and every part, thinking it'll finally give me whatever it is I need, I know better. The hole doesn't fill. It only gets deeper.

"I don't know, Tam, but I need a break. A long one."

"Well, you've got a few weeks coming up that aren't too busy. Why don't you go through the scripts this weekend, get back to Sammy about the ones you're interested in before you unplug?"

I wouldn't call it "unplugging." I've got an interview, a photo shoot, and prep for my next project, which includes working out twice a day. It won't be back-to-back 14-hour days of shooting, but even a few weeks at quarter speed won't be enough.

"This weekend's for me. I doubt I'll get to them until after Claire's baby is born."

"And when's that again?"

"Soon." I owe my sister a lifetime of debt, and at 36 weeks pregnant and on her own, she's come to collect. "I'm good, Tam. Don't worry." I slide along the leather backseat and open the door, welcoming the rush of fresh air. "I'll get to them soon, I promise."

But after five years as my manager, she knows better than to believe me. "Get to them this week, *please*. And by the way, I told Cady to prep the place, so there should be the usual in the fridge."

The usual. Great. Forty-five hundred calories of plain chicken and leaves. "Thanks for the ride."

"See you." With one last wave, she drives off and leaves me at the door to my hideout for the weekend.

* * *

Cady knows to book me a spot with a pool. It's how I prefer to recharge: floating as the water laps away the stress and grime of the day.

But that only works when I'm alone.

For the thirtieth time, my eyes pan across to the adjacent rooftop balcony. A young woman with long black hair and dark clothing lies on a lounge chair, face turned up towards the sky, eyes closed. I'd seen her on the way into the pool, but from here, I doubted she'd recognize me if I kept my face turned away. Plus, every time I look over, she's always in the same position, not shifting, hardly moving.

Very, very still.

But I can't stop staring. Because on the table next to her sits what looks like a handle of liquor, and next to that, a distinctive red and white bag.

Shrimp chips.

Crispy, salty, umami chips, the same size as my fingers back when I was a kid.

I can taste their baked little bodies on my tongue.

The water bubbles as I slip back under, holding my breath again. *Keep it together, man. It's not a cheat day. You have a fitness plan to stick to.*

But...*shrimp chips.* Seeing them was a shock to the system, like coming across an old, explosive flame. The one you could never resist, if only for a night.

God, that hit of dopamine from eating junk food. There's nothing like it.

The calorie count is probably colossal. The salt and carbs will make me bloat. But I can cut harder tomorrow, right? Drink a lot of water, skip the almonds on the counter in exchange for a handful of shrimp chips now?

Just a handful. That's it.

My lungs tighten, glitching out, and I flounder to the surface, gasping. I pull myself up out of the pool and approach the railing, my wet feet burning against the sun-soaked wooden deck. Our two balconies are separated by maybe a few feet, a single step for my long legs.

But I turn around, clutching my face. What am I doing? I'm supposed to be hiding. And asking some random chick for chips is ridiculous. I should just...

What? Go get some? Tam dropped me off. I don't have a car, and I don't want someone else to have to drive around, burning gas, searching for this specific brand of chips. And I don't want to see anyone right now anyway. I don't want to deal with being Darien Fucking Lee.

But if I want the chips, won't I have to turn on the charm for *her?* What if she's an obsessed fan or angry hater, or worse, an aspiring actor?

I should calm down, go chug a liter of water. It's not a big deal. The craving will go away like it always does.

But another pang of nostalgia hits me, and I'm desperate for a taste of my childhood, of a time when things were simpler. When I could be myself, and no one cared what that meant.

Besides, when was the last time I'd had *any* chips, let alone *shrimp chips?*

If I ask, chances are she'll recognize me, flip out, say yes, and after a brief interaction, we'll go our separate ways. Fans have given me all kinds of things: designer goods, basketball tickets, restaurant reservations...

A bag of shrimp chips is nothing.

I take a deep, steadying breath and approach the balcony again. She appears to be Asian, with long lashes and red-painted lips, the only real color in her otherwise black ensemble. She's on the thicker side, tall, dressed in what looks like a pair of many-pocketed utility pants and a strappy mesh halter top that reveals the outer edges of her breasts, her sides bare down to the curve of her waist.

Pretty, I guess, in her own way.

The important thing is, I've met thousands of girls like her before. I'll be fine.

I put on a smile and give her a, "Hey," in a loud, pleasant voice, like I'm greeting an old friend.

She doesn't answer, doesn't stir. Nothing.

My eyes catch on the vodka bottle. It's more than half empty.

There's no way that she drank all of that, right?

...right?

I give it one last try. "Hey!"

Her eyes snap open, and she turns her head to look at me. Alive.

But her eyes flash murder as she removes an earbud from one ear. "What?"

Her voice is deep and rich, like that one word was coated in thick, melted layers within her chest. And with her eyes open, she looks older than I thought. Closer to my age.

But I'm in for a penny, so I sweep my hands through my wet hair and give her my signature smile—the Lee Special. "Hey there. Could I have some of your shrimp chips?"

Her lips part, and her brows knit together in a *Really?* look. But I adjust my smile and nod towards the chips. *Just imagine how it'll feel when she says yes, when I've got a fistful of salty chips in my mouth.*

Unnnnh.

My knees go weak, and I have to lean against the railing for support.

She turns and looks at the bag on the table, then back at me, frowning. "Why don't you go get your own?"

"Oh. Well, I would, but..." I lean further over the railing and make sure to flex my pecs straight into her eyeballs. "I can't go out right now."

I have to fight to maintain the smile when she stares without even a hint of recognition, or appreciation. The pecs have failed me.

If I'd done this to literally any other person, they'd have come in their pants and I'd be halfway to shrimp-chip heaven already. But this girl doesn't crack an inch. She tosses her hair behind a shoulder and says, "Is your mom home? Maybe she can get you some."

I blink, and she blinks back just as slowly. I may be Asian, so maybe I don't look 32, but it should be pretty obvious to her that I'm not a fucking *kid*.

"Uhhh...no? That's not what I mean." My grand vision of a shrimp chip mouth-orgy fades to black, replaced by the sudden reality of how dumb I must look to this vampire-wannabe. "You know what, never mind. I'll figure something out."

Maybe there's oil in the house. Maybe I can shred the grilled chicken breast and salt and fry the strips until they're crispy and close to chicken chips. Though if Cady did her job, she would've stashed those kitchen staples away. Nothing for Darien except the healthiest of foods.

But as I turn away, she takes out the other earbud and sits up straighter. "Why did you ask me that?"

Uhhh... "Because I want to eat them." *Obviously.*

She picks up the bag with delicate fingers. Brings it onto her lap with a gentle crinkle, the sound of hope and happiness sealed into plastic. "And you yelled at me from across a balcony and thought I'd give them to you because...?"

...I'm hot and famous and people give me things when I ask?

...because I'm a fucking idiot.

She knows. She's got this stony, almost haughty look on her face, telling me exactly how much of an asshole I am. I haven't always been this dumb or entitled, but recently, as a celebrity, it really has been *ask and you shall receive.* So why not ask when I want something?

But that's just it. Does she really not know who I am? "Look, if you want me to pay you, I'll pay you. But I don't have a car right now and I can't head out anyway."

And this chick—*this chick!*—has the balls to tear open the top and begin to eat. To crunch, and munch, and lick her lips and swallow, right where I can see.

My mouth floods with wet, hungry lust. From this distance, there's no way that I can physically smell the chips, but my brain fills in the gaps.

And yet she sits there, eating those baked, golden chips like it's her job.

Her eyes are cold and calculating as she asks, "How much would you pay?"

So that's how it is. "I don't know? It's like three bucks at the store, right?"

She eats another chip, eyes flat, not even tasting them. "Yeah, but you can't leave, and this is the only bag here. Supply and demand."

I roll my eyes at her bullshit econ lesson. "*Fine*. Ten bucks."

She eats another chip and nods towards the house, assessing it over my shoulder. "That your place?"

"No, it's not." *Nice try.* Though honestly, my house would make this place look like a tool shed.

She eats another chip, and another, without saying a word. My stomach whines at the injustice of it all.

"God, how much do you want?"

She eats another one. "Fifty."

"Fifty? Are you out of your mind?" After the slew of blockbusters I've starred in over the past six years, fifty dollars is nothing, but it's the principle of the thing. No bag of baked flour snacks is worth fifty dollars, full stop.

Except that this is a bag of childhood bliss, and it's right here, slowly getting lighter and lighter.

She eats another chip. And another. Shrugs.

"Ugh." I turn around, unable to watch her eat, but I can't close my ears to the sound of crisp chips falling apart and melting on her tongue. The crackle of the bag as she picks up another one. *Another salty, crunchy, puffed up—*

I whip around. "Fine! I'll pay. But you have to stop eating right now."

She stops mid-chew. "Fine. Here." She holds the bag up from her seat, as if she's too lazy to get up and walk it over to me.

I swing my leg over the metal railing, holding on tight, and reach over to the other balcony. I'm tall, so I make the transition over easily, and soon my feet are on hot cement and I'm close enough to snatch the bag and sit down on the lounge chair next to hers.

Finally. Mine. Even if the Scrooge who sold them to me is now squinting like she's trying to figure out whether I've gotten a nose job.

Whatever. I wiggle my natural nose and savor the sweet, salty taste of victory.

Chapter 3

Darien

Airy, oily, shrimpy essence fills my mouth, electrifying my tastebuds. She watches like I'm a leprechaun or something, but damn do I feel lucky.

"I'm on a diet." She hasn't asked, but my mouth runs away, high on umami and carbs. "I'm not usually allowed to eat these."

One well-drawn eyebrow sweeps upward. She's got the kind of curves that would normally require hours of squatting and donkey kicks per week, but seem natural on her tall, thicker frame. Maybe she doesn't understand what it's like to eat chicken and vegetables every day for weeks on end.

Nor does she care. "I'll take cash or Venmo."

"I'll get my phone in a second." I eat another, and another, fighting back groans until my tongue warms up to full-speed chip-eating mode, an endless plateau of salty pleasure. "Thank you. Seriously."

She eyes my bare legs, my torso, my face. I return the favor. Like I said, she's pretty. Not in the taut, polished way that's endemic to this part of town, but with extra little details that draw you in. Her nose is soft and rolling, a gently sloped roof above full, luscious lips. And under thick lines of black eyeliner, her eyes are wide and double-lidded, though asymmetrical, with one lid folded ever so slightly deeper. Before draping down her back and across her shoulders, her long black hair frames and lengthens her round face, giving her a somewhat youthful look.

But her expression is that of an old crone, like a Miyazaki villain.

"Do I know you?" she asks slowly.

Finally. "*Do* you?"

She crosses her arms over her ample chest and raises the other eyebrow at me. "Should I?"

"Yes." With all of the *Icarus* ads, my face is everywhere right now. Unless she lives inside a bunker, she's probably seen my face at least four times today.

"Okay, then who are you?"

Really? *Really?* I've had dozens of people mistake me for the lead actor in *Mad Affluent Asians*, even though we look nothing alike, but to not even have a guess is a new low. I open my mouth to answer—

But my brain kicks to life and I shove a chip in instead. I wanted a vacation from Darien Fucking Lee, so why am I telling her who I am? And after charging me *fifty bucks* for this bag, she doesn't deserve my real name.

"Hayden Chu," I say, and the name is so light compared to my real one. It's the name of my stunt double from *Icarus*. At least if she looks him up, he'll vaguely resemble me.

"Doesn't ring a bell." She watches me eat handful after handful, but doesn't reach for any herself. Good. "Did you seriously think I would give you my chips because you're famous or something?"

It sounds even dumber out loud. "You weren't eating them, so I thought maybe you didn't want them, or weren't hungry. And you look like a nice person. I thought you'd be willing to share."

She looks at me like I've just said the earth is flat. "*I* look like a nice person?"

Well...her clothes belong somewhere between *The Matrix* and *Underworld*, like she's headed to a 90's underground techno rave. And there aren't any laugh lines on her face, but there *is* a small shadow of a crease that's permanently visible between her brows, and a severe set to her pouty lips. A few tattoos peek out from her shirt, but I can't make out what they're of without staring.

But I stick to my guns. "Yeah. You do."

She quietly huffs and looks away. "Well, I'm not."

She isn't screaming in my face or throwing herself at me, so actually, I'd say she's plenty nice. But she might have friends inside who aren't as chill. If this house is anything like the one I'm staying in, it's meant for a dozen people. "Anyone home besides you?"

She casually picks up her phone, but the way her radioactive-green fingernails curl around the edges tells me she's ready to call the cops depending on my answer. Or maybe throw it at me. "Why, are you thinking of murdering me?"

"Only if you taste like shrimp chips." Though by this point, I've shoved most of the bag into my face and the greasy sea flavor is starting to wear on me.

I almost drop a chip when her lips twitch and her mask flickers, the iridescent flash of something lovely swimming underneath. She's probably even prettier when she smiles, the way her cheeks would curve and her eyes would tilt and her lips would thin and spread like...

Hm.

Anyway, I know better than to comment on that kind of thing. She'd probably try to kick me off the balcony if I did.

After so much salt, my mouth is dry and the last of the chips tastes like sea ash. I'm already breaking my diet, so I pick up the vodka and toss it back. It burns and waters my eyes, but it does the job and cleanses my palate.

Still coughing a bit, I hold it out to her. "Want some of your own vodka?"

Her lips do that little twitch again before she grips the bottle and takes a healthy mouthful. She dips her head back, and her hair slips over her smooth shoulders, revealing her long neck, the tantalizing edge of her breast, large and shapely.

Braless.

I catch myself staring.

There was some dry bedroom choreography in *Icarus*, but the last time I'd genuinely touched a woman, and not on camera...

Not since the last time, months ago, with—

"Here."

I snap out of it and accept the vodka back from...

"What's your name?" I ask before taking another swig.

"Di."

"Die? As in death?" Jesus, maybe she *is* a vampire.

"Di, like Princess Di. My mom was a big fan of hers." She looks down and brushes her lap.

"Wow, *Princess* Diana. Is that your job, too?" She doesn't seem like a socialite, but you never know who you'll meet in L.A.

"No." She clears her throat. "I'm a designer."

I almost ask what kind of designer, but the way she says it, that grimace that flickers across her features, reminds me a little too much of my own career.

And fuck work, anyway. I'm off the clock.

"Well, nice to meet you, Di. And thanks for sharing." I glance down at the vodka bottle. "Unless you plan on charging me for this, too?"

She taps her chin. "You know, now that you mention it..."

I groan, and she lets out a small, muted laugh of plush velvet. And the wry smile she gives me, that warm glow across her cheeks? Cuter than I'd imagined.

But then she frowns as if to herself, and the next second, it's cloudy again.

More than ever, I want to see what's underneath.

"I'm kidding. Vodka's on the house." She picks up the joint on the table and offers it to me with a shrug. "I guess this, too, if you want some. I don't want to smoke the whole thing by myself anyway."

I shouldn't. A few hits of that and I'll wake up covered in Cheesy Gordita Crunch wrappers.

But when I weigh my options—cute girl with snacks versus another long-ticking night of suffocating alone—the choice is clear. "Thanks. Got a light?"

"Yeah." She pulls a silver crescent-moon-engraved lighter out from one of her pockets and cleans in, flicking her thumb and hovering her hand until the tip of the joint burns orange. I can't help but lean in, too. Her scent is sweet and herbal, like honeyed tea, and there's a gorgeous view down her plunging neckline. I look up just in time to meet her gaze above the flame, her eyes widening for one glowing second before she pulls back and puts the lighter away.

One puff is all it takes. The air feels thin and thick and shimmery, but it's not just from the weed. It's...her, it's us, it's all of it. The fact that she doesn't know who I am. The fact that I'm snacking and drinking and hanging out like a normal person, a regular guy. We're strangers, alone, and she watches me through the curtain of smoke as if waiting for something to happen.

And for the first time in a long while, I'm free to wonder: do I *want* something to happen?

She *is* pretty, and with those curves and that attitude, she'd probably be fun in bed.

Plus, it's been months since I've been with someone, and this whole time, Eliza's been fucking Ethan.

Once again, I force that nauseating image from my mind.

On the lounge chair next to mine, Di brings the joint to her lips. She takes a hit and exhales, her eyes partly closed, watching me coolly, but her movements beg for attention. The curve of her back as she tucks a leg underneath her and turns to face me just so, or the graceful crook of her wrist, her long fingers as she hands me back the joint. In the dusky light, her skin practically radiates against her dark clothing, every bare inch a beacon to my lonely hands.

She doesn't smile, doesn't flirt, doesn't lean in to touch me. She looks away, pretending like I'm a part of the chair I sit on. But I study body language for a living, and I recognize a challenge when I see one.

And you know what? I think I *will* rise to this challenge.

I'm half-risen already.

Maybe an anonymous night with a stranger is exactly what I need.

Puffing on the joint, I give her a once-over and don't hide it, admiring the deep cut of her top and the way her pants mold to her hips like dark chocolate on an almond. She said she was a designer, right? It makes sense. "Did you design what you're wearing right now?"

"I did."

"I like it. It looks good on you."

It would look good off of you, too.

I mentally shove myself. Too strong, too cheesy, especially for an alt-girl like her.

She nods. "Thanks."

I turn my chair to face her more directly and cross an ankle over my knee. "If you were going to design an outfit for me, what would it look like?"

"Hm." She accepts the joint back from me and takes another puff. "I would make you something warm. Because you look cold."

The light *has* nearly faded, and the cool evening air is starting to get to me. I run through any number of *maybe you could warm me up* lines and reject them all, but can't come up with anything less clichéd.

I settle for, "It's not that cold." A lie. A bad one.

She huffs in quiet amusement. "Yeah? Well, I hope you're not an actor, because you're terrible at it."

To say that it feels like a slap would be an understatement. A sucker punch, maybe. Et tu, goth girl?

"Sorry," she says quickly, blinking. "I didn't mean that."

"Forgot where we are, huh?" I try to keep my voice light, but don't quite succeed. "But nah, it's true." I pick up the vodka again and throw it back, shame and liquor burning my throat. "I *am* a terrible actor."

Her comment shouldn't matter. Acting isn't the same as pretending or lying—it's rooted in truth. A scene is something you prepare for by tapping into real emotions and filling yourself with them ahead of time. It's something you do with intention, and it's exhausting. I don't do it when I don't have to.

I wasn't trying to act just now. I was lying on the fly, as myself.

But that doesn't change the fact that she's right. I'm *not* the greatest actor, especially not when the only roles I seem to get these days are written for cardboard cutouts. And hearing it from *her* makes it hit a thousand times harder. This woman doesn't even know me, but she can smell the failure on me like I've been steeped in it. Ten years, in fact. Ten years and I still can't act, can't flirt, can't...fuck. Without my fame, I can't even seduce this random chick.

She touches my forearm. "I'm sure that's not true."

Great, and now she feels bad for me, too. I'd rather have her cold and aloof again than to see the empty pity on her face.

But as she leans towards me, my eyes are pulled down to her wide, black-rimmed eyes, her red parted lips, her half-exposed breasts.

Her big nipples, poking through her shirt.

She's cold, too.

God, sinking into a girl like that after all this time. Losing myself between her thick thighs.

I should go back to my place and go to bed before I mess this up even worse. Maybe work away the extra calories in the gym. That, at least, I'm good at.

But the truth is staring me in the face: the only thing that will make me feel better is fucking the shit out of her.

And I don't know what happened to make her so joyless today, but she seems like she could use a good fuck, too.

I put the vodka bottle down and flash her a look. A real one, pure and simple. "Should we go inside?"

Her gaze shutters. "Depends. What do you want to do in there?"

I lean in close.

She doesn't move.

"Honestly?" My lips brush the shell of her ear as I whisper, "*You.*"

Without a script.

Without any direction from anyone, except you and me.

She sucks in a slow, tremulous breath, and too late I realize that I've overstepped. She's going to slap me or shoot me down with an insult. Maybe push me back and send me over the balcony.

Instead, she lets out a quiet, "Yeah?"

Relief, something just short of triumph, floods through me. "Yeah. You down?"

It's barely perceptible in the dim light, but her breath quickens as she nods, then nods again more vigorously. My hands, unleashed, rush to touch her, brushing her hair from her ear, cupping her head, her neck, tilting her face towards mine. She shivers and blinks up at me with soft surprise, eyes widening as I lower my lips to hers.

Our lips meet, and it's simple at first, a gentle kiss. But as our lips move and meld together, it begins to feel like the slow crash of waves from two different oceans, building into something torrid and wild.

I've kissed a lot of strangers in my time, but it's never felt like *this*. Like lush, intoxicating warmth, so rich and potent that you linger in the first sip, head swimming, rocked in a sea of time.

Whew, that's some strong weed.

But it's not the same for her. She stares at me and doesn't react, doesn't move, and for a second, I wonder if she's going to change her mind. But when her eyelids sink and her tongue flicks against mine with cat-like acceptance, my doubts evaporate in a rush of heat. She presses herself into me in a full-bodied *yes*, wrapping her arms around my neck as I gather her to my chest, warming myself on her silken skin. She kisses me back, slow and deep, massaging her fingers into my hair. I run my hands all over her, her back, her waist, slipping one up her side and along the edge of her soft breast—

She captures my hand and stands, pulling me with her. "Let's go."

Her voice is even thicker, almost muddy, and I know it's not just me anymore. We're in the same hazy bubble, the same buzzing energy coursing through our limbs. The same need.

But when Di leads me into the house and turns on the light, the sudden brightness is a splash of cold. I blink and take in our new surroundings, all immaculate whites and pale birches with flecks of jewel tones here and there from a menagerie of glass-blown figurines against the wall. Not at all what I would've expected for her.

Oh, wait, there's a painting in the corner of a bunch of bat-people fucking, and a skull-shaped bong on the mantel. That's more like it.

"This is my friend's house," she explains, "and her boyfriend's. He's a veterinarian."

In the far corner of the living room, there's a black wire pen on the wooden floor. "Is there a live animal in there?"

"Yeah, my friend's rabbit. I'm pet sitting for the weekend."

I walk up to the edge of the pen, and like she said, there's a loaf of amber fur in the far corner with two tiny feet sticking out, almost like the handles of a bellows. "Aww."

"Yeah. She's cute, but she sucks. Kind of a demon rabbit. *Loves* biting me."

I don't blame the rabbit. With skin that smooth, I'm tempted to leave a mark on her, too.

Di looks at me, lips parted, eyes slightly wild, as if she still can't believe what's happening.

That makes two of us.

I close the distance between us and tilt her head back to kiss her lips, her cheek, the spot just under her jaw. She lets out a ragged breath and grips my shoulders, melding her soft, decadent body to mine. I grasp her tight, drinking in the sweetness of being warm and wanted. Of spark-filled touches and shining newness. Of her, here, and real.

But as she grinds her hips against me, I'm hard, too hard. It's been too long, feels too good, and every rough brush against my dick snaps a whip of searing pleasure through me.

I take a step back and make a split-second decision. "I want to take a shower first, rinse off this pool water. Is that okay?"

She frowns, but then her face lights up and she nods. "That's a good idea. You should do that."

"Where's the shower?"

"There's one right here." She walks past the large kitchen island and pulls open a door. "There's a towel already in there. And soap."

"Thanks."

But before I head into the bathroom, I pull her close and kiss her again, slowly this time. She melts against me, squirming, driving me to the brink until I have to take a step back yet again. I almost laugh at her dopey, kiss-drunk expression, but when it morphs into a sweet, embarrassed smile, my heart thumps and I can't help but smile back.

With one last nod, I head into the bathroom.

It's time to make sure that I last.

Chapter 4

Di

The memory of his words, his hot breath on my ear, the press of his dick into my lower belly...all of it plays on repeat as I watch him saunter into the shower, leaving my body simmering with need.

Would I date him?

Not with that attitude.

But would I *do* him?

I'll take three orders, please and thank you.

After retrieving a fistful of condoms from Mischa's nightstand, I rush to the bathroom that's connected to my guest bedroom, yank off my clothes, and throw my hair up into a messy bun on top of my head. If he's going to be clean for our sexy times, then so am I.

Holy shit, I'm about to have sexy times with an actor.

Holy shit, I'm about to have sexy times!

My last random hookup was pre-dinosaurs, three hundred million years ago when the first large herbivores roamed the land. Meanwhile, he's so hot, I assume that he...he—

Oh, shit. Does he do this all the time? Is he full of diseases? Will he stick it in and expect me to come ten times right off the bat? I've never been with a guy like him before, but Mischa has this theory that the hot ones give the worst dick because they don't have to work as hard for it.

Please please *please* let her be wrong.

I do a quick rinse in the shower, carefully avoiding messing up my makeup, then pull on my favorite black hemp and cotton robe while brushing my teeth like I need to pee. I barely have time to dab at the oil on my face, touch up my makeup, and fluff out my hair before he gets out of the shower with a towel wrapped around his hips. I'm sitting on the couch, waiting for him, heart ringing like an alarm clock. Because thank the gods, it's Business Time.

A cloud of steam escorts him from the shower, dewing on his golden hills of muscles. It's completely unreal, a scene straight out of a 90s music video, and yet I can smell his clean scent, feel his warmth as he bends down with hungry eyes, cupping my head to give me another spine-buckling kiss.

My pussy is *meowing*.

Or maybe it's the deranged yowl of a cat in heat.

I almost whine when he pulls back. He's got this impossibly white, cocky smile, like he knows exactly how wound up I am. "Bedroom?"

I take his hand and lead him past the spiral stairs and into my guest bedroom. A large TV is mounted in the corner, and the bed has plain white sheets and about a thousand pillows. Mischa, that sloppy sylph, likes to be able to trip in any direction and hit something soft.

I shove a bunch of pillows aside and turn just as he leans in and pushes me back against the bed, pinning me down with his body. It's hard and hot and *oh god,* I want him inside of me yesterday.

But I whisper, "Go slow."

Please don't be a one-minute man.

Please know what you're doing.

Please don't be a shit-cherry on top of the massive shit-sundae that is my life.

He nods and shifts onto his side, and I follow his lead. He rises onto his elbow to kiss my lips, letting his free hand rest on my belly, warm and anchoring. I moan into his mouth and kiss him back, my hands sliding up his chest to cup the back of his head. I want to swallow him, all of him, but like I asked him to do, he goes slow, lightly nipping at my lips, kisses shallow and sweet, until I can't take it—I slip my tongue into his mouth and say *bonjour!* to his.

His hand wanders through the gap of the robe and slides it open, the fabric floating over my skin until my tits are bare. I arch my back and let the robe fall from my shoulders, and his fingertips trace the under-curve of a breast, spiraling up to the stiff bud of flesh at the top, each flick and twitch of his finger pulsing my insides to hot mush. When he lowers his head and takes a nipple into his mouth, I whimper.

"This okay?"

"*Yes*. Harder, please."

He scrapes my nipple with his teeth, tugging, plucking that invisible wire that connects my pleasure centers. I gasp my approval, and he repeats the motions on the other nipple before kissing a line down to my navel, down *past* my navel, down...down?

Holy shit, is he about to go down on me?

But he stops and stares, and I hold my breath, waiting.

His fingertips trace the rooster tattoo that's below my left breast. "It's like watercolors."

I warm with a headier kind of pleasure as his fingers trail down to the snake that graces my right hip, the tiger that's leaping out of my left thigh. The nine other creatures that dance across my skin. "I designed them."

"They're beautiful." He says it in hushed tones, as if viewing the Sistine Chapel instead of my unholy body.

Well, if he wants a place to worship...

I let my knees fall open, and his eyes go from my tats to my pussy. It's so wet, it's dripping down my butt cheek, twitching. Waving at him shyly.

But he doesn't touch me. He goes as statue-still as David with a towel on.

"What's wrong?" Is it my cellulite? My flab? My bush? I try to keep it neat, but maybe the women he's used to are all razed-to-the-bone size-double-zero Barbies.

He doesn't respond except to rub his jaw, as if in regret.

I shrug my robe back on and sit up. "If you don't like what you see, you can leave."

"No." He pins me with a stare and a hand on my thigh. "That's not it."

"Then what is it?" I steel my spine, waiting for the blow. For the litany of awful things I imagine whenever a man's eyes slide away, or when I'm out with Mischa and people talk to her like I'm not even there.

"I just...I need you to sign an NDA. I should've made you sign one earlier."

"Seriously?" He's a mediocre actor, right? How famous could this guy be?

"Yeah. It's a pretty standard thing, but also..." He trails off with a sigh. "I'm such an idiot."

My skin goes cold. *Yeah right.* If he's famous enough to need an NDA, he can have whomever he wants. He doesn't need me.

I huddle deeper into the sheet, hiding every inch of myself until I look like Frosty at the end of March. "You don't have to lie to me. Just get out."

But he stares at me, silent, and won't leave.

Well, I don't back down. I can read him, and—

He tugs the towel off his hips, and my gaze drops to the most mouth-watering dick that ever watered a mouth. Three Michelin Stars. Bouche, amused.

"If you promise not to tell anyone, I'll keep going." He takes my hand and guides it to his cock. It's scalding hot against my palm, and smooth and shiny like brand new. "And honestly? I love what I see...if you can't tell."

The sheet slips away from my shoulders, but I hardly notice. I have some random actor's Golden Globe in my hand and he's fucking ready to *put it in me.*

My pussy clenches in response. She's ready, too. He can't hear it, but she's yelling like Scorpion, "GET OVER HERE!"

So I whisper, "I promise."

"You won't tell a single soul?"

Mischa doesn't have a soul, so... "Yes."

The word unlocks him, his hips moving so that my hand pumps his cock. *Fuck.* I continue the motion on my own, loving the hard, silky feel of him, his labored breathing.

"Do you have a condom?" he asks in a strained voice.

"They're right there."

He grabs a foil packet from the pile on the nightstand and straightens to kneeling to roll it on. His abs are cobblestones, with a V-shaped gutter pointing the way to heaven. No wonder he's not allowed to eat shrimp chips.

Again, I don't understand how a real-life underwear model has appeared in my hour of greatest need, but I am very much here for it. His lips cover mine, and he's back to kissing me deeply, hungrily, his fingertips teasing the tops of my thighs. I open my legs and urge his fingers to go lower, which they do. And when I'm not-so-silently begging him to touch me at my core, he does, sending showers of sparks up my spine.

"So wet," he whispers as he kisses my neck. I turn my head to give him better access, cupping my own breasts, pinching my nipples. Meanwhile, his fingers have found my clit. I spread my legs even wider, and he drops his hand, palming me, sliding his fingers in and out to the beat of my hips.

"Yes. *Yes.*"

He presses harder but not deeper, teasing the outer edges of my pussy. His fingers find some magical spot, and at my gasp, he presses it again, eases out, then back, over and over. The pleasure builds, effervescing, heating my skin, the edges of me stretched and straining. I clench and hold my breath, fighting the tide, holding it back until I can't, I *can't*...and I'm drowning in it, washed jend wrung. I gasp, and air and light return.

His hand is gone, and my hips buck as he fills me to the core.

"Oh, *fuck.*"

He stops. "Is this okay?"

"Yes..." I'm breathless, stuffed, still tingling. "Keep going."

He nods and begins to move, a slow glide that quickly builds, in and out, faster and faster. I move with him, locking my legs behind his back, scraping my nails down his shoulders, his taut, rounded biceps. My hands sample every part of him, every inch of his hot skin.

"Do you like this?" he asks. He grits his teeth, hard at work, carefully studying my face.

"Fuck yes."

He drops his head and kisses me, his tongue sliding along mine with a sweetness that leaves me breathless again, and giddy. I arch further into him, moaning, loving the—

"Is there anything else you want me to do?"

I blink away the haze a little. "No, this is great."

"Yeah?"

"Yeah."

He moves and I move with him, building up momentum again, a steady thrum of pleasure at my core. My body starts to shimmer with sweat—

"I want to make you come again."

I stop moving. "Oh—okay?"

"Is there a better position to do that?"

"This is fine, just...keep going."

His thrusting stutters, and he gives me a questioning look, which I return. It's nice that he wants to make me come again, but when it comes to P-in-V orgasms, it usually takes some *very* specific conditions that I'm not sure we're ready for, and I'm not faking a damn thing. But this is fine, and I'm not complaining, so what's with all the bangxiety?

He gives me a shaky smile. "It's just...*fine?*"

I stroke his cheek and slip my hand into his hair, lightly parting the strands. "Just do what feels natural to you. I'm enjoying this."

He nods slowly, but there's a tightness in his expression that makes me frown. And when I stop moving, he stops moving.

We exchange puzzled stares.

With a quick, heavy breath, he pulls out and rolls away, sitting and facing away from me.

"Hayden?" I rise to my knees, folding them under me.

"I need a second."

"Okay." My hand itches to reach out and ask him what's wrong, or what I did wrong, but he's bent like a roly poly, tense and closed off. A stranger. I can't tell what he wants or needs in this situation: some space, a hug, something else. He's out of the moment, and I don't know how to bring him back.

I fold my arms over my chest, shivering, waiting. Dreading what's coming next.

"Sorry," he says at long last, staring at the backs of his hands. "There's a lot on my mind right now."

"I see." I replay the last few moments, trying to understand what it is I did. I'd told him he was doing fine, that I was enjoying it. Did he not believe me?

The first time with someone always feels like a game of Marco Polo, where both of us are It and we're trying to tag each other's orgasms. It's awkward as fuck, and sometimes it sucks. But somehow, this feels bigger than that.

He doesn't move, doesn't get up to leave. And I can't see his full expression, but he lets out this quiet sigh that slumps his shoulders even further, like someone's just dumped a fifty-pound bag of rice on him, or possibly sent him an email with the words *We're sorry to inform you...*

It's a familiar pose. And as disappointed as I am, I can only imagine what he must be feeling.

I don't overthink it. I place my hands on his shoulders, and when he doesn't flinch away, slide them down his arms until my breasts are smushed into his back. Mischa says my boobs have healing properties. "Do you want to talk about it?"

He takes a slow, deep breath. Pressed against his back, I can feel my own chest fall and rise. "I'm not sure if that's a good idea."

"Why not? Just pretend I'm a horse."

"What?"

"Equine-assisted therapy? Ever heard of it? Just pretend I'm a horse and talk it out."

I'd heard about it on a podcast, but I've never done it. I'm not really sure if there's any talking involved, or if it's just the quiet reassurance of a large, gentle animal. But the idea captured my imagination, and it seems to capture his too. "Does that actually work?"

I let out an affirmative snorf. He smiles, but it quickly fades, and he becomes a quiet orchestra of breathing, blinking, and swallowing. But I've got time. I lie across his shoulders and enjoy the movement.

Finally, "You're not mad at me for fucking this up?"

I think of all my worries earlier, about his skill or stamina or Mischa's theory about hot guys. But in the face of his raw dismay, I'm not disappointed so much as ashamed. He's a person, not a dicking machine.

"Why would I be mad? I wouldn't want you to keep going if you're not feeling it for some reason."

Just as I'd expect the same courtesy in return.

On his lap, he opens and closes his hands, flexing his fingers. "It's not that I'm not feeling it. You're everything I could've wanted for tonight. There are just a lot of...thoughts in my head that I can't shake."

Everything I could've wanted for tonight. I swallow the sweet, poofy compliment and focus on him. His needs. "Like what?"

He doesn't respond, and I get it. I wouldn't spill my beans to a naked stranger, either. But I massage his arms, rub my head against his, trying to communicate with him the way I do with Attila. *I'm here for you. I won't hurt you. You can trust me.*

And because he's not a demon rodent, it works.

"I've disappointed a lot of people recently. I didn't want to add you to the list."

Something inside me cracks and shifts, and hot, shining goop spills out. I wrap my arms around his neck and perch my chin on his shoulder, maximizing boob contact. "You haven't disappointed me. You're the hottest guy I've ever touched and I was ready to cream all over you and die in a blaze of fireworks. I really *was* enjoying myself. And I'm still enjoying myself, talking to you like this." I turn my lips into his shoulder, kiss-whispering the rest. "Honestly, before you showed up, I was begging the Universe for a sign that I don't suck. So you have no idea how lucky I felt that you were feeling snacky."

It takes him a moment to respond. "Are you calling me a gift from god?"

"No, I'm calling you a man who should shut up and quit while he's ahead."

His warm, quiet chuckle is everything. He covers my hands with his, tilts his head forward to press a kiss to my wrist that sets off a flutterfall in my chest. "Thanks, Di."

I love how he says my name, like it's a sigh of minty cool relief. But I can't tell him that, so I whinny. Or try to, anyway. How do horses do it?

He full-on laughs, and it's perfect, just like his smile. "Weirdo."

"Thanks."

He tilts his head into mine in a kind of *boop*, the hardness of his skull mellowed by the softest skin. He may be hot as fuck, but he's human, alright.

I close my eyes and take him in: the clean scent of his smooth neck, his warm back, curved into my chest, rising and falling with mine. The broad strength of his shoulders, so firm and yet so slumped. What other burdens do they bear? And what's with this mad-dog urge to help him lift them up and toss them away?

"You really don't watch movies, huh?"

I lower my head onto his arm so that I can look up at him. "Only ones my friends make me watch. Or *creepy* ones." And I widen my eyes when I say *creepy*.

His smile grows. "Par for the course."

"Why, should we watch something?" I ask. "Maybe one of your movies?"

Aaaand his smile goes rancid. "Let's not."

"Oh, okay. I was joking." Mostly.

"I don't want to watch anything." He says it in a rush and lurches to standing. Without him, the room feels colder than before.

"Sure, yeah, I'm okay with that." But if we're not going to Netflix and chill or Netflix and *Chill*, then what should we do? Is he going to leave?

Again, he makes no move to go. Again, I'm glad. But he shivers, I shiver, and neither of us are wearing enough clothing. I walk to the dresser where my suitcase sits open and put on an oversized tank, my usual sleep outfit, then grab the black robe that I was wearing before and bring it to Hayden, who's rubbing his arms and looking at the photo on the bedside table. It's a Polaroid of me and Mischa from high school, both of us looking like bargain bin mannequins from Hot Topic.

"Here."

He eyes the robe askance. "Isn't that a women's robe?"

"No, it's just a robe. More importantly, it's warm."

He pulls the robe on and ties it shut. It's a tiny bit short on him, lengthwise, but where the sleeves sat past my shoulders, they fit his. "Do you only wear black?"

"Not *only* black, but a lot of it."

"Are you emo or something?"

"Goth, actually."

"Huh. I thought that was a phase in high school."

"It's not." I tamp down my annoyance, swatting away echoes of my mother asking when I'm going to grow up and start dressing like a woman. "I *was* goth in high school, and I still love the music, but I rarely go out to the clubs or shows anymore." Not that I'd be opposed to it, if I had the time and money.

"Is music a key part of being goth?"

"Um, yeah? It's the most important part. You didn't know that?"

He shakes his head. "What kind of music is goth music?"

What kind of music is goth music?

What kind of music is *goth music?*

I give him a wild-eyed smile. "Get in the bed. It's time for your initiation."

Chapter 5

Darien

I toss away a few pillows and find a comfortable spot on the bed, adjusting the robe so that it's square on my shoulders. The material is thick and smooth, weighted, but not clunky. Best of all, it smells like her, this…strange, friendly human who's been nicer than I deserve.

"Put this on." She drops an earbud into my hand, which I slip into my left ear. An electric guitar and fevered drumming kicks off what sounds like rock from the 70s or 80s.

"This," she whispers on my right, "is Siouxsie and the Banshees."

Her well-deep voice weaves through the music, guiding me through decades of goth rock, death rock, dark wave, cold wave, post punk, and so on. All the while, she's curled up on my arm, leg thrown over mine, her once-heavy scowl now light and animated. Like a kid sneaking icing on his birthday, I nuzzle her hair, sniff her skin, stroke her arm with my thumb. It's been too long since I've experienced closeness like this, and there's something about *her* in particular that I can't get enough of. The subtle sweetness of her scent. Her toasty curves under the blanket, the sensual tilt of her neck, her long fingers and soft wrists. The way her eyes flash when she—

"Do you like any of these songs?" She hits me with her headlights. Caught. "Am I boring you?"

"No, not at all. It's cool to hear how the sound has changed throughout the years. Or hasn't."

"Right? It's still pretty intact. Though there are new sub-subcultures that have grown out of it, too."

"You said you still identify as goth?" A haunting chant sounds over a deep, rhythmic synth. According to her, this is ethereal wave.

"Yes, but not as much. I don't really go out these days, but I still enjoy the music. And even though I'm not teasing my hair or wearing band tees anymore, it's influenced my style a lot."

"So in high school, did you go full black and white makeup? BDSM? Drive a hearse?"

"First of all, hearses are a pain in the ass to own, so no, I didn't drive a hearse. And I wore more eyeliner, but I didn't do the white foundation. You can be goth with any skin color. My best friend was a Black goth, and she was fucking *goth*, okay? Though you wouldn't really be able to tell these days. And the stereotypes about kinky sex, tattoos, devil worship, none of those applied to me or my friends. Any kinks or tattoos that I'm into are because *I'm* into them, not because I'm goth."

I've seen the tattoos. But the kink? My mind goes to all kinds of possibilities.

Di, tied up, ass red with my handprints, begging me to fuck her through a gag. I'm half-hard again, though I've never done any of that before, only seen it in porn. Could Di be my first experience with it?

But she snuggles closer and looks up at me with bright, rounded eyes, her thoughts worlds away from mine. "I take it you didn't really hang out with goths in high school?"

"Me? Not really. I was a theater kid."

"And what was that like for you?"

"Hanging out with a bunch of awkward introverts who finally had an excuse to interact with each other? It was great." Though I was the most awkward and introverted of the theater kids, at least at first. Back then, my family members hardly ever touched each other, and they never talked about feelings. So when I met the theater kids—when they started massaging my shoulders and sharing shockingly intimate details about their families and relationships—I didn't know what to do with myself.

It was Eliza who helped me out of my shell. Eliza who—

"Hm. Awkward introvert, huh? When I first met you, I thought you were a douche."

The creeping panic recedes. "I guess I deserve that. Honestly, I was hoping you would swoon and give me your shrimp chips for free."

She lets out a deep chuckle, the warm crackle of a beloved record. "So what happened? *Are* you a douche, or is it all an act?"

She sucks in a breath as I lean over her and brush her cheek with my fingertips, parting her thighs with a leg while giving her the Lee Special. For once, it feels forced, and I almost don't want to show it to her. Can she see the raw edges, how the smile has burrowed into my skin like a foxtail? "You tell me."

She purses her lips, fighting a laugh. "You're so full of shit."

"Am I?"

"Yes." The corners of her eyes crinkle softly, close enough to mine that I have to switch my focus between the left and right. There's a small brown freckle in her right eye.

Like a fish into water, I let the smile slip away. "So what do you think I'm really like?"

She tilts her head to look up at me through her lashes. "Hmm. I bet…that you're an ugly duckling who grew up and surprised himself. But you're still a big, anxious softie who's worried that people will see through the hot alpha act and judge you for it."

I huff at her answer, but my pulse beats loudly in my ears, echoing every doubt-filled, sleepless night or bungled encounter. You'd think that after ten years in the business, I'd have rhino hide for skin, but with enough exposure, thick skin still burns.

At the beginning, I wasn't hot enough, talented enough, or well-enough connected, and even Asians laid into me for accepting a few roles that, I'll admit, were problematic. But they were the only kinds of roles available to me at the time, and I wasn't going to let perfection get in the way of progress. But even now, getting roles that are the complete opposite of how I began, I'm still not good enough. There are those who believe that I don't deserve what I've earned, or that I'm no better than a passing trend—a diversity hire instead of a talented actor.

The guy who set off an entire petition for #notmydarcy.

But she's heard enough of my sad interior monologue for one night. I let it all go on a breath and say, "So you think I'm *big* and *hot?*"

"Loser." She laughs and playfully shoves me, but I pin her down, making her breath hitch.

"Just trying to understand your point."

She slips her arms around my neck, wrapping her legs around my waist and pulling me down. The robe rides up and loosens, raising the curtain between me and her warm inner thighs.

"Tell me about the real Hayden. What are you into?"

The real Hayden is probably in Burbank with his wife and kids. But me? "Um… I like reading. Literature, classics, sci-fi. And I play video games." Things I don't broadcast widely. I don't need more associations with nerdiness.

"Oh yeah?" Her eyes widen briefly like a swell just swept through. "What do you play?"

"Mostly shooters."

"Do you play *Unhunter*?"

Now *my* eyes widen. "You know *Unhunter*?" Not what usually comes to people's minds when I mention shooters. It's a weird, spooky game that true fans never stopped playing, even though it came out years ago. Instead of playing as a soldier like in most modern shooters, players choose among creatures from myths and folklore, like ghosts, vampires, werewolves…

Yeah, now that I think about it, if she were going to play any shooter, it'd be *Unhunter*.

"I don't play as much anymore, but I used to."

"No way."

"Way. Why are you so shocked?"

I shift my hips, and my shaft glides against her wetness. Beneath me, her eyelids flutter, and she adjusts her hips, too, centering me between her legs. Her skin is soft as velvet, and after months of hardly touching anyone, my brain crackles like butter on a griddle. "I've just never met a girl who played *Unhunter* before."

"Well, now you have."

"Yeah, but did you get into it because of a guy, or because you actually liked it?"

Her face turns dour. "Because of a guy. But I played FPS games before him, and I kept playing even after I dumped his ass."

"Right."

She pulls the robe from my shoulders, peeling the edges down my arms before letting her hands drift down my back, tracing the points of her fingernails along my spine. "Don't believe me? I'll play you sometime. I bet I could hold my own against you."

My body holds its own against *hers* as we slowly start a fire between our hips—one with wet wood. "It's cute that you think you could beat me at *Unhunter*. There was a full month between projects that I played everyday. My goon levels are all maxed out."

"Yeah?" She sighs as if I've just told her how much I want her. Too much. "Me too."

"Then I guess we should play sometime." I kiss her neck, nibbling gently, and she lifts off the bed, arching into me while her hands hold me down. "Not tonight, though."

"Mm." With her low, breathy voice, it sounds like a purr, one that prickles the skin on the back of my neck.

Pushing her tank aside, I suck her nipple into my mouth and dip a finger into her slick, ready warmth. She raises her hips, angling them, swirling herself on my hand.

"Take off your shirt."

She sits up and tosses the shirt across the room like it's on fire. With a small bouncing flop on the bed, she's back in the same position as before, watching me with hooded eyes, her long hair a calligraphy stroke above her.

Barely hovering, I taste her lips, plump and soft like fresh mochi, and press her legs apart with a hand. The robe slips the rest of the way off as I lower my face to her stomach, her generous hips, kissing her thighs on either side. Our eyes lock just before I use my thumbs to spread her wide and lick her down the middle, up and down, again and again. She bucks as I suck her clit—gently, gently...*harder*—before dipping my tongue inside. I press down on her abdomen the way that Eliza—

Don't. "Is this okay?"

Di's hands slip into my hair. "If you stop, I will murder you."

I smile against her thigh and keep going. This, at least, I know I'm good at. Especially with how wet and swollen she is, the quiet burn of her gaze, the desperate pressure of her fingers on my scalp.

"Hayden..."

I lick deeper, curving my tongue, tasting her richness. My fingers tease the edges of her, up and down, slipping past my tongue, inside—

She groans and her hips buck, pushing my fingers in deeper. "*Please* fuck me. If you...if you want."

There's a question in her voice, like she's not sure if I can. And for one heart-stopping moment, I'm not entirely sure either.

But the pure, unbridled lust on her face leads the way, along with her soft curves and sweet sounds. I shut off my thoughts and let instinct take over.

Di sits up and kisses me, tasting herself on my tongue, drawing me down to her. I groan as her hand finds my cock, as she strokes me, slow, tight.

"I want you so much," she whispers, and her eyes offer a plea. She lets go of me and spreads herself out below, showing me exactly how much she wants me, an ocean of want.

I grab another condom from the nightstand, roll it on. She spreads her legs, and eyes wide, searching mine, I sink into her, inch by slippery inch.

"Di..."

Her eyes squeeze shut, her fingernails dig painfully—clarifyingly—into my shoulder. "*Yes.*"

We move together, her hips rolling with mine until she can't keep up and she yields, gripping my wrists as I squeeze her waist, her face twisted in soundless ecstasy. I'm pounding into her, centered on that rhythmic connection between us, the winding rapture of sliding into her again and again and again.

But beyond the slapping of flesh, there's nothing. She's quiet.

I thrust, and thrust, and thrust into the silence.

Why isn't she saying anything?

Why isn't she making any noise at all?

It's almost like—

She gasps for breath, panting.

"Don't stop," she rasps. "Please don't stop."

Again, she tenses, neck straining. Her pussy clenches, sending me soaring to new heights, floating, waiting for her to catch up.

Except something's not right. I can see it on her face, the tangled web of frustration there.

She sucks in another breath, panting, almost exasperated. "Do me a favor?"

Panic slams into me, slowing me to a stop. Am I doing something wrong? Is this not—

"Put your hands here." She takes my hands and places them high on her collarbone, at the base of her neck, one thumb and four fingers each to a side, like a killer bird with its wings spread. "Don't move them up or down from here, okay? And just press along the sides of my throat. Lightly."

She says the words in a rush, as if trying to outpace her fear.

"You want me to choke you?"

"It's not choking exactly. More like putting pressure, just a little. And focus on the sides of my neck, not the middle. If it's too much, I'll tap your hand like this or say the word stop." She taps the back of my hand twice, her brows drawn into a frown. "Is that clear?"

She watches me like I'm a flight risk. Like she's just told me she's got a cannibalism fetish instead of something I've seen plenty of in porn. But have I ever *done* it? No, no I haven't. All of my partners were as vanilla as they come.

Her pulse thuds against my fingers, waiting.

"Can you repeat what I just said?"

"Yeah. You want me to put pressure on your neck, on the sides, and you'll tell me to stop if it's too much. Or tap my hand."

"Yes. Don't try to choke me, just...light pressure." Her eyes soften in plea, and a drop of uncertainty leaks out in her voice. "Are you willing to do this for me?"

The music still plays in both of our ears, a wild medley of dark, pounding, sensual sound. And suddenly, she's not a random chick, but a woman, bare, standing at the edge of the dark, asking me to follow.

"I'm willing."

She melts back into the bed, relief washing over her features. "Thank you."

I press my hands against the base of her neck, just above her collarbone. "Here?"

"Yes. But only put pressure on the sides."

I close my fingers, barely pressing into the skin. "Like this?"

"Tighter," she whispers. And it's like she's said it to herself, because she squeezes so sweetly on my dick. I increase the pressure until she nods. "Yes, like that."

She can still talk with my hands like this, which implies that she can still breathe and tell me to stop. Good. I keep my hands in that position and begin to move my hips. "This okay?"

"*Yes*." Her head falls back, and her throat muscles snap taut against my fingers. I watch her, fascinated, heart pounding like I'm walking along the edge of a cliff. I'm almost choking her, lightly holding her throat as leverage as I move against her, and with the way she shifts her knees and takes me into her, she's fucking loving it. She feels so good, so fucking hot and slick inside, and I'm so close, so close, so—

"Tighter," she whispers again. I oblige, and she whimpers as I pound into her, clenching around me so that I have to grit my teeth against the growing tide. Her breasts move with each thrust, bouncing almost up to where my hands grip her throat.

There's no real danger here, as I maintain the same firm, yet comfortable pressure about her throat. But the unfamiliar gesture, the significance of it, becomes a potent rush. Something primal begins to rise, all-consuming like anger, almost triumphant. Possessive.

I want to close my hands even tighter...but I don't.

I want to grip her hips until they're bruised, suck her light brown nipples until they're dark and swollen.

I want to come *inside of her*. I want to let go and fucking *take her*.

Her eyes bore into mine, reflecting every one of my base desires, every shadowy half-formed thought that skitters away when you look too close. Her fingernails dig crescents into my arms, and I drive my hips into her even harder, desperate, returning her sharp little gifts on my skin with *more*.

I'm so fucking close.

She's close, too. She's gasping, squeezing, slick as cream. And I'm not stopping until she gets what she needs.

She lets go of me, goes rigid, fingers clawed around the bedsheets. Silent. As if to make up for her lack of breath, I breathe even harder.

Two seconds. Five seconds.

Longer.

Her face turns red—

I jerk my fingers away.

"*Fuck*," she cries out, and her hips buck against mine as she convulses, her legs clamped around my thighs. I let go and pump my own hips until I'm cursing, too, lightheaded, awash in shimmering pleasure.

As I catch my breath, I check her face. The angry color has started to fade. "Are you okay?"

"Yes," she says, wheezing lightly. "But next time, don't stop until I say stop or tap you. Please."

A flicker of annoyance, then shame, burns my throat. She knows her limits better than I do.

Still. Next time. The promise of this, again. "Sorry. I'll keep that in mind."

She nods and adds, "Thank you."

It's such a simple thing, but I have to close my eyes. I'm the one who's grateful.

That was new. Different. Intense. I want to turn it around and examine it more closely. But right now, I can hardly think, and my limbs feel like wet concrete.

I slump into bed next to her. "Do you do that with everyone?"

"No. I don't just trust anyone with that. I'm not looking to get strangled to death or have brain damage." She lets out a weak laugh. "I shouldn't have even asked for it tonight because we were drinking and smoking."

Strangulation. Brain damage. It hadn't felt that dangerous. I'd been in control, and she'd been able to talk. But when I think about those shadowy thoughts, how easy it would've been to go a bit further, it's clear how, with the wrong person, something could've happened.

"I'm just glad you're not one of those guys who thinks that I like it all *gag-face* because of how I dress."

"All gag-face?"

"Yeah, like, *rough*. I don't like it *all* rough. And I don't like being completely choked out. I like what I tell you I like. But some guys see my dark clothes and makeup and they assume that I want to be abused. I don't."

There's a sharp edge to her words, and she closes her eyes as if remembering something she'd rather not. My hands fist involuntarily, wanting to strangle whichever fucker thought they could treat her like a sex doll, or anything less than the soft, kind human that she is. Which is easier to see now, given the way she's looking at me. So unlike the mace-laden scowl she'd hit me with when we'd first met.

She's like a hissing cat, fierce, but fragile. Helpless when scruffed, and cuddly when she feels safe.

"I see. Then why'd you trust me?"

"Because I'm dumb." She turns and settles her head onto my chest, and lets out a warm sigh. "But also...I dunno. A feeling."

Her low voice is soothing, and when her eyes drift closed and she throws a leg over my hips, the walls of my chest relax.

"A horny feeling?"

She smiles and wraps her arm around my torso. "Yeah, obviously."

"Obviously."

And even though we've just had sex, there's something even more intimate about the way she kisses my chest and snuggles into the crook of my neck.

Or the way she says—barely audible, like a child whispering a secret—"I like you, Hayden."

I pull the blanket up around us and wrap my arms around her. "I like you, too." Surprisingly.

I debate whether or not to tell her that it's Darien, not Hayden, but...not yet. Not right now.

Tonight, I'm Hayden. Tomorrow...

Well. We'll see.

* * *

Beside me, Di's long hair forms a river of black with tiny flecks of pale morning sun. She removed her makeup before bed, and there's a strange, gooey warmth that fills me to see her bare, serene in sleep, all signs of gnashing vampirism exorcized. Her eyebrows aren't as thick or long, and her real lashes are short and straight. But the canvas of her—the full lips, wide eyes, and soft, smooth skin—is the same.

It's her, the real her.

Even with a stranger, she's unabashedly herself.

No wonder I couldn't fake anything last night, no matter how hard or embarrassing. It's like trying to act beside a natural. You don't act. You *re*-act. You take what they give and you give back.

And she'd given a lot more than I'd thought I would get.

If I know what's good for me, I should make Di sign an NDA as soon as possible, but I don't keep them lying around like Tam does. It's like she's always got one tucked into the huge bun on the back of her head. I do have a copy on my phone, but it's all the way back at the house next-door.

And of course, Di thinks I'm Hayden, but once she googles his name, she'll realize that I lied.

I need to tell her the truth. Bits of it. The right version.

But first, I'm starving. We never got to the Taco Bell portion of the night, and it's time to raid the fridge at my mini-vacation rental, even if all that's in there is my usual fare.

I slip out from her arms and ease off the bed. She doesn't stir except to curl up tighter around the pillow she's holding, her plump lips parted and shiny with drool.

I haven't left yet, but already my instincts are telling me to go back to bed. To go back to *her*.

Soon.

I pull on my swim trunks in the bathroom. On my way out, I hear a tiny thump from the living room, where I find the rabbit at the edge of her pen, cute little thing. Not sure what Di's talking about; she hops swiftly towards me when I offer my hand, then sits there, quivery, awaiting my touch. I give her soft head a few gentle strokes before sneaking outside, where the city is already wide awake, buzzing with noise.

Literally. A drone zips by and I avert my face, but not before I see it cruise towards a house further up the hill, where a group of people are gathered. The sweet sound of violins drifts down from their deck.

I cross the distance between Di's balcony and mine and head to the chair where I'd left my towel and phone, grabbing both and hurrying inside.

With a deep breath, I check my messages.
Bad decision.
Bad decisions all around.

Chapter 6

Di

I'm not disappointed that he's gone.

I mean, I am, but it's not his absence that I'm annoyed about. I just...I'd thought that we'd agreed with our eyes and smiles and bodies that we were going to wake up and spend the day together. My subconscious had already painted the plan so vividly: lazy, swirling kisses, a bedside brunch buffet, and a reformed Attila, happily munching on hay in my lap. We were supposed to stay in our weekend bed oasis, whispering secrets about our pasts, sharing a dragon's hoard of shining intimacies with our lips and hands.

But the bed beside me is empty, and all that's left is a dull, lovely ache.

I don't dwell long. On the nightstand, my phone is buzzing with a call. Mischa.

I swipe. "Hey, what's—"

"What is going on over there?"

Spoken like a parent busting a rager, but nothing's been trashed. As long as I wash the towels and sheets, I'm sure she'll be happy for me. "What do you mean?"

"How do you know him? Did you guys have sex in *my* house? Oh my god, tell me tell me tell me!"

I relax into the bed. She's not angry, she's excited. "Yeah, I—wait a sec." Her words register. From almost three thousand miles away, she's hit the bullseye, and my brain is dunked in icy water. "How did you know?"

"I have a camera in the living room, remember? To check on Attila? I checked the footage, and like twenty minutes ago, *Darien Lee* was petting her, so I checked the old footage and you guys were half-naked and making out. Are you two hooking up? I'm so confused and like..."

She keeps talking, but it's a garbled, tangled knot of noise. My brain is caught on two things.

One: camera. Mischa has a live-feed camera to keep tabs on Attila. She'd told me a while ago. I'd forgotten.

Two: *Darien Lee?*

"Wait wait wait," I say, and manage to slow Mischa's train. "Darien Lee?"

"Um, yeah? The guy who was palming your ass and sucking your face—"

"His name was Hayden. He told me that his name was Hayden." And why did *Darien Lee* sound so familiar?

"Are you kidding me? Google him, right now. Darien Lee."

I put her on speaker and do as she says. When the search results finish loading, each photo, each headline, each page of hits makes my stomach drop further and further, until it weighs down on my aching vaj.

Darien Lee...

...Agents of Icarus...

...Prince Charming...

...fiancée, Eliza de Santis.

"Tell me what happened! I need to know how this happened."

"Is he engaged?" My voice is so quiet, I'm not sure if she hears.

"Yeah, and that's why I'm so confused. I thought they were total sweethearts."

It sure looks like it, huh. Maybe his hair's a bit different, but that guy and *my* guy...I'm pretty sure that they're the same. And if that's the case...

The warm-hazies evaporate in a flash of bloody lightning.

He's *engaged*.

He cheated on his fiancée.

He's a lying, cheating piece of flaming shit!

Promise me that you won't tell anyone.

I promised. I fucking *promised*.

But that was before I knew the truth.

"Di? Are you going to tell me—"

"Yes, we did, okay? We fucked." I grip my hair by the roots, as if clamping my hands to my skull will keep me from unraveling. But it's not working. My thoughts spiral. 'Cuz I fucked a famous guy and I liked it but he's engaged—he's engaged?—he's fucking *engaged...* "Did you delete the footage?"

"No? Do you want me to? I can do that right now—"

"No, can you send it to me?"

"Um, yeah, I can. What are you going to do with it?"

"I'm not sure yet. But I want to see it."

"Babe, just hold on! Okay!" Her voice is muffled, as if she's talking to someone else. Probably John Davis, adventure enthusiast and celebrity pet doctor, her long-time boyfriend. "Hey Di, I gotta go. I'll text you the login info for the footage. But next time we talk—"

"I'll tell you everything. And please don't say anything to anyone else, not even John. Not until I sort this out."

"Of course. I'll talk to you later."

"Yeah."

I hang up, my stomach tight and tense like I've learned my identity might've been stolen. Except it's not *my* identity I'm worried about, and the consequences aren't that dire, but last night's big, beautiful bubble is popping and splattering into a soapy mess.

Mischa sends me the login info. I pick up my laptop and finger-stomp around until the video footage from Attila's camera is ready for me to scrub through.

Thirty minutes ago, dressed in his swim trunks, he stopped by Attila's pen and gave her a pat. And that faithless, long-eared rat, she let him! Something squeezes in my chest at the tender, soft-hearted way he looks at her, the small smile on his face as he smooths his hand along her head like she's the sweetest thing he's ever seen.

Is that really the face of a cheater?

Every fiber of my being, past, present, future, says no, but I've been wrong so many times before.

I scrub even further back. Hours, back to when we were last by Attila's pen together.

There. A bit grainy, but it's him in his swim trunks on the edge of the frame. Video me steps up next to him, and after a second of major eye-fucking, we start making out and humping hard enough to make Attila hop away and face the corner.

I pause the footage and close the laptop, but the images linger on, shuffling in with my memories of last night, of him, here, kind, embarrassed, rough.

Was that why he'd had problems fucking? Guilt? And was that why he wanted me to sign an NDA?

I've known my fair share of cheaters, maybe even an unfair share. Given my record, maybe it's more surprising if Darien *isn't* a cheater. But in my experience, cheaters are slippery, charming little fuckers who've got an obvious tick: their eyes keep sliding sideways, usually to their phones. Last night, Darien didn't even have his phone. His eyes had slid inwards, not sideways, as if he were preoccupied with something deeper than lust or guilt.

It doesn't make sense. What am I missing?

I ask my magic mirror to show him to me, and there he is in a wall of squares: a smug, boring mass of muscle surrounded by suits, sunglasses, watches, cologne, gym workouts, beaches, red carpets, and of course, a stunningly gorgeous fiancée, too perfect to credit only Photoshop. Photo after photo of them together, movie after movie, Hollywood's hottest, most unstoppable couple, with a high-fructose corn syrup kind of love.

It's definitely, one hundred percent, *him*.

Which means that that fucker cheated on his fiancée, with *me*.

He knowingly lied to my face and told me that he was someone else. Did he lie about everything else last night, too?

But I know what I saw, I know what I *felt*. There has to be more to the story.

What if Darien has a twin named Hayden? What if he's got like an open-relationship thing going on? What if there's a simple explanation that I'm missing, and the glasses were on top of my head all along?

A quick Google search turns up nothing to support my conspiracy theories, and the pictures I find of "Hayden Chu" feature a man with thicker brows, a smaller nose, and a softer jaw than the guy I was with. Not him.

He lied.

And if he lied, he probably cheated.

Which means that Darien Lee is really, really, really fucking dumb.

He's so famous. How could he have thought that he could get away with this? And if he's so rich and powerful, why not find a starstruck, willing accomplice? Why lie and waste his time and effort on me? Why touch me so tenderly, and kiss me so deeply, and listen with such cozy patience to my music and stupid horse noises?

I blink away the mist and stand, hands curled into fists. There's only one person who can give me the truth right now, and he's staying next door.

After slipping on the black robe that he wore last night, I step out onto the balcony to see if—

What the actual fuck?

Up in the sky, a soft, fluffy question, written in pure white capital letters.

WILL YOU MARRY ME?

Seeing it sets off a supernova in my chest, flooding my head with light and heat that threatens to leak out of my eyeballs. But it only lasts for a few seconds, or however long it takes for me to realize that the message is already beginning to dissipate, the letters slanted like willows in the wind.

Around me, there's buzzing. Drones, several of them, right overhead, flying away. I glance up the hillside, following their flight path. They're centered around a house that's just up the hill, covered in garlands and white balloons.

Obviously the message isn't for me. No one would propose after just one night, no matter how lovely it was.

Especially if they're already engaged to someone else.

Fucker.

I head towards the neighboring house. His balcony is only a few feet away from Mischa's, but it's three stories up, and I have to take a few calming breaths before I'm steady enough to climb over to his side.

"Hayden?" It's Darien, I know it's Darien, but I stupidly give him the benefit of the doubt and use the name he gave me while knocking on the glass door to the house. "Hello?"

I try the sliding door. It's not locked, so I head inside, shutting the door behind me.

"Hey. Hayden."

No answer. I check the rest of the house, which is furnished like a Crate and Barrel catalog spread, all woods, grays, and browns. But there's no Hayden, no sign of him anywhere. The house is still and quieter than a coffin, and as devoid of life. Unless he's deliberately hiding in a closet, he's not here, and I'm wasting my time.

When I head back outside, the air is thick with buzzing. The drones are back.

Wait. Drones.

With flashing red lights.

Oh my fucking god, drones have cameras don't they?

I hurry across the gap between the balconies and run inside, pulling the curtains closed and slumping against the couch. Is Hayden—Darien—gone because of the drones? Is he hiding from the paparazzi? Have they gotten me on camera, too?

I check my messages on my phone. There are only a few texts from Mischa from earlier. But as I go to slip my phone away, it starts to buzz. My younger sister.

I send it straight to voicemail.

She calls me back immediately.

"Hana, I can't talk right—"

"YOU'RE ON YOUTUBE, DI. LIKE JUST NOW."

Her voice is deep like mine, but right now, she sounds like a honking goose. "What?"

"My favorite YouTubers just got engaged and they were live-streaming the event and YOU WERE IN THE BACK-GROUND CLIMBING OVER A BALCONY—"

My skin ices over.

"And now they're saying that DARIEN LEE was there earlier this morning, climbing across the same thing but in the opposite direction, and now you're there so what the what is going on?"

I press my palm into my cheek like I'm kneading dough. Calm, warm, smooth dough. "Where's Mom?"

"She's out with Arul. But Jeje, I need to know—"

"Wait, what? Who's Arul?"

"Her new boyfriend. But—"

"What? Since when did she get a new boyfriend and why didn't you tell me?"

"They just started dating, like literally *just*. He's nice, okay, he's not like the last guy."

Shit. Hana's razor sharp when it comes to math or books, but she'd accept candy from a stranger if they said please and thank you. My mother is the skeptical one. If I've got resting bitch face, she's got resting murder face, and she uses it to deter suitors and solicitors alike. But the last time my mom dated someone, she'd fallen like an Olympic diver, head-first into the deep end, and didn't surface until he'd scammed her out of thousands of dollars and we'd nearly defaulted on our rent and insurance payments. After that, she'd sworn off men like I'd sworn off meat, and our lives were better for it.

So, new boyfriend? No, not now, not on top of all this other shit. I shake my head like a wet dog, willing the air to wobble and the hallucination to dissolve. This can't all be happening at once.

But my sister keeps going. "So Darien Lee is—"

"Just drop it about Darien. Don't tell anyone anything, don't say a word. Tell me about Arul—"

"I already said it was you on the livestream."

I blink. I check the date on my phone. It's not April first, but it's close. "What?"

"Everyone already knows it was you. I commented on the livestream as soon as I saw you. I said, THAT'S MY SIS-TER! And I dropped your social media links to prove it."

I take another deep breath. Maybe it's not so bad. What kind of livestreams would my nerdy sister watch anyway? Ones that nobody cares about, surely. "How many people were watching the livestream?"

"I dunno, maybe a few hundred thousand?"

Yeah, I'm ready to throw the phone. I have no idea where I am or what's happening. Might as well just throw the phone away and start over.

What's next, a UTI?

At this rate, I wouldn't be surprised. Because what were the chances of this happening, and to me specifically?

But it makes some sort of stupid sense. It's L.A., it's the Hollywood Hills. Rich people love filming every second of their lives, don't they? Every single moment is caught on camera and monetized. I'm just collateral damage.

"Jeje, tell me, please? I can keep a secret. Are you hooking up—"

I hang up. I hang up on my own damn sister and turn off the phone.

I just...need a moment. Quiet. Peace.

Why did I stay here again? Why didn't I third-wheel it in Miami with Mischa and John? Because a sunny beach full of hot strangers sounds pretty great right about now.

I inhale. Exhale.

Okay. So. What the fuck is happening?

My mom has a new boyfriend? What?

More pressingly, I've been caught on camera, trespassing next door. I have no idea whose house it is.

Darien Lee—presumably—has also been caught on camera, here, at Mischa's, and possibly next door.

Neither of us were wearing much clothing.

The whole internet, I assume, now knows these facts.

What the internet doesn't know for sure is that Darien—definitely not Hayden—and I banged last night, hard. The private pet-cam footage of us makes it pretty clear what was happening, while the drone footage was more ambiguous, but still shady as fuck.

Normally, I wouldn't give a shit if people knew I was banging someone, but the shitty thing, again, is that Darien Lee is *engaged to someone else.*

And that fucker left without saying goodbye, or paying me my fifty bucks.

I sink deeper into the couch, staring up at the ceiling, lost in a sea of milky white. Have those seashell imprints always been there? I try to focus on their details, the ridges radiating out from the bottom edge, the little spirals along the...um...

It hits like a kimchi slap: cold, heavy, wet, and salty.

Everything last night was a lie.

Chapter 7

Darien

The car screeches to a halt in front of the hospital, and as promised, I tip the driver a hundred bucks. "Thanks, Caleb."

"You're welcome, Mr. Lee. I hope your sister is okay!"

"Thank you."

Outside the car window, the hospital entrance looks far away, blocked by a sea of milling bodies. I take a few deep, calming breaths, preparing to step out of the car and into a scene. I exit, the car pulls away, and I'm on my own.

With a neutral, smile-ready expression, I keep my gaze pointed forward, away from the widening eyes of a dozen patients, doctors, and nurses. It doesn't work—a young woman stops me and asks for a photo and an autograph, and once it starts, it doesn't stop until everyone's gotten a piece of my patience. I grin through it all, shaking hands and listening to the stories of a few clinging patients before my throat is too tight and I have to excuse myself to head inside. Stiff and sweating, I barely stop to check in with the front desk before walking as quickly as could feasibly be considered normal towards the privacy of my sister's hospital room.

I don't make it that far. In the family waiting area, my mom squints at her phone, her blue, thin-framed glasses creeping down her nose as she tilts her head to read instead of moving the phone. With her dyed hair and bird-like diet, she looks like a retired ballerina, all elbows and legs. Next to her, my step-dad, Carl, reads a local newspaper, his plain blue tee tucked down into his khakis. Both of them must've driven over early from La Jolla.

Sitting down beside them is *him*, Ethan, my half-brother. It's taken months for me to be okay occupying the same room as him, but I still have to hold my knuckles away from his face in case they accidentally connect. It feels like wanting to punch myself, a version of me but watered down, with longer lines and wider proportions. And these days, he looks so sad and sorry, like a puppy who doesn't understand why he's in trouble. But Ethan knows full fucking well why he's in trouble.

He's slightly shorter than me, paler, a bit skinnier and less shredded, not bad for an assistant professor. He's got the physique I would have if I didn't keep up my diet and fitness regimen, which is another reason why my little bender last night was a mistake.

"Mom. Carl. How is she?"

They all look up, but Ethan speaks first. "They had to perform an emergency C-section, but she'll be okay. They're preparing her room for visitors now."

"And the baby?"

"Eliot," says Carl. "She named him Eliot. They're monitoring him in the NICU."

My mother skewers me with a look, and in that moment, she looks just like Claire. It's a power they both possess, the Asian Eye of Sauron. "Why are you so late? We couldn't get a hold of you all night."

I want to argue, but can't. So I say, "I was busy," and pretend like I don't know why she's surprised. I'll wallow in my own guilt later, alone. "Have you eaten yet? Do you think I can grab a quick bite before they're done prepping her?"

My mom gives me a curt nod. "The cafeteria is downstairs."

"Okay. Does anyone else want anything?" I look at my mom and Carl, and only them.

"Coffee," from all three of them at once.

"And could you get me something simple, like a pretzel?" adds Carl. Translation: a pastry.

My mother throws in, "An apple. Or banana." Translation: another pastry.

"Got it."

"I'll come with you," says Ethan, lurching to his feet.

"I'd rather you didn't."

"Let me help you. That's a lot to carry."

Mom and Carl watch our exchange from over their glasses, their eyes shifting between the two of us, waiting.

I grit my teeth and don't respond except to start walking.

People stop and stare when we walk by, frowning as if they aren't sure it's me. It's probably my hair, which I didn't have a chance to style this morning, so it flops against my head, a few stray strands poking into my eyes. I sweep my hand through the flat sheet, hoping it doesn't look too ridiculous, and hoping that anyone who sees me remembers the context of where we are. *I'm at the hospital. My business is private. Leave me alone.*

They don't.

In the elevator, I get asked to autograph a prescription slip and a cast. One person pulls out their phone to take a video, following us down the hall. I keep a small smile stapled to my face and ignore our shadow, but Ethan peers over his shoulder repeatedly, his scowl growing deeper with every pass until he turns around and asks the woman to give us some privacy. She puts away her phone, but continues to follow at a distance, a starving mountain lion whose prey is too big.

"I don't know how you deal with it," Ethan mutters.

Poorly, which is why I hardly go out in public, except on quiet nights so stale and stifling that I've been forced to leave my house in disguise, in search of somewhere I can feel alive without being seen. Watch without being watched. But with my face on every corner and this big physique, it's no easy feat.

Thankfully, the cafeteria is mostly empty except for a few stressed-looking medical staff who look as eager to be alone as I do. I select some oatmeal and fruit to eat while Ethan picks up two cheese danishes and two large coffees for our parents. But just in case we're wrong, he gets a banana, too. And he pays.

I haven't said a word.

It's like when we were kids. I never had to ask him to cover for me, he just did. He was good at reading situations and looking out for me, often in the background when I wasn't aware of it. It'd taken years—and college, and our mom's accident—before I'd realized how much I'd come to rely on him to take care of things at home when I couldn't, to tell me what was going on when I was busy or distracted.

Until the night he *thought* I was busy and distracted and he fucked my fiancée.

After paying, we sit down at a table by ourselves. There aren't too many people around, probably because the cafeteria smells like wet eggs and bleach. I force myself to eat—slowly, not shovel down—two tiny cups of plain oatmeal, even though I'm tempted to snake-swallow the entire stack of soggy, pale breakfast burritos from the hot food bar. But bad burritos and the regret that comes with them are the last thing I need.

"So, Darien, what were you—"

"No."

"Right." He leans back in his chair, fiddling with a spoon, his fidget spinner stand-in for today. The guy never could keep his hands still, or to himself, apparently. "Anyway, Claire was pissed."

Obviously she was pissed. I'd have been pissed, too. I *am* pissed, at myself. But I'm more pissed that *he* was the one who was there for her instead. The same sad story.

I force another spoonful of mush down my throat. "Thanks for taking care of her."

"Yeah, of course." He taps his fingers against the table with no apparent rhythm, each tap-a-tat sending my blood pressure higher. "She's my sister, too."

The plastic spoon bends under my thumb. I leave it in the empty oatmeal cup and push it away. "I've got it from here."

"Sure. But I'm available if either of you need anything."

"I've got it," I repeat, and pick up my apple, waxy and dull and wholly unappetizing. Penance, I guess, for cheating on my diet last night.

God, what I wouldn't give to be back there, warm and in bed with Di, smelling her softly sweet skin instead of clinical brunch food and disinfectant. Claire and Eliot come first, obviously, but if not for them, I would've wanted to wake up with Di, and to see her secret little smile one more time before figuring out how to tell her the truth.

As I bite into my dry, bitter apple, my phone rings. Tam. I send it to voicemail, but when she calls again, I swipe to accept. "Hey, I texted you, I'm at the hospital—"

"Did she sign an NDA? She didn't, did she?"

I blanch. There's only one *she*. "Tam, slow down—"

"Tell me that you have her contact information."

"What's going on? How do you know about her?"

"You and this girl—Diana *Ho*—were caught on camera."

Di. Camera. Caught.

Like surfacing from a dream, it takes me a moment to sort out each detail. "Caught? How?"

"Tell me everything, and I mean *everything*."

I ignore Ethan's concerned look and walk towards a corner where I can whisper and tell Tam all of it, start to finish, including, at her insistence, a high-level rundown of what happened in the bedroom. And, of course, the fact that I haven't made Di sign an NDA.

"So how were we caught? What does that mean?"

"There was a livestreamed event in the area this morning, and both of you were recorded by different drone cameras, jumping across to each other's balconies."

Oh, shit. The drones.

"And now everyone thinks that you've been cheating on Eliza."

"No."

"Yes. Which is why I need her contact info ASAP. You don't have it, do you?"

"No, but...maybe you could slide into her DMs?" *Fuck.*

"Oh god." She mumbles something to herself. "Alright, whatever, I'll figure it out. You're at the hospital? Well, leave. Get to somewhere private. Try to keep out of sight. The next few days are going to be bad. And whatever you do, do not contact that woman. She's a major liability right now, so don't make things worse."

Tam's words make sense, but they don't feel true. Because what comes to mind is Di's guarded expression, her quiet judgment, like even when she's shorter and looking straight on, she's still looking down her nose at you...at least until you get her naked and on a bed. She'd promised not to tell a soul, yes, but she'd made no effort to hide her disdain for my bull-shit when I'd tried to charm my way into her shrimp chips. My looks and fame mean nothing to her, which is why I'm positive that it'd be better for me to clear the air as soon as possible.

Except that I don't have her contact info.

Good job, Darien.

"What about Eliza?"

But Tam has already hung up.

"Fuck."

I walk back to the table, where Ethan watches me with battle-ready eyes. "Everything okay?"

I lean against the table, palms flat, hanging my head. If anyone's filming or taking photos right now, it will come back to haunt me later. I can't afford *not* to care. But for fuck's sake, when will I get a break? There's a spotlight on my every move, and I want to bash it in and stomp on all the shattered glass. Be alone in the dark for a while so that I can take care of the ones I love.

It's always work that gets in the way, and it's always Ethan to the rescue—

No, not this time. This was all me. How could I have been so stupid? A little self-pity and suddenly I'm rolling in bad decisions. The tabloids must be having a fucking field day.

"Darien Lee? Could I get a—"

"Not now," says Ethan to the young man at my elbow. At first glance, he looks white, but there's something about his brow and nose that make me think he could be mixed.

That's what it is. He reminds me of Ethan.

I straighten, but can't summon a smile. The most I can do is nod. I scrawl my signature on his napkin and wait for him to scurry off before turning to Ethan, who's sitting there with something suspiciously like pity in his gaze.

What a joke.

"I need to go see Claire." I get up and walk as quickly as possible to the elevator, without making it seem like I'm in a panic. He grabs the snacks and coffees for Mom and Carl and follows.

"What happened?"

I call the elevator. Get inside. Tap my foot against the floor instead of kicking the walls like I want to.

"Are you about to have another press emergency?"

Fuck. The last time I was truly stalked and swarmed by paparazzi, the paps had hounded me for days and whipped up a fake media frenzy. Everyone close to me had been followed and harassed, too.

"Darien. Darien, don't do this to Claire."

The elevator doors open. I hurry out. "I promised her I'd be here for her."

"But can you really be present if all of this press stuff is happening in the background?"

"I'll be fine." I have to be, don't I? *Because there's no way in hell I'm letting you replace me in Claire's life, too.*

"And what about when you leave? They'll be camped outside the hospital, ready to ambush you, or possibly us. Remember that time they pushed Mom?"

How could I fucking forget? "I know, okay?"

"Then go! This isn't the place for you. We'll take care of Claire. I know you made her a promise, but you staying is just going to force all of us to deal with your drama. Stop being selfish and *go*."

My hands curl into hard knots. It's Ethan to the rescue all over again. When our Mom got hurt, when Eliza got lonely, when Claire gave birth and I was nowhere to be found.

Hiding.

"I'll tell Claire you tried to stop by, but couldn't. I'll explain—"

"*Fine*. Tell Mom and Carl I had to go." I almost ask him to tell Claire that I'm sorry, too, but I'll do that later. I don't need the two of them talking about me behind my back.

Ethan nods and hands me the hoodie off his back and his keys. "Take my car. It's three rows to the right and up a few from the main entrance."

I almost toss the keys back in his face, but I already dismissed the private chauffeur and who knows how long it'll take to send another. Ethan's car is the fastest and most discreet getaway I have. Gritting my teeth, I pull on his hoodie. It's a tight fit. "I'll have someone drop it off to you later."

"Sure."

Keeping the hood up and my head low, I sneak out a side entrance and hurry to the car. Once inside, I look for Di on social media. She's got over eight thousand followers, so it's not too hard. Most of her photos are of clothes or plants, lightly curated in alternating frequency, all edited to be slightly grainy and with deeper shadows. I stare at the few that are of her, posing beside models, scowling, laughing, flipping the camera off, taking in these sides of her that I haven't seen yet.

How did someone like her get caught up in this?

I hesitate for only a second before DM-ing her with my number, asking her to call me when she gets a chance. I tack on a belated, *Sorry*.

On the road, I call Eliza, who's in New York for a press tour. She doesn't pick up on the first try. Or the second. She doesn't answer until halfway through the third.

"What do you want?"

"I want to explain—"

"I think it's pretty clear what happened."

I'm surprised her words don't burn my ear off. At the same time, the long-seething monster inside me is glad that she's gotten a taste of what I've been choking on for months. It wonders if any of that venom is a result of jealousy. Hopes it.

"You're jumping across balconies in your boxers, what else are people going to think?"

"They were swim trunks. There was a swimming pool on the deck, I was swimming."

"It doesn't matter. You fucked her, that's obvious—"

"So? You've been fucking Ethan this entire time."

"That's diff—"

"Do you expect me to be celibate while you sleep with my brother? If we're over, we're *over*. Don't drag me along like a spare tire."

She lets out a soft, derisive snort. "I don't care who you fuck on your own time, but you promised me four months. Thanks to your little fling last night, I have to come back and smooth this over."

Four months. Four months of hiding what she did to me so that the scandal doesn't ruin her new movie premiere, even though *she* ruined my life.

Four months to put it back together again.

Only two left.

"Look. I just wanted to call and admit that I made a mistake. I'm telling you, I'm owning it, and I'm going to fix it."

"You'd better fix it. Or else I'm going to let everyone believe what they want to believe."

I huff, amazed, but at this point, why am I surprised? It's like once she showed her true colors, she couldn't stop flashing them in threat. "You're not going to throw me under the bus, Eliza. Not unless you're more of a hypocrite than I thought."

To be honest, I'm not sure. Despite our history, I hardly recognize what we've become. Over a decade of warm-hued memories, memories of high school dramas, followed years later by on-screen romances and off-screen dates. Six years of dating, much of it immortalized on film. Six years of days when I wanted to give up, but Eliza wouldn't let me, or days when she picked at her sweaters, fretting over a part, and I had to hold her still to keep her from ruining her wardrobe. The nights when we hid our faces and ran from the cameras, holding hands and laughing, or spent hours together, running lines with each other, cuddling, kissing, making love after.

And now, this.

It takes her several seconds to respond, and when she does, her voice is tight. "I'll be back tonight."

I sink back into the driver's seat, all the fight rushing out of me, but this is far from over. Our publicist is always on our asses for maintaining appearances, making sure that we look more in love than anyone else. Our fans can't get enough of it, and that's why, for two more months, my image is not my own.

But that's also why I've often wondered how much of our love was for them, and how much for us? Like two characters in a plot-heavy script, how often did we choose each other for the sake of the story, and not for ourselves?

I try to remember the way she looked at me in private, whether she looked at me the way she did in front of the camera: a cozy cottage with all the lights on, a *Welcome Home* mat by the door.

But my brain has blurred the image to dull the pain.

"I'll see you at home."

She hangs up, and I know better than to call her back.

Chapter 8

Di

Coffee happens first, then a shit, then a shower. It's the ultimate order of good mornings, and I desperately need a good morning today.

But the coffee is instant because John and Mischa are mutants who don't usually drink caffeine.

And the shit is disappointing because I didn't have my usual strong coffee.

And the shower...

Well, the shower is actually pretty nice.

Fresh, clean, and dry, I start to feel more human than moldy potato, but that nearly gets derailed when I turn on my phone. My hand goes numb from the long chain of vibrations as dozens of texts from friends, old acquaintances, even a guy I sold a sewing machine to through Craigslist, come through. Everyone wants the dirt on me and Darien Lee.

Worse, the DMs have started coming. Death threats. Insults. Propositions. People telling me how I should feel for ruining Hollywood's cutest couple.

Maybe the coffee was a mistake; my stomach's churning like Mauna Loa.

I should make you sign an NDA.

If you promise not to tell anyone, I'll keep going.

Ass. I'd said I wouldn't, but he lied to me first. Cheaters don't deserve a cover.

I turn off notifications for all of my social apps and pick out my armor for the day, a black backless leotard with silver chains hanging from the collar ring like shiny ribs, and my usual black utility pants. But as I'm dressing, the doorbell sounds. Shit.

I finish pulling on my clothes and tying my hair up in a high, fierce ponytail. All the while someone's ringing the doorbell like they're trying to button-mash their way into the house. On the video display by the door, there's a woman, average height, bronze skin, flawless black talk show host hair.

"Diana?" she says through the speaker. "I'm Tam, Darien's manager. I'd like to talk."

Darien. There goes the secret twin theory.

Then again, is *she* really who she says she is? What if she's a reporter who figured out where the house was based on the footage. Maybe the paparazzi are on their way here this very minute.

"Diana? I know you're there. Darien told me everything."

I debate whether or not to ignore her and hide, but shake myself and press the button to respond. Partly because she *does* look like a Hollywood manager, but mostly because she appears to be holding a tray of coffee in her hands. "How can I trust that what you're saying is true?"

She tilts her head back and rolls her eyes. "You have a pet rabbit in there. How's that?"

Hmph. Lucky guess? "Fine. What do you want?"

"Could we talk about what happened?" She holds up a pink box in addition to the two to-go coffee cups in a cardboard carrier. "I brought you some donuts and coffee from Leap's."

Leap's Donuts. They always sell out by noon, which is why I've never tried them before. This lady knows what she's doing.

I bulge my eyeballs out trying to make sure there's no one else out there before opening the door. "Come in."

"Thank you. Shoes off?"

"Uh, no, this is…" Ehhh, it's probably not a good idea to bring Mischa into this. "Shoes are fine."

She nods and sweeps past me into the house, up the stairs and all the way into the living room, as if she's been here dozens of times. Her eyes catch on Attila's pen before she gracefully lowers herself to the couch and places the box and drink tray on the coffee table. She's dressed in a long pollen-yellow shift dress with pointed white cap sleeves and two huge pockets on the front, and chunky white sandals on her feet.

"What a lovely home. Is it yours?"

It's not the most unreasonable question to ask, but it sends me into a quiet panic. Is she being polite, or trying to get information? "I'm just here for the weekend."

She curves her lip and glances thoughtfully at the porcelain skull-shaped fruit bowl on the mantle. "I see. Well try a donut. And I got one plain drip coffee and one mocha, just in case. Both for you."

Ooh, she's *really* good. I pick up the one marked M—I assume for mocha—and take a sip. Rich, decadent, but not too sweet, my tongue smiles in my mouth. I can't wait to see what the donuts are like. "Okay, I'm listening."

Tam leans towards the couch back without quite touching it, hovering, threading her fingers across a knee. "So. He didn't get you to sign an NDA."

"No, he didn't."

"I assume you understand the difficulty of the situation?"

"That Darien is," ...*a lying, cheating douche-hat...* "engaged to someone else? Yes."

"Have you told anyone about what happened between you two? Anyone at all?"

"No." Not anyone who would blab.

She smiles. "And there's no footage or images of the two of you together, correct?"

"Actually, I do have footage of us together."

Her smile drops like a bowling ball, knocking her mouth open. "Prove it."

"No." The word comes out automatically. She's got this predatory look on her face, and a grainy black and white film plays in my head of her leaping across the table and wrestling the laptop from me to delete the video. I'm taller than her, but her thick arms would make Arnold proud.

After a long stare-down, Tam's smile returns, but it's pointy this time. "If you don't prove it to me, Diana, I can't—"

"It's Di, not Diana." I point to where the camera sits on the mantle, just under the arm of a giant octopus candle. "That's where the camera is. We were in this room together. Remember the bunny? It's a camera meant for monitoring her whenever...whenever I'm away. After we're done talking, I can send it to you."

She stares at the camera, then Attila's pen, before uncrossing her legs and leaning towards me. The smile is gone. "Right. Well then, let's assume you have the footage, which you *will* show me later. What do you want?"

"What do I want?"

She cocks her head at me. "Don't act dumb. You seduced him in front of a camera. You got him. So now what?"

"I didn't *get* him. That's not what happened."

She performs a slow, exasperated blink. "Do you or do you not have footage of him being intimate with you?"

"I do, but—"

"Then there are two scenarios. One: you sign an NDA and agree not to say a word about what happened. You say what we tell you to say, and that's all. In exchange, we give you money."

I'd thought that something like this could happen, but my brain still struggles to process her words. "You're bribing me to sign an NDA?"

She pulls a packet out of thin air and places it, with a pen, on the table in front of me. "Unless you'd like scenario two: you sign it for free?" She leans forward, eyes narrowed. "But I think we both know what you want, don't we?"

No, I want to say. *You have no idea what I want.* I only wanted...what? A night with a hot guy. To forget about my problems for a while. I didn't sign up for *this*. And yet she's accusing me of plotting the whole thing, of blackmailing Darien when I didn't even know who he was. Did he think that my ignorance was all an act? I *am* terrible with names and faces, and I hardly watch movies, but even if I'd known who he was, I wouldn't have cared.

Except for one thing. "I didn't know he was engaged, but now that I do, I'm not keeping quiet. I want it known that he's a lying, cheating, sack of shit."

"You don't know what you're talking about. The situation is complicated, to say the least. And—regardless of what you think of him, think about the consequences to *you*. If you speak out about this, you're going to get a *lot* of unwanted attention. The tabloids will paint you as a home-wrecker, the woman who broke up Hollywood's most beloved couple."

"I didn't do anything. Darien's the one who did that."

"No," she says firmly. "*You* will be painted as the one responsible."

Her emphasis is unmistakable. "Is that a threat?"

She nudges the packet and pen towards me. "Think. Do you really want people poking into your private life?"

"No, but his fiancée deserves to know what kind of man she's agreed to marry. And his fans—"

"She knows what kind of man he is better than you do, and she's asking for privacy at this time. You talking to the press isn't going to warn her, it's only going to drag them both into an unwanted scandal. Is that what you want? To ruin their careers?"

"I...no." But will his fiancée truly understand what he did from today's footage? Or has Darien already confessed to her? "I just don't want him to get away with this."

"He won't, I promise, not from Eliza. I manage the both of them, I would know." She closes her eyes and exhales, resetting her face with a patronizing smile. "Do the right thing.

Let them handle this privately. In exchange, we'll pay you for any inconvenience this may have caused."

Inconvenience? He's a fucking cheater! I don't want his stupid hush money, even if it *would* be nice to get a huge payout right now. Yes, I'm so broke that I had to pet sit the Rabbit of Caerbannog instead of partying in Miami with my best friend. Yes, my sister's about to go to college. So what if I can barely afford to live in L.A. anymore? Even with all of that, I would never sink to taking cash just to—

"Two thousand? Would that work?"

I blink. Two thousand dollars just to keep my mouth shut.

But money can't buy a conscience. "I'm not interested in—"

"How much would you need to start your own fashion line?"

The words land like a punch to the gut. "My own fashion line?"

"It's all over your socials. Your dream is to start your own line of alternative streetwear. Well, we can give you enough for that, *if* you don't say anything."

Thousands. Thousands of free dollars, right here at my fingertips, no bullshit gate-keepy application needed.

Thousands of free dollars, straight out of his pocket.

And what better way to punish him? As rich as he probably is, he was still so stingy about paying fifty bucks for a bag of chips! Cheapskate! It's not like he needs all that money for himself. I could do so much more with that money than he ever could. I'd be like Robin Hood, stealing from a heartless prince and giving it to people who are more deserving: my mom and sister.

The more I consider it, the more it makes sense. Maybe Tam is right. This is Darien and Eliza's private business, and assuming she really does know what happened, I should let them handle it. I certainly don't want to be the center of attention.

And if I can walk out of this with something for the "inconvenience"—something to help my mom rest a little easier—then even better.

Still, it feels icky, like getting paid to shove a slimy toad down my throat. I'll have to keep my mouth shut and hold the secret inside. And as nice as it would be to get a reprieve from our financial worries, I have never asked for help from anyone, not Mischa, not boyfriends, not my dad, no one. Why start now?

But what's more important, helping my mom and sister and punishing Darien, or my pride?

I know what my mother would say.

"How much would you be willing to give me?"

Something smug lights her eyes, and I can almost hear the clang of the trapdoor slamming shut. "How much do you want?"

Negotiation 101: let them give the first number. Two thousand wasn't an earnest offer. "You tell me."

Tam throws an arm out along the back of the couch. She studies my face, all emotion gone from her own. "Five thousand."

I bark a laugh. "Have you seen my designs? Read about my work? I want to create a sustainable brand with fair labor practices, not another throwaway brand."

"Then how much are you asking for?"

I have a rough estimate in mind from all of the grant proposals I've written, and I almost open my mouth to give that number, plus maybe ten thousand more for good measure. But is that too much? Too little? There's something weird here, something I can't quite put my...

Ah. She's trying to anchor me on the price of starting my own line. But what I should really be asking for is the worth of his reputation. Of this secret. If he's willing to pay fifty dollars for shrimp chips and he's a world-famous actor, then why not add a zero or two and see?

"Three hundred thousand."

I expect her to swat me down like a fly, but all she says is, "Fifty thousand."

Decades of RBF have trained my muscles to keep scowling, but my stomach is doing backflips. I almost yell, *YES!!!* but her reaction has told me that my first number wasn't extreme. I should've gone way higher. "Three hundred thousand. It's his reputation on the line."

She scoffs and shakes her head. "That's too much."

"No, it's not. Three hundred thousand." The payout restructures itself in my head. Fifty for me and my line, the rest to pay for Hana's cottage-sized tuition, plus taxes. Can't forget taxes.

But Tam doesn't budge. She frowns at the wall, thinking for a moment. I can see the exact moment the lightbulb goes off. "You won some prestigious fashion design competition?"

"No. Third place." Though I might as well have come last, for all the good it did me.

"How about this? Assuming that you truly haven't told anyone, you get fifty thousand, *and* you get to dress Darien for the Met Gala."

"Fifty thousand and—" Her words register, and I stare, dumbfounded. "The Met Gala?"

She tips her head forward and gives me a *you're-kidding-me* stare. "It's only the biggest fashion event of the year—"

"I know what it is. But Darien's going?"

"Yes. Eliza is going on behalf of one of the fashion houses. Darien is her guest. So if you dress Darien, if we spin a story where you two are old friends of some sort and he wanted to help you out by wearing your clothes and promoting your new line, that kind of deal...that could help to explain why Darien was here in just his boxers. You were fitting him for something. It will give us both a cover."

Swim trunks, not boxers, but whatever. Most people wouldn't know the difference from the footage. But the idea is so stupid. If that's the story, then why were we jumping back and forth across balconies? And if he was the one getting fitted, then why was I also half-clothed, barefoot, and hopping back and forth? If we're old friends, then how come we've never been seen together in the past?

She misreads my expression. "You *do* know how to make men's clothing, correct? Suits, tuxes, et cetera?"

"Of course." And anything I don't know, I'll figure out. "But will the public really buy the story?"

"You'd be surprised at how absurd celebrity lives are. The story has enough mystery to cause a stir, but just enough plausibility for people to accept it at face value and move on." She leans in and drives the deal home. "Especially once he walks out on the red carpet in one of your designs."

My mind reels. Me, designing a red carpet look for Hollywood's It guy. The Met Ball. The Super Bowl of Fashion.

Gr...oss?

I love clothes, and I love the language of clothes. But the Met Gala celebrates the kind of fashion that's elitist, that puts on an exclusive spectacle of wealth and celebrity when inequality is higher than ever. It's the kind of fashion that promotes unhealthy images and unattainable standards, that perpetuates the idea that you need to eat less and buy more. It's the kind of fashion that would scoff at me and my clothing for falling stagnant, when that's precisely what I strive for—longevity, economy, sustainability.

But it's also the biggest fashion stage there is, and my design in that space, as conspicuously different as it would be, could send a message. This is my opportunity to make a statement, or at least cause some buzz as I work to launch my own brand.

Darien, however, is not the right ambassador.

While drinking my instant coffee that morning, I'd rage-scrolled through photos of Darien and Eliza, picture after picture of him holding her up in fun poses on yachts and beaches, hiking in the woods together, smiling at each other with enough sweetness to make my teeth rot. Their social media captions are the worst.

She's my cup of tea. #madteaparty #disneyland

He steals my fries, but also my heart xoxo!!
We woke up like this. #twinning

If I ever need to throw up, I'll know exactly where to look.

Worse, they dress like classic Hollywood stars, all flattering cuts and neutral tones and safe styles, like if Cheesecake Factory served people. Either way, neither of them would be caught dead in my shadowy, gothy techwear.

"What's Eliza wearing?"

"I'm not positive, but I know that it took over two thousand hours of labor to create. Last I heard, it was something like a pastel-pink gown with Swarovski-detailed epaulets and a long train. A custom Dior."

My jaw drops. Dior is worlds away in every dimension that matters to Fashion people. It'd be like putting Paris next to the grungy Jersey suburb where I grew up. Still...if I can get a mega-celebrity to wear one of my designs at the *Met Gala* next to the face of Dior, it would be a huge marketing opportunity for me. My design might be out of place, but everyone would talk, and hopefully my brand would find its way onto the right screens. But...

"Isn't it a month from now?"

"Yes."

"He doesn't already have an outfit lined up?"

"We've been in discussions with a few designers. Jill, Eliza's stylist, has been handling it for the both of them, but she's been busy. Nothing has been agreed upon yet. Darien's an easy customer, so she usually handles his look quite late. Her other clients are more demanding."

Well, no shit. Jill Bergendahl—I assume that's who she means—is the hottest celebrity stylist in L.A. Even *I've* heard of her.

And if so, "What makes you think she'll say yes to me?"

Tam gives me a strange look. "Because what's best for Darien and Eliza is best for her."

We go back and forth until we agree—two hundred thousand and one red carpet look for Darien. I'll have to meet with Jill to get her approval on some ideas in the next couple of days, and then the initial fitting is two weeks after that, the final fitting a few days before the Met.

I've competed in a design competition. I know what it's like to make high-fashion looks under time pressure. But this is different. I won't have my pick of model. I won't have full control. And it won't just be some viewers on the internet watching—it'll be the entire fashion world.

God, that gives me chills, and not the good, spooky kind. But I'm doing it, right? I'm doing *something*, and that beats doing nothing and rotting in angst-jail.

By the late afternoon, I've sent the footage to Tam, their lawyers have sent me the final paperwork, and everything is settled. Tam and Darien's publicist have "leaked" the news to the media: Di Ho will be designing a look for Darien Lee. Apparently, I'm an old friend of his who reconnected with him recently. He heard about my upcoming line and offered to help.

It's complete bullshit and the media crawls all over and bites holes into the story, which causes a frenzy around which story is right: the one where Darien is innocent, or the one where Darien's a cheating bastard. I hope everyone sees him for what he is, but I've signed my voice away for a big fat check, and don't say a word. I ignore all calls and messages and get to work.

It's only later, as the glow of excitement fades, that I'm left wondering what the hell I've gotten myself into.

Chapter 9

Darien

"Drop your hand so I can take it," I say, doing my best ventriloquist's smile.

Eliza does as I ask and raises her eyes to mine, laughing. "I hate this."

We swing our hands together like lovers on a stroll. Like we used to, months ago, when what passed between us was warmth and sweetness, not just cold sweat and lilac hand cream.

"Well, tough luck," I tell us. "We're here."

"We wouldn't be here if you hadn't messed around and gotten caught."

I laugh, and it's almost funny. "I could say the same thing."

Her smile widens, but from the tight corners of her eyes, I've hit my mark.

We fall into lockstep, and with two bodyguards and the paparazzi a few feet ahead of us, pretend to look at each other like dogs gazing at their owners. Her eyes are ringed with the longest natural lashes I've ever seen, drawing you into irises that are a striking shade of silvery green. So few people get to study them up close. Even fewer get to witness their full range of expression. Hurt. Jealousy. Contempt. Resentment.

I break our gaze and pretend to study my ugly, oversized watch, which I'm contractually required to wear as a spokesperson. It's excessive in detail, like a small robot vomited its insides into a gold monocle, and it costs more than my mother ever made in a year.

As much as I'm steeped in it, I will never understand capital-F Fashion. If I didn't have so many sponsors, I'd probably walk around in the same black outfit all the time, because isn't black the safest color?

Di wears a lot of black, but it's not to be safe. Does she understand Fashion?

I wonder what she's doing, or why she hasn't responded to my DMs. Or what she must think about—

"Ethan and I are completely different from your little one night stand, okay? We're in love."

Christ, the B.S. that comes out of this woman's mouth. How did I ever think of her as the start and end of my days? "Whatever helps you sleep at night. But when all is said and done, you and Ethan are going to come out of this looking like terrible people."

Eliza laughs, and it's rainbows tinkling on glass. Fake rainbows on fake glass. "People date their ex's siblings. It's not illegal."

"It's not illegal, but it's messed up, and the timing is suspicious."

"Let me worry about the timing. You just keep your word."

My word. Agreeing to lie low for four months, until her newest movie is no longer news. Agreeing to the most milquetoast breakup announcement ever, that we've gradually become more friends than lovers. And finally, agreeing not to say a word about them when Eliza announces her relationship with Ethan, assuming they even last that long.

In short, agreeing to cover up their mistake.

They'd gotten me to sign a piece of paper while I still had any feelings at all for Eliza, any sympathy or hope that she and Ethan might break up, or that she might come back to me.

Shouldn't we be able to handle this in private? she'd asked, tears in her beautiful eyes, and I'd caved like the sucker that I am.

I place my hand on the small of Eliza's back, on that gorgeous dip that was once for my palm, and shepherd her into the kitschy French cafe—*Oui Love You?* What?—that we've picked for our public outing. The warm buttery scent of fresh croissants greets us at the door, briefly forcing me back to Paris, to the time when she'd broken the heel of her shoe and I'd given her a laughing piggyback ride along the Champs-Élysées. When the crowds had gotten too thick, we'd borrowed a pair of bikes and rode along the Seine, stopping for espresso and croissants at a tiny bakery where the owner didn't give two shits about who we were.

I shake the memory away. There's no use in holding a rotten apple and remembering what it used to taste like.

She takes the seat opposite me, lowering herself as gracefully as a snake, tilting her face to examine the menu before her. "I've apologized a million times, so here's a million-and-one: we're sorry for hurting you, okay? But I don't regret my actions, because it's clear now that you and I don't belong together."

Pretty sure that any apology that comes with an *I don't regret my actions* is moot. Which is why I've never been satisfied with her answers as to what happened at the end. Maybe we didn't call each other as often as we used to. Maybe I didn't send as many bouquets. But it's because I was busy developing my career to keep up with her, to be the type of person she belonged with. Yet she felt like I was distant, that we weren't spending enough time together.

Which is why she had to fuck my brother behind my back, I guess.

And true, they've apologized a million times, but they've also offered a million excuses.

They hadn't meant to cheat...

He'd had feelings for her since high school...

I wasn't meeting her needs...

She'd felt alone in our relationship...

He'd tried to stay out of my way...

Perhaps I'd fallen for someone else...

I wasn't right for her...

I'm sorry, and I'll always be your brother and your number one supporter, but I'm not giving her up.

I'm sorry, but I choose him.

A shutter click sounds—a pap is outside the window. They're all here on Karen's invitation, so they're theoretically on our side, for now.

We bought out the restaurant for the day just to stage this shoot in privacy. It's disgusting, the lengths to which we'll go to reinforce a lie...which was true even when we were together. Things were good between us, but not nearly as good as we'd made them seem. There were days where I couldn't quite tell what was performative and what was real. How much we liked the idea of our relationship versus how much we liked each other, like we'd gone method for too long.

Well, it's unambiguous now. Eliza leans in with a smile, which to an outside observer would seem flirtatious. But I see it for what it is: bloodthirsty. "Tam thinks she set you up. Your blackmailer."

"She didn't." I was the one who invited myself over. She didn't know who I was until later. And if Di's small touches and playful smiles—or that writhing orgasm with my fingers around her neck—were anything but genuine, then she deserves an Oscar, not Eliza.

But that's exactly why I hadn't expected Di to ask for money. She'd promised not to tell anyone, and yet she'd hustled two hundred thousand dollars out of me after the fact. I *did* lie to her, and it was my fault for not getting her to sign an NDA in the first place, but that's like her finding my wallet on the ground and stealing some cash before giving it back. A good person wouldn't do that. Just like a good person wouldn't have charged me fifty dollars for a bag of shrimp chips.

"Was she worth it?" asks Eliza, pretending to stare at her fingernails. But her ears are perked.

"She was." I say it softly, easily, even though I would never pay that much for one night with anyone. Two hundred thousand dollars could've funded two years of that solar energy project I was looking into. Instead, it's going to fund—what, the local goth clubs? The kink scene? What a waste.

Then again, Eliza's expression is priceless. She eyes me over the top of her menu, eyebrows raised. "I don't believe you."

"It's true. I had an amazing time with her."

She purses her lips.

"Look happy," I remind her with real glee.

Her lips snap into a smile, as if someone has yanked the puppet strings on the corners of her mouth. "Why don't you keep it in your pants for the next couple of months, until we're done?"

Hah! "Why? It's not like you're keeping it in your pants."

"Yeah, but I'm not the one getting into trouble for it. You almost blew our cover over some woman who ended up blackmailing you. And anyway, Ethan's your brother, not a stranger. We can trust him." She reaches across the table, puts her hand on mine, which I guess is supposed to be a comforting gesture. I want nothing more than to yank my hand away, but the cameras are still nearby. "I know you don't believe me, but I still care about you. Given our public relationship, the only people who would hook up with you are opportunists. I don't want to see you get hurt."

"If you actually cared about what happened to me, then—"

"Hold on." A waiter walks past with a smile. She snaps the menu shut. "And you'd better not have told your blackmailer about us, either."

"Of course I haven't." Our lawyers, publicists, managers, everyone and their mom have warned us not to rely on NDAs. They're difficult to enforce if you can't prove where the leak came from, and while they might act as a deterrent, accidents happen, and an NDA won't keep the sharks at bay once the news is out. Too many friends and colleagues have been tripped up by leaky networks, including Eliza's parents, whose divorce was announced before they'd even decided to go through with it.

Tam puts it this way: when someone signs an NDA, it's a ticket to one movie, whatever it is they paid for, and not the whole theater, or else you'll be out of money, fast.

The less Di knows, the better. Which is why it's a good thing that she hasn't responded to my DMs, even though I check them every evening before bed. It feels like opening the fridge every night, scanning the shelves, knowing that all that's in there is chicken and kale or some variation thereof.

That's the one saving grace of this fake date: a real meal, though I still have calorie limits.

The waiter approaches, and Eliza turns to him with a dazzling smile. She's got the classic Hollywood look, the Audrey-Hepburn-slash-Grace-Kelly face with large, innocent eyes from her British mother, actress Dame Anne Marie Klein. But she's half-Spanish on her dad's side, which means she has warmer skin, poutier lips, and dark brown hair.

Sexiest Woman of the Year, apparently.

Her profile is sharper now, settled into its ultimate form, but still the same general outline as when I first met her back in tenth grade Chemistry. Still the same lines as when we started dating years later on the set of *Pride & Parallax*.

She's the reason why I'm where I am today. Prince Fucking Charming.

I won't let her be the reason for anything else.

After we place our orders with our overeager waiter, the paparazzi retreat, so I open up social media and start scrolling through Di's pictures again. She doesn't post very many of herself, but the ones she does post are silly or candid, no model poses for her. She's fluid and free, not forced to live within a flipbook of poses.

There's one photo of her in a swimsuit next to a tall Black woman who looks like she could be a runway model. Seeing the two of them together, side by side, only makes it clearer how strange of a couple Di and I would make. The model is more my speed. Di's got great curves and a keen sense of humor, and there's something naughty and exciting about her smile, almost daring. But by the light of day, out from the fog of sadness, alcohol, and weed, it's obvious that we're two halves of completely different pictures.

Still. She was exactly what I needed in the moment...

"What are you smiling at?" asks Eliza.

...and she might be what I need now. "Nothing."

As predicted, her lips thin, while mine curve with real pleasure.

Chapter 10

Di

"I knew that even if you were the last humanoid in the universe, I could never marry you!"

Mischa bursts out laughing. "What the fuck? How did this get so popular?"

"No idea."

But that's not true. We both see how. It's because of *them*.

Playing on my laptop is the movie that launched Darien's career and his relationship with Eliza: *Pride and Parallax*, an epic retelling of *Pride and Prejudice* that takes place in the farthest reaches of space. The writing is cheesy and over the top, but their lingering looks and sparkling laughter make you feel like you're in on the joke. There's an easiness to their banter, a slow-breathing wonder between them that's palpable in every scene, even through the layers of alien makeup and elaborate headpieces.

I'd thought that watching one of his movies might help inspire a design, but so far, all it's inspired is heartburn. I close my laptop and focus on sketching my fifth attempt at something to show to Jill tomorrow. Nothing feels right, not for me nor for Darien, because there's no middle ground between us. I'm techno-chic; he's like if protein powder and a yacht had a baby. Way too preppy and buttoned up for my tastes.

If I'd met him while he was dressed in anything more than his swim trunks, we wouldn't have hooked up.

I'm not sure if that would've been a good thing or a bad thing.

"I kinda like this one." Mischa picks up a drawing of a trench coat with raw edges, a simple, sleeveless, slim-fitted shirt with pants inside, and an oversized hood. "It's so dark. I love the black with those blood-red edges. Very Di."

"It's not very *him*, though. And honestly, it's boring. Not Met-Gala-worthy."

Sitting on the edge of the desk, she leans over me, watching me draw, her thick cloud of curls shading my sketch. "But isn't that how it is with men's clothes? It seems like most guys at the Met wear suits or variations on suits. Anything that's not a suit is already a win."

My pencil scrapes to a halt on the paper. "I guess. But I want something special for my big debut."

"I get it. You want to give it that *Ho factor*."

"Exactly."

She nods as if she knows what that *Ho factor* is. If she does, that makes one of us.

"I guess I'll head out. I know you don't like it when I throw ideas at you." She eases off the desk, gently rattling the large metal tumbler of Rock-It Fuel, the fancy, ultra-caffeinated coffee that she came by to drop off. "But let me know if you need anything at all. You know I've got your back."

The pencil starts to move again. "I know. Thank you."

Mischa's always been there for me, all the way back to the time I'd passed her in the hall at school and she'd complimented me on my new "NIN" shirt, a thrift store find. I hadn't known that it stood for Nine Inch Nails, or that they were a band. I'd just liked that the shirt looked dark and an-gry.

"Hey, you like industrial music?" Overriding snide comments from her friends, she'd reeled me in with a black-banded orthodontic smile and pulled out a CD from her locker. "Listen to this and tell me what you think. You're Di, right?"

The nickname had stuck, and so had she.

Though not quite. Her curls and freckles are still the same, as well as her glowing ochre skin, but her brooding dark-elf energy's been replaced with something less angry, more playful. More at ease with responsibility. She's glided into adulthood like a disco dancer on skates, while I've bumbled in different directions and sucked the whole time, like a Roomba.

I've got a lot of catching up to do.

I chug the tumbler of coffee and glare at the blank paper, hoping to spook some lines out of the void.

Nothing comes. Nothing of worth, anyway.

In the morning, I'm a mess. I'm hardly able to get out of bed in time, so my hair gets thrown up into a ponytail and my falsies don't go on. I barely finish folding up my futon before there's a knock on the door.

My studio apartment is bright and sunny, but tiny. The kitchenette has the least amount of space but the most charm, a white and royal-blue nook with just enough counter space for a hot plate, microwave, and hot water kettle. Steps away are my burnt-orange fold-up futon, white plush chair, and oak dresser, all of which I got from a failed scriptwriter for a steep discount. A few lush, happy plants line the giant windowsill against which I've placed my sewing machine and drafting table, and next to that stands a sewing mannequin. The only thing ruining the vibe is the various bolts of fabric shoved into the corner, beneath the futon, under the desk, everywhere, like we're in an episode of *Hoarders: Crafter's Edition*. Not the most professional space to meet her, but she offered to come by and it's more efficient this way.

I throw open the door. "Hi, Jill, I'm—"

A pang, as if my soul has stumbled out of my body. Darien—wearing a black polo, dark-washed jeans, and a baseball cap with sunglasses—smiles and raises a hand. "Hey."

Nothing comes out of my gaping mouth. It's been a few days since I last saw him. I thought I had gotten him out of my system, but my heart starts kicking like Chun Li. I close the door and watch as he enters my apartment and takes it all in, bringing with him a cloud of some spicy, musky scent that he wasn't wearing before.

Last time.

Naked, thrusting, sweaty—

"Where's Jill?" It comes out harsher than I intend.

"I let her off the hook." He takes off his shades and his baseball cap, and it's him again—cut cheeks, back-swept hair, piercing eyes, teasing lips. Lips that I've tasted, and touched, and *ground myself against—*

Asshole. "Why?"

He picks up a sheet of paper with a few discarded sketches, but I snatch it away before he can really look. I face him, keeping my back to the walls as if he's a wild bat who's gotten in by accident.

"Because she's busy, and expensive, and because then she won't be blamed if I look terrible. It'll all be my fault."

He doesn't have to say it, but I hear the "and yours" at the end of his statement.

"You won't look terrible."

"I know. I won't." He smirks like he's fashion-invincible, as if he thinks he could make a plastic shower curtain look good. Unfortunately for him, that's not how fashion works, though a shower curtain might be an improvement over his current alpha-Chad getup.

What happened to the weird theater kid who liked shrimp chips and video games? The guy in front of me screams L.A. narcissist.

But I guess this is the real Darien, not Hayden or whoever he was that night.

Not who I'd hoped.

He cranes his neck like a museum visitor, seeing what else there is to look at. I reach out and turn him to face me, my hand flinching away from the hot, smooth skin of his forearm, but I need him to look me dead in the eyeballs and tell me the truth. "Seriously, though, what are you doing here? I agreed to talk to your stylist, not you."

His eyes drift up from my hand to my face. "Why didn't you reply to my DMs?"

"Uh, why did you lie to me and cheat on your partner?" Though, actually, I hadn't seen any DMs. I'd muted my notifications, because the only thing they'd notified me of was more verbal dysentery from Dariza stans.

He lets out a huffed laugh. "You're one to talk." He takes a step closer, and though my anger is front and center, searing the air between us, the room tilts forward. I have to lean back to avoid falling into him, and it's only then that I realize I can hear my own breaths, rasping over the silk of his voice. "As soon as you found out who I was, you demanded hundreds of thousands of dollars from me."

"Your manager approached *me*. And the only reason why she had to *bribe me* was because you're fucking engaged to someone else!"

I'm close enough to see the pores on his face. Not so perfect after all. But he leans even closer—close enough to head butt, or lick—and says softly, "Don't judge me when you don't have all the facts."

God, he's warm, and much too close. But I focus on his words. The facts? They're engaged, he lied about who he was, he put his dick in me. Case closed.

But his gaze is solid, clear, and I'm back in a sea of doubts. It's a familiar place, one that I loathe with all my heart. I've scared off more than one person with my suspicions and accusations, but can you blame me when I've been cheated on three fucking times?

And now, *this* guy. If he didn't cheat on her, then why all the secrecy? "I signed an NDA, remember? So enlighten me. What are the facts?"

He stares at me for a moment, scanning my face, but then there's a pinch of something raw, a painful thrash beneath the surface before his gaze slips away. It reminds me of the slump-shouldered, sighing man from that night. He's in there, trapped in this caricature of a dude-bro, this overinflated sausage casing.

But before I can cut him free, Darien closes his eyes, and when they open again, they're vacant and boarded up. Dude-bro has won. "It's better if you don't know."

"Better for whom?"

"For everyone."

Bro, really? Why hint at *the facts* and then give me nothing? We fucked and signed a contract, so I think it's better for *me* to know what he's dragged me into. And after what we shared that night, doesn't he know that no one wants to believe in him more than I do?

But if this is how he wants to play it, I'm not going to beg. "Fine, don't tell me. But I'm going to keep assuming that you're a liar and a cheater."

He opens his mouth as if to argue, but instead, takes a deep, shuddering breath and pauses—unsure or unwilling to say what's next? "For what it's worth, I *am* sorry. I didn't mean to leave that day without telling you who I was."

I cross my arms over my chest and lean into a hip. "Then why did you?"

"My sister went into premature labor. She doesn't have a partner, so the plan was for me to be available these next few weeks to help take care of her. You know, drive her to the hospital and get her anything she needed. But by the time I checked my messages in the morning, she was already at the hospital getting an emergency C-section."

My face unscrews itself, wiped smooth with shock. "Is she okay?"

"Yeah, she's fine now. But I should've been there for her, you know? Instead, I was...distracted." Again, that ghost flickers in his eyes. "Anyway, I'm sorry for not telling you who I was. Though I'm not sure how you didn't know. My face is plastered all over the city."

I walk to the kitchenette, three apartment-rattling steps. "Your hair is shorter in those images, and I'm not good with faces. And even if I had known who you were, I wouldn't have treated you any differently."

"Ah, so you still would've charged me fifty dollars for a bag of chips?"

"Yes." I pour myself some coffee from the French press and take a long, noisy sip. "Which you still haven't paid me for. And honestly? I would have given them to you if you'd just said *please*."

He frowns as if trying to remember our conversation. "I never said please?"

"No."

"You sure?"

"Yes, I specifically waited for it."

"Huh. Well, I'd hope the two hundred thousand covers the cost, at least."

The tips of my ears go hot. "It doesn't. Those were separate agreements."

"I see." But he glances around the room again, taking in the worn furniture and cramped environment with a passive, almost clinical expression. Is he judging me, or trying to understand?

I lift the mug to my face with both hands, covering my mouth. Printed on the side of the mug is a grizzled woman holding a shovel and smoking a cigarette: *Gravedigger Barbie*. An old gift from Mischa, the perfect thing to hide behind as I ask the question I've wondered most.

"That night...what you told me. Was any of it real?"

Our gazes lock over the mug.

"I do like shrimp chips," he says after a moment. "That's real."

I'm surprised his skin doesn't boil and explode under my glare. But then he continues, "So is everything else I said. I meant every word and...everything. Except my name."

Everything. The way he says it, it almost aches, like he's thought about that night as much as I have.

Slowly, my shoulders relax. I lower the mug to the table. "But you're actually engaged."

The tiniest pause. "Yes."

"But you didn't cheat."

He starts to shake his head, but says, "I can't tell you anything."

"Are you in an open relationship?"

He frowns, but doesn't respond.

"I signed an NDA. If I tell anyone *anything* about you, I'd have to sell my organs just to pay you back."

"Exactly. Can you honestly say that you haven't told a single soul about what happened between us? No family or friends?"

"Yeah, I can." Mischa doesn't count. She's not family or a friend, but something in between. And she would never, ever talk about my business to someone else.

Still. My kidneys twitch, and I think he can sense it.

"I know it must be frustrating for you," he says finally, "but I'd be grateful for the privacy. I don't get much of it these days."

I straighten and turn away from him, disappointed. "Yeah, well, I'm getting scrutinized, too, thanks to this."

"I'm sorry," he says quietly. "Really. But that's why I'd rather not tell you more than you need to know. In this day and age, even if you mean well, accidents happen, and in this case, we can't risk it."

Whatever. I kind of get it. The fact that he's hiding anything at all implies that it's not sunshine and rainbows between them, and with millions of people watching their every move, I'd probably be careful too. It's not personal, it's just business, and at the end of the day, after all I've seen and heard, he doesn't seem like the kind of guy who would do something to hurt his fiancée.

Then again, Attila looks like a puff of sugar and not Frank from *Donnie Darko*.

"Anyway." I chug the rest of the coffee and put the mug by the sink. "Do I need to make a new appointment with Jill, or are you going to make the call on this look?"

"I'll do it."

"Fine." I gesture for him to sit down, while I end up shuffling piles of pattern books and papers around, kicking bolts of fabric back under the futon, working to refocus my energies. He's not here for me, he's here for work, and I won't forget it again.

I take a slow, bracing breath and turn around, handing him the three best sketches from last night. Or, you know, the three least shitty. "About the look. I know that you usually wear a tux, but I took the liberty of putting a few new ideas together. This year's theme is the Military Conquest of Fashion, so these all—"

"Don't look anything like what I usually wear."

I blink down at the three drawings: a jacquard military-style jacket with flowing trousers, a shredded asymmetrical cape with faux-bloodied suit, and Mischa's favorite, the Gothic trench coat. "And?"

"Didn't Tam tell you that I wanted a tux?"

My neck prickles. Bad prickles. "She said the word tux, but I thought she meant that generally, like she was referring to a men's look. I mean, it's the Met Gala, so the point is to meet the prompt, right?"

He dares to raise an eyebrow at me, but I stare him down, channeling Mrs. Axe. Mrs. Axe didn't take shit from us in third grade.

But none of us kids had ever been on magazine covers, or had a gaze that turns my insides to hot jelly.

"The prompt is optional. More importantly, tuxes are my thing."

"Your thing?"

"Yeah. They're classic, simple, and I look good in them. I always wear a tux."

His mouth is moving, but all that's coming out is hot air. "I was told to design *a look* for you."

He shrugs and crosses his arms and ankles, effortlessly taking up half my apartment. "There are plenty of ways to customize a tux. The fabric, the details, like the cuffs or a pocket square. Won't making a tux be easier for you, too?"

Am I speaking another language? Why are our words sliding past each other? "The contract says that I'm designing a personalized look for you. Me. You don't get to tell me what to make."

"Did you read the contract?"

"No, I didn't, I just signed my life away without checking."

"Okay, well, did you see the part about designing a look to specifications?"

To specifications. The phrase sounds familiar, so it's probably in there, like he says. But I'd assumed it meant that I had to tailor the design to his correct size. If they meant to specify the design itself, then...

Anger simmers on my skin. "If you're saying what I think you're saying, then that's not fair. I get to design a custom look for you. It's my design, not yours."

"Read the contract again."

"But—"

"Read it."

Stifling a groan, I pull up a copy of the contract on my phone and begin to read the fine print.

...agrees that garments will meet all specifications as required by Darien Lee and parties authorized to act on his behalf...

And his requirement is that I make *a simple tux.*

A tux.

The problem is, I don't *want* to make a tux.

"I'm not making you a tux."

"Then don't, I guess. But if that's the case, then I won't have to wear it."

Is that really how it is? The contract was long and full of legalese, but I couldn't have misinterpreted it that badly, right? "The story is, I'm your friend and you're helping me, right? How am I going to debut my fashion line with something that's the exact opposite of my aesthetic?"

He shrugs. "Those are my requirements, and you signed the contract."

I want to take him by the collar and shake him, wipe that stupid placid look away...but he's right. My signature is all over that document. I'm the one who signed it without asking for clarification. I'm the one who was too excited to spot the trap. Me.

So instead of shaking him, I turn my gaze from Broil to Off and take a deep breath. "I can make you something better than a tux. I promise, you'll look great, just...please. Tuxes aren't *my* thing."

There's a brief flash, a shooting star of empathy across his features. But he only says, "You read the contract. You signed the contract—"

"Then what can I do to change the terms? There has to be a way."

He shakes his head. "You already signed it," he repeats. "And I know it's not ideal, but I have to protect my brand."

"Come on, Darien. Please." I sit down next to him. There's a caring person in there, I can sense it, the same way my mom believes that dogs can sense ghosts. "There has to be something I can do."

Something. Anything.

Anything at all...

Oh so slowly, his eyes drift down to my lips. I have to fight the dry, itchy urge to lick them, to ask him if any of the filthy, sweaty, writhing possibilities flashing through my head will help change his mind.

But I'm being ridiculous. Sex never solves anything, except horniness. But if he keeps staring at me like that—

He blinks and shakes his head. "My team and I work hard to curate my brand. I need a tux."

His brand. His stupid, pointless brand. Rom-Com Default? Asian Alpha Bro? Barbie's Booty Call? It's not even who he really is—

Lightning strikes. I turn towards him, knocking my knees against his thigh, but I need to get this out too much and don't care how incredibly hard and...and hot it is. "What if you give me a chance? Let me design something for you, the *real* you."

He begins to shake his head again, but freezes when I take his callused hand.

"You'll get to approve it. I'll make sure you look good, and it will meet the prompt, too. But let me make something true to both of us, to me *and* you. Let me try, and..." I squeeze his meaty hand, trying to squeeze even a drop of warm compassion out of him. "If you don't end up liking it, you can wear a tux by some other designer. Or whatever you want."

Regret hits as soon as I say the words. But he needs to believe that I can do this even more than I do. He needs to see how serious I am. Dead serious.

A miracle: he cracks a smile, and his fingers close around mine, warm and familiar. "You really hate tuxes, huh?"

"No, I just don't want to compromise on my vision, or my taste. And I honestly believe that I'll be able to make something you'll like that won't embarrass you. But you have to give me a fair chance. You have to trust that I can succeed."

I hold my breath, suspending the flock of doubts from flying in, but I can see them hovering, waiting to strike.

Slowly, he begins to nod. "Okay. Fair."

"Yes! Thank you." I jerk forward and just barely stop myself from hugging him. *Keep it professional.*

"I'll consider your design. If it doesn't work for me, I'll wear someone else's." He looks down at our hands and squeezes once, almost regretfully, before letting go.

I fold my hands back into my lap. "You're going to love it, I promise."

But the doubts still hover nearby. Because a month isn't long, and how well do I really know this guy?

At the very least, I have to try.

When I look up, he's studying me like I'm a CAPTCHA test, and he's scanning my face for bridges or traffic lights. I wipe my feelings and give him a determined nod. But it must not be convincing, because on the way out the door, he turns and pins me with his gaze.

"I want you to know that no matter what happens, I'll do my best to help you with your business. I know some people in the fashion world. Maybe I can introduce you."

A tiny stitch in my heart gets pulled tight. "Thank you, Darien."

He leaves soon after, but it's like a fighter jet has flown through and my body still vibrates in the wake of him.

He was so...so *close*. And almost reasonable. Kind. Like, yes, he's hiding stuff from me, and his chosen persona is Kirkland Boneless Skinless Chicken Breast - Pack of Six. But I saw it, the outline of him. The sweet, funny person I'd cuddled and listened to music with is still in there, hiding behind layers of muscle and contracts.

Completely inaccessible...and it's for the best.

Chapter 11

Darien

"Something wrong?"

I snap out of it and glance across at Tam. It's my private home office, but I gave her the chair behind the desk instead of in front, as always. "Sorry, I'm back on the two-a-day workout plan. Still adjusting my sleep schedule."

"Yeah, well, try to pay attention, I only have thirty minutes."

"I know."

She taps her pen on the paper, a *tat-tat-tat* that counts the seconds of our meeting. "Sammy said you still haven't gotten back to him."

"I haven't had a chance to." Not with all the working out, video games, and napping I have to do. "I'll get back to him next week."

"Good. It's important. You need to have something lined up before July so that we can pre-empt the scandal."

"You mean, distract people from the news?"

"Yes. But also, to demonstrate that there are no hard feelings. You're landing jobs, dating, et cetera. Carrying on as usual. Not depressed."

Oh yes, rising above and moving on. Like six years and betrayal are just dog turds on the sidewalk.

Tam gives me a sympathetic smile. "Just focus on work and you'll be back to normal in no time."

She tells me to focus on work like there's anything *to* focus. Like there's any mental or emotional energy left that isn't used up by doing the bare minimum, eating and exercising and lying down.

She gave me the same advice two months ago, back when I'd wanted to cancel the press tour for *Icarus*. So I'd worked, filling my time to try to numb the pain. But there's plenty of time to pick at scabs while sitting on planes, waiting in cars, and eating in hotel rooms alone. Being on set will likely be better, but harder, because acting isn't like other jobs, where you can half-ass a smile and get by. Half-assed in 4K resolution, 24 frames per second means millions of angry notifications, a parade of ant bites that continues well after your carcass is clean.

Tam turns her phone around for me to look at. "I have the list of scripts here, I marked the ones that—"

"Honestly, I looked at them already. And I'm not interested in picking up work right now."

She blinks with studied patience. "But you'll miss out on these opportunities."

"I'm not missing out on anything. I skimmed through them and there's nothing new, nothing exciting."

"What? What's more exciting than that *Batman* reboot?"

"You mean *Batmen*, the one where Batman has to fight *himself*? No thanks. How many *Batman* reboots do we need?"

"You know the answer: however many people are willing to pay to see."

"It's been done a million times. Maybe not with an Asian Bruce Wayne, but I don't really care to have that privilege."

Tam gives me a knowing look. "It won't be another Darcy debacle, if that's what you're worried about."

"It would definitely be another Darcy debacle, but that's not why I'm not interested."

The Darcy debacle, #notmydarcy, a campaign that started years ago when I was cast in the starring role for *Pride and Parallax*. I wasn't the original actor cast as the alien Darcy, I was a replacement for Jacob Beauford, British heartthrob, a gangly, pasty, tousle-haired man with piercing blue eyes.

The response to the announcement was utterly predictable.

I wanna give whoever thought this was a good idea a punch in the face #notmydarcy

Stop trying to be wOkE hollywood, you won't get my money that way. #notmydarcy

Why do they feel the need to make it so historically inaccurate #notmydarcy

My good opinion once lost is lost forever. F this movie #notmydarcy

I was criticized for being too "modern," not hot enough, not broody enough, and also...Asian. People sent explicitly racist messages directly into my inbox, telling me in no uncertain terms that I didn't belong in the movie, in America, on this planet. Which is funny, because the retelling took place in space, for fuck's sake. So white aliens are okay, but not Asian ones?

An Asian Bruce Wayne would crack the internet.

Anyway, I'm not looking to stand where white people once stood. I'd rather go somewhere no one's ever been.

"What about that rom-com adaptation, the one about rock climbers in New York City?"

"No. The main character is too perfect. Boring. I'm tired of playing that kind of guy." The role fits like a cashmere sweater that's been through the dryer. Better for someone smaller and younger.

Tam snaps open another can of Diet Pepsi, probably her third today. "Which is why it'd be easy for you, and why your fans would love it. Classic Darien would be a nice palate cleanser after all the new roles you've been trying. And besides, you'd be starring opposite Madison Lin, who by the way, is *single*." Her eyebrows jump Double Dutch.

"I don't need you to find me a new girlfriend."

"I know you don't need me to, but as your manager, I feel obligated to tell you that Madison would be a great candidate. She's pretty, popular, a bit new in her career, but I see her going places. And the two of you would make a cute couple."

Because we're both Asian?

I brush away the thought. Tam doesn't think like that. First of all, she's Indonesian, so she probably gets it. Second, she's the kind of manager who specifically seeks diverse talent. She knows the industry inside out, but she's the best at her job because she knows how to steer her clients.

I've just been thinking about that part of my identity for too long, like it's the only thing that matters anymore. Like it's all anyone ever sees.

"She's from SoCal, just like you. She likes musicals and the Lakers and running in the mountains. You two would get along great."

My frown grows deeper with each item on the list. "I don't know. I'm sure she's nice, but I'm not ready for that yet."

"Yeah? You're ready to hook up with some random fashion designer, but that's it?"

"Yeah, actually." Though hooking up with Di hadn't been much of a choice. It was more like she was a shiny EV station that appeared just as my car rolled to a dead stop. It didn't matter whether she liked musicals or the Lakers or running in the mountains. What mattered was that she was funny, and caring, and everything I needed to get away.

"I know you might not be ready for a while, but it'll be better for you if you move on quickly. And I've told you this a thousand times, but make sure you date someone else in the industry. Doesn't have to be an actor, could be a musician or some other celebrity, but they need to be able to understand your lifestyle. The pressure, the public, the privacy concerns, all of it."

"Yeah, I know." Though I wonder if she gives Eliza this advice. Aside from his association with me, Ethan the astrophysics professor is as far from fame as you can get.

Tam steeples her fingers and slides them through each other like carving forks. "Then why do I get the feeling that you're still thinking about that clout-chaser?"

"I'm not." But Di's smile and quiet laughter replay in my head, as easy and pleasant to recall as the taste of shrimp chips.

"Good."

"But can I ask you a question?"

"Shoot."

"Before you were my manager, back when you only represented Eliza...did you think that I was a clout-chaser, too?"

Tam lets out a surprised laugh and taps her pen on the paper again, a quick staccato. "No, of course not. Why would you think that?"

"Just wondering."

"I wasn't worried about you being a clout-chaser. If anything, I was worried that you didn't want it *enough*."

"It's not that I didn't want it. At the time, I was more interested in indie films."

"Right—"

"And I still am. The indie films, I mean. Which is why, at some point, I'd like to talk to Sammy about putting my name out there for smaller, more interesting projects. Maybe later, after I've had a few months to cool down."

"Oh, psh. For someone of your caliber, there will always be indie movies. You'll have your chance later. Trust me, if you want to weather this announcement with Eliza, you'll have to come out strong. You won't want to look like you've lost any momentum at all. Get people excited about your next project, don't let them grieve. You get it, right?"

I open my mouth to object, but let out a sigh instead. Tam's the best of the best, and if she tells me a big project is the only thing that will help me weather the storm, then I need a big project. "Yeah, I get it."

She smiles. "I'm excited to see where you'll go from here."

That makes one of us.

* * *

The Bel Air house that I own with Eliza is a glass and stone monstrosity, sold to us as a "contemporary architectural triumph." It's listed as a six bedroom home, but with nine bathrooms, a home theater, wine cellar, game room, gym, and two open terraces, it could fit two or three of my childhood home inside, for ten times the cost. Eliza had insisted on as much space as feasibly possible. The plan was for us to have at least one, at most three kids, plus room for guests, room for hosting, and room to roam. When we'd gotten it, I'd thought it'd be big enough to host a cult, but with two bitter adults inside, it feels more like a Blood Dome. Though Eliza has left to resume her press tour, so it's just solitary confinement today.

I've already worked out, swum in the pool, and half-heartedly flipped through the scripts again, but I have the attention span of a bird in a swarm of bees. My vision feels gray and flat, and when I stare at my phone, contemplating the few people I can talk to, my breath comes fast and shallow.

There's only one person on that list who isn't Eliza's friend, too.

Darien: Hey, just checking in. How's it going?

Di: good. making progress on your look

Darien: Nice. What's it look like so far?

I shatter the silence with laughter at her response.

Di: it's a leather bondage suit

Di: there's a mouth hole

Di: for shrimp chips

Di: why, what are you up to?

Di: swimming in a pile of gold?

Darien: I'm not Scrooge McDuck.

Darien: I have an interview today. Last one where I have to promote Icarus.

It's the end of the press tour, so I've already been asked every possible question about *Icarus*. I've honed my answers and filled my quiver with witty one-liners. But this is the first time I've spoken to the press since Di and I became "friends." Like always, Karen, my publicist, has coached me on what to say, but I usually spend hours obsessing on my own before these types of events, shaky and on the verge of throwing up right until the moment I put on my smile and go on.

But with every new text from Di, my thoughts go sideways.

Di: I saw an ad for that movie on a bus bench today

Di: how does it feel to have all of LA sitting on your face

I burst out laughing, and before I can think, type, *Been thinking about sitting on my face?*

My smile slowly slips as I imagine Di staring down at me, biting her thick lower lip and riding me. The taste of her, the softness of her thighs, her deep whimpers, riding, riding—

Followed by another two-hundred-thousand-dollar invoice.

I delete the message and send something else.

Darien: How does it feel to have the last name Ho?

Di: oh god. I've heard every Ho pun under the sun

Di: hated that Ludacris song

Darien: I forgot about that song

Darien: "ho-asis" and "ho-zone layer"

Darien: Inspired lyrics

Di: ugh

Di: I once got into a fight with a girl who wouldn't stop singing that first line at me

Di: "who's a ho? ho!"

Darien: Like a real fight? What happened?

Di: I sang back "who's a bitch" to the same tune and she pushed me

Di: I pushed her back

Di: but before I could break her face, my friend Mischa came and pulled me away

Darien: Good friend.

Di: I dunno, sometimes it feels like she holds me back

Darien: lol

My thumbs leap from letter to letter, and soon we're replying to each other's messages out of order because we have too much to say, too much to joke about. She's only being polite, or maybe trying to get ideas for her design, but I make a point to ask her questions, too. I've spent the last few months like a bird in a cuckoo clock, coming out to do my job but hiding otherwise. The push and pull of our conversation feels like the gentle sway of a hammock, and not the one-sided yanking of an interview. It feels *normal*, which is a rare thing in my life these days.

Di: can I just call you? it'd be faster to talk

Di: unless you're one of those anti-phone millennials

I wander down to the warm, sun-filled living room where the cell service is better. She picks up on the first ring.

"I'm not an anti-phone Millennial, but I sometimes wish I had a dumb phone instead of a smart one."

"That almost sounds like Boomer talk," she says, and my eyes sink closed to better listen. "Do you also prefer vinyl records over streaming services?"

"Obviously. Kids these days don't know how to listen to *real* music."

She lets out that distinctive crackle that has me nestling my neck into the couch cushions. It takes me back to the bed we shared, to the teasing, half-veiled smiles and helpless laughter, the unique static-like tingling conjured by her voice.

"Can you sing, Di?"

"Me? No. I sound like a wheezing toad."

"Really? I would've thought you'd have a beautiful singing voice."

Her chuckle tells me I'm tragically wrong. "No. Total toad. Why do you ask?"

"No reason." Though I still don't believe her. We'll see. "What did you want to ask me?"

"Oh, um..." She pauses. "Could you just, like, talk about yourself? Like, what are the most important things I should know about you?"

"Why don't you look at my Wikipedia page?"

"Are you saying that's all you are?"

"No, but it's a good place to start."

"I read it already. I know about your movies, your philanthropy, your...relationship with Eliza." She says that last bit almost through her teeth. "Was she really your only long-term girlfriend?"

My eyes slide open, and I'm back in a huge, empty house that smells of lilac perfume. "Yes."

Not for lack of trying. Dating had felt like swimming in a race, with some women too slow, some women too fast. Eliza kept pace. She understood where I was going. She was just right, at the time.

"I see." Di clears her throat. "So…there's one thing I've been really curious about."

She's going to ask me about Eliza.

She's going to question why we got together, how we lasted for six years, why it ended—

"Why did you agree to pay fifty dollars for a bag of shrimp chips? Do you really like them that much?"

I let out a surprised breath. "You've tasted them. You know how good they are."

"Yeah, but enough to ruin your day by talking to me?"

"You didn't ruin my day. You made my night." When she doesn't respond, I continue, "I guess maybe my actions were a bit extreme, but shrimp chips are special. Every Sunday, after going to the Asian grocery store, my dad and I used to split a bag on the car ride home. It was our thing."

Which is why, for a long time, I couldn't eat them. It took years before the flavor brought me comfort rather than pain.

There's a smile in her voice. "For me, it was those chocolate-filled pandas. Though my mom and sister prefer the strawberry ones."

"Oh, I do, too. Strawberry's better."

"What, really? What about Pocky?"

"Same. Yan Yan too."

She clucks her tongue. "Well, now that I know your disgusting snack preferences, I guess I have everything I need to make your look. I'm thinking a trash bag filled with actual trash?"

"You mean, filled with chocolate Pocky?"

"No, I mean filled with your current wardrobe."

"Ooh, ouch." Though honestly, my wardrobe is ninety-nine percent sponsored and one percent ugly sweaters that Claire's knitted for me. The trash can have it all.

She asks me about the music that I like, famous people I know, what it was like to become a famous person myself. I tell her about the indie bands I wish I could see in person, my actor and musician friends, and getting used to going out with a security detail, the loneliness of having no privacy except at home.

"...even when I was at the hospital, people mobbed me. Like, give me and my family a break, you know? No one wants to have their privacy invaded, especially in such a sensitive space."

"That sucks. Does that mean that, except for work, you never leave the house?"

"These days, pretty much. I only leave when I need to."

"Well, what about yesterday, when you were here at my place? Was there a security guard somewhere?"

"No, it was just me. I do go out on my own sometimes. There are ways for me to hide in plain sight. But I'll admit, I was anxious driving over, and I was checking up and down the street before I got out of the car."

"Then why'd you risk it?"

"Because. You weren't responding to my messages, so I needed to see you again. To clear the air."

"Oh." She clears her throat, but when she speaks again, she's strangely subdued. "I'm glad you did."

"But…?"

"Oh, I'm just imagining what it must feel like to never be invisible. And I get pretty pissed when my family gets too nosy about my life. I think I'd lose my shit if there were millions of people prying instead of two."

"Now you know why I was so happy when you didn't know who I was, and why I didn't want to tell you the truth."

"I see," she says softly. "Not because you were cheating?"

My smile fades. The conversation's been smooth sailing, but that comment hits like an iceberg. "I wasn't. But also, no comment."

"Right."

She drops it. We move on. We talk a bit longer, until I have to head off to Fairfax for the interview.

On the way over, in the backseat of yet another black Escalade, I replay our conversation in my head. Each detail I'd shared fills my stomach with more lead.

She treats me like a normal person, and it's too easy to forget that I'm not. Too tempting.

I need to be more careful.

Nothing is likely to happen, but as Tam reminded me, laypeople don't have the same awareness or sense of priorities that other celebrities do.

Ninety percent of me trusts her.

The other ten percent, waits.

Chapter 12

Di

Mischa gives me a narrow-eyed look. "Sounds fishy."

I agree. But whatever the reason is, at least it hasn't been a burden. Chatting with him this afternoon had actually been kind of...fun? And while I still have no idea what's going on with Eliza, there *were* social media photos of him at the hospital recently, so his story about why he left checks out. Maybe he's telling the truth, about everything.

Or maybe he's a better liar than I thought.

"I just don't understand what the deal is between him and Eliza," continues Mischa, crossing her arms. She's dressed in a black wide-legged jumpsuit with geometric cutouts and dozens of silver bracelets. I spot a few anatomical body parts among the thick chains.

"I tried to get it out of him, but he wouldn't say. He was pretty adamant that he hadn't cheated on her, though."

"Do you think they're not really dating?" Mischa shakes her head. "And it's been years! Do you think they could have been faking all this time?"

"Maybe something's changed. And they *are* actors." I sit down at my desk and stare at a fresh page, waiting for the lines to draw themselves.

"Maybe they broke up," says Mischa. "Maybe he's using you to make her jealous."

I almost snort. "*Me?* Why would the Sexiest Woman Alive be jealous of me?"

"Who even votes on those things? Creepy internet dudes? They're meaningless. You're sexy as fuck."

I strike a pose, eyes flat, shoulders raised, bending my elbows to cup and lift my tits. "What, this?"

"Unngh, girl, *work it*." Mischa pulls out her phone and snaps a pic. "Hawt."

She shows me the picture and we both laugh. "This is going in as your new profile pic."

"Wow, thanks."

She taps her phone a few times, smiling. Mischa always had the most gorgeous smile, with even teeth and cheekbones to die for, literally die. *She* should be Sexiest Woman of the Year, not Eliza.

Actually, no, *no one* should be Sexiest Woman of the Year, because women shouldn't be rated and ranked on their sex appeal.

"I just hope that you don't get blamed for whatever drama is happening between them. Dariza stans are not a nice group of people."

"Yeah, I know. They sent me some friendly warnings. By which I mean, borderline illegal threats."

In graphic detail. After Darien mentioned his DMs to me, I'd taken a peek and gotten stabbed in the eyes with every insult under the moon. Ugly. Bitch. Slut. Whore. Synonyms, misspelled, lobbed in different languages even, like they'd enlisted the help of Google Translate to make sure my "oriental" ass got the message loud and clear. English is my first fucking language. I'd typed out one scathing response with perfect fucking grammar, but then erased it, the cursor whisking the words away like a magic wand. What was the point? Why waste my time on any of them?

And even if I'd wanted to, I couldn't. Not when I'd signed my voice away like Ariel for a pair of useless legs.

Thank god for weed gummies.

"Ugh. People are such shit-heads."

"Yeah. Anyway, I'm sure it'll blow over soon." I hesitate over my next question, spinning a pen across my fingers, watching as she taps around on her phone. I'm a thousand percent positive that she's checking my socials for troll-holes and preparing to wreck them. "I know that you wouldn't, but I have to check because Darien was acting all weird about it—you're not going to tell anyone about what we've discussed, right?"

She gives me a flat-eyed look. "You asked me not to tell anyone and I haven't. Not even John. I'll take it to the grave."

As I'd thought. "Thank you. Sorry to ask, he was just being a pain about it. And if it gets back to me, I'll have to sell my feet."

"You mean, feet *pics?*"

"You heard me."

She laughs. "If it comes to that, I'll get you the hottest pair of studded leather peg legs that money can buy."

"Aww, thanks, babe." I beam her a wave of undying love. "Anyway, I only need to deal with him until he wears my look to the Met Gala. I'll launch my line that night, and then we'll be done."

"Really? That's launch night?"

"Yep."

Mischa looks around the living room, frowning. "Wait, but I thought you said you weren't done with the samples yet? How are you going to get inventory ready in time?"

"That's the thing—I'm going to make samples and do pre-orders. Everything will be made-to-order and sent out later. It's more sustainable that way."

"Will people be willing to wait that long? And won't the clothes be expensive?"

"Yeah, but these garments are meant to last forever. They'll be worth it, unlike all that cheap crap at the mall. And with the money I got from Darien, I can afford to offer slightly lower prices, at least for this initial run, and possibly hire an assistant to help me once the pre-orders are in." I just hope that my instincts are right and people have become eco-conscious enough to put their money where their mouths are.

If I'd opted to go the usual fast-fashion route, I could've had a line long ago. Multiple lines. It's so easy to start your own fashion brand these days, which is why social media is clogged full of ads for cute, trendy stuff that costs a few bucks to make overseas, which then inevitably ends up in the dump. But I'm not interested in creating a line like that. One of the cool things about having a mom who sews is that I learned how to fix and alter my own clothing, to create clothes that are almost modular, transformable. And with the goth-inspired streetwear that I make, trends are much slower, and vintage is always in. My clothes will be made to last and last, and hopefully, so will my brand.

Which is why I need to make headlines with Darien's look at the Met. If I can finish my samples, design and finish

Darien's look, and set up my website, all before the Met Gala in three weeks, maybe it'll be enough. Maybe it'll mean I can stay in L.A. with my best friend and keep doing what I love.

"Do you need a photographer for the website photos?" She gives me an expectant smile. Now that she's in her 30s, she's transitioning out from in front of the camera to behind it.

"Yes. And all your model friends, please. In a variety of sizes."

"You know I've got you," she says. "I'll ask everyone. And I know just where to shoot it, too..."

Everyone. Alan, Carina, Ella, Opal, Donny, et cetera, her charmingly over-the-top colleagues from modeling. I'd met them at dinners and events that Mischa's put on, her glamorous friends who party way harder than I do, who dress in dazzling colors and flaunt their tiny flaws like prized jewels. She and I make a point to see each other at least once every couple of weeks, but *they* go out for drinks all the time, and she sees them often for work, either modeling beside them or building up her portfolio by shooting them. I have an open invitation to join for drinks, but eighteen-dollar cocktails and feeling like the old pair of boots on the shelf is not my idea of a good time.

Whatever, it's fine. Mischa deserves a happy, healthy social life. She's cut out for it; not all of us are. Some of us are destined to become scary plant ladies like Poison Ivy.

My phone buzzes and pops the mental image of me cackling in a scarlet wig and green body suit. Darien's sent me a list of "I'm so goth" jokes. I'd worried that I might've said something wrong last night, but after texting him this morning with a listicle about why chocolate Pocky reigns supreme, he seemed fine.

Not that it matters to me what he thinks.

I read a few out loud to Mischa. "I'm so goth, I menstruate oil."

"Hahaha, ew."

"I'm so goth, I make onions cry."

"Eh. I feel like that's more emo than goth."

"I'm so goth that I'm not goth."

"*Ahhh*, nice. Where are you getting these from?"

I turn away so that she can't see my face. "Darien sent them to me."

She leans over the desk and lowers herself until she can study my expression. I keep calm and focus on drawing random clothes-like lines on the sheet.

"Holy shit, you like him!"

I give her my deadest stare. "He's a liar and a basic bro. Why would I like him?"

"Wow. Di! He's so not your type."

True. He's not a Japanese tattoo artist or Argentinian metal drummer or any of the other cool bad boys I've fallen for in the past. Which is how I know that this itch will pass, and scratching will only make it worse.

"He didn't care that you almost-kinda-unintentionally blackmailed him?"

"Not that I can tell." After finding out that he maybe *didn't* cheat, that maybe he *is* a decent person, I've alternated between shrugging it off and feeling like I've eaten a bucket of fried guilt. But besides that one time, he hasn't mentioned the money. Surely he can afford it, right? "And I'm not an idiot. He's cute, and funny, but he's fucking *engaged*. I know better than to get caught up in whatever bullshit his life is."

"Do you?" she asks softly. "Seems like you're already caught up in it."

I don't respond except to pick up my pencil and start to sketch again.

But I can't help but worry that she's right.

* * *

Wrong. It's all wrong.

My pencil's a stub, my hands are cramping, and nothing is coming out. Every time I draw something, it echoes garments I've already made in the past. No matter how much I stare at Darien or look for inspiration, my well is bone dry.

The more I see his smile—the same smile, over and over, always tilting his face as if he favors his right—the more plastic he seems, so unlike the warm, fleshy human from that night. And I've never seen him wear anything even remotely interesting. He always looks like he's just left a dinner or a garden party, which is probably because he's paid by dozens of companies to look that way and sell their products. And of the two years that he's been to the Met Gala, he's always worn a black tux. One of them had a black dress shirt, which is at least a slight improvement over a classic tux. But as hard as I fought for it, I have three weeks to complete a non-tux look, and nothing is fucking coming out.

I open my laptop and go over to YouTube, where I type his name into the search bar. The top results are recent interviews he's done on late night shows to promote his latest movie, *Agents of Icarus*. I listen to one for a minute, scrub through, then click back to find a different video, and another one, skipping over the ones with both him and Eliza.

One called "Darien Lee's Private Pickle Obsession" catches my eye. It's from a couple of months ago, and it takes us through his path to stardom, from high school theater club to landing random gigs in college, including as a pickle addict in a commercial for *Happily Ever After* brand's "Spicy Dill Big Boys." It wasn't until after college that he became famous, starring opposite Eliza in *Pride & Parallax*. People loved them so much that the director of *Pride & Parallax*, Don Michelle, brought them back together for *The Moonlight Saga*, which appears to be some sort of epic cross between *Sailor Moon* and *Twilight*. Which, not gonna lie, I'm mildly intrigued by.

"What does it feel like to be one of the hottest Asian actors in Hollywood today?" asks the interviewer.

In his chair, Darien blinks, his smile frozen. "Ah...well, I'd like to think I'm one of the hottest *actors* in Hollywood today, no qualification needed—"

"Well, yes, *that*," sputters the interviewer, "of course, but—I guess I didn't phrase that well. I meant, what does it mean to *you* as an Asian actor to be one of Hollywood's hottest leading men?"

Darien laughs outright and says jokingly, "Do you ask this question of all hot actors?"

The interviewer almost agrees, but then catches himself, frowning, and waits for Darien to continue.

"I'm kidding. It means a lot. Early in my career, the only roles I could land were those of awkward nerds or foils to more traditional love interests. You know, the types of roles that have long been relegated to Asian men, both in the media and in the real world. I set out to prove that men with faces and features like mine could be so much more than a stereotype. It feels good to have succeeded, to demonstrate that we're just as desirable and badass as everyone else."

The interviewer smiles too broadly. "Bravo! So true! What do you think has contributed to that success? Do you think Hollywood is trending towards greater diversity?"

Darien chuckles and gives his signature smile. "I think my dietician and personal trainer are the ones who've contributed the most to my success. And Eliza, of course." He says Eliza's name straight into the camera, as if personally thanking her.

"Ha, right, right. But then, have you also seen an increase in the number of roles available to Asian actors?" The interviewer gives him an expectant look.

Darien's still smiling, but he says the next words slowly. "Hollywood recognizes that it needs to do better. That's a start. But it's not just the number of roles for Asian actors that needs to go up, but the types of roles, the types of stories. I'm glad that we've broken some barriers, but there are always more."

"I see. Then what would you like your next role be?"

They're magical words that turn Darien's smile real. "Something no one's ever seen before."

The words echo in my head, drowning out the rest of the interview, which ends soon after.

Something no one's ever seen before.

Then why is he playing it safe with tuxes? If he wants to break stereotypes so much, then why not embrace being different? Why not *be* someone that no one's ever seen before?

I look for more answers on YouTube and stumble upon an older interview, one from seven years ago, when Darien was rounder, softer, more bright-eyed. Still handsome, but less seamlessly smooth. The interviewer this time is a mature Japanese woman.

"Do you find yourself in roles that make you uncomfortable?"

"You mean, because they're racist or because there's a sex scene or...?"

"The former. Or maybe both."

"I'm just kidding, I never get offered roles with sex scenes." Darien's smile isn't the plastic one, but an amorphous one that twitches and wiggles. It's like he hasn't dialed it in. "As a relatively unknown Asian actor, it's not like I really have much choice. I need to get paid, don't I? And no one's going to rewrite a script just because I complain. I need to take the part, or else someone else will, and then they'll get paid and I won't."

"That sounds almost like crossing the picket line, doesn't it?"

Darien lets out a nervous laugh. "I guess so. Don't get me wrong, every time I have to speak with a fake accent or get snubbed by a girl on camera, it hurts. I hate reinforcing these stereotypes. But the hope is that someday, I'll get big enough that I won't have to play these stereotypical roles anymore. That I'll be able to help steer the conversation."

"We hope so, too. It's a familiar dilemma..."

After that video, I watch a couple more recent clips, but I get the gist. He's passionate about breaking the worst stereotypes about Asian men. Is that why he's so uptight about only wearing a tux? He's afraid of being embarrassed or emasculated?

I get it, at least somewhat. As an Asian woman, I've been fetishized in all kinds of fucked-up ways, but also criticized for not being as thin, demure, agreeable, feminine or whatever fucking sexist-racist adjective you want to throw in there. I love being myself and telling a different kind of story—that Asian women can be thick and goth, and look and act like me. But I don't hold onto that identity as a fuck-you to racists. I look and act the way I do because that's who I am.

And I know, it's different because Darien's famous, so people look up to him or whatever, but it must be exhausting pretending to be a Ken doll all the time.

I like the real Darien better, and I want to present him to the world in clothes that suit him.

Di: Durian

Di: whoops, autocorrect. I meant Durian

Di: DURIAN

Di: oh well, I guess that's your name now

Darien: Are you implying that I smell bad?

Di: you said it, not me

Di: but yes, you smell bad

Di: and you should be banned from hotels and airports

Durian: Whatever. At least durian tastes good *smirking face emoji*

Di: ...

Di: durian tastes like ass-flavored ice cream

Durian: Wow. I'm not sure if we can be friends anymore

Di: well, too bad. legally, you have to be my friend, at least until May 1

Di: anyway, wanna go for a walk?

Di: I have more questions

Di: need more inspo

It has to be done. I have questions, it'll be more efficient than texting, and if I see him in person, maybe my eyes will be able to draw the lines that my hands can't.

But if we meet here in my hot, stuffy apartment, the room is too small for the two of us, alone.

Besides, I haven't left my place in three days and it's starting to feel like a coffin.

Durian: A bit late for a walk, no?

Di: I'm a night person

Di: and won't it be easier for you to hide now that it's dark?

Di: let's go lurking

Durian: By "night person" do you mean vampire?

Di: I wish. I love garlic way too much

Di: pickled garlic with congee

Di: garlic noodles

Di: garlic sticky wings

Di: garlic crab

Durian: Alright, settle down, Bubba

Durian: I'll go for a walk if I can choose the place

Di: ok. where should I meet you?

Durian: I'll send a driver over

Durian: Be ready in 20

Twenty minutes is barely enough for me to put on a full face of makeup, style my hair, and throw on a sheer, low-cut tank and Doc Martens. But I get it done, because it's common courtesy to look your best for a walk with a client-slash-friend-slash-guy-I-definitely-don't-find-attractive.

Chapter 13

Di

I creep out of my apartment with my hood pulled up and head towards the only car idling on the street, then peek my head into the tinted windows of a Prius...? "Darien? You're the driver?"

"Hurry up and get in."

I open the door and throw myself inside like we've just robbed a bank. "Why did you say you were sending a driver?"

"I *am* a driver, aren't I?"

"I guess?" I say as I click in my seatbelt. "Weird to refer to yourself like that, though."

"I was going to send a different driver," he says, speeding off. "I changed my mind."

"I see. Well, I never would've expected a Prius."

"What did you expect? A Lambo?"

"I don't know. Something more than a Prius." Not that that's a bad thing. If I had the money for more than my mom's old Honda Civic, I'd buy a Prius, too.

"But that's why it's perfect. No one looks twice at a Prius. I could easily pass for a normal person right now."

A normal, jacked fitness model, but I guess that's not uncommon in L.A. And with that baseball cap and pair of fake glasses on, he really doesn't look like a star. More like a kidnapper.

"But if you wanted, you could buy a starter Lambo for the amount you got out of me."

I freeze. There it is, my own greed back to slap me in the face.

Before I can explain, he continues, "I'm kidding. With taxes and fees, a Lamborghini would cost more than that."

"I didn't mean to record you, I swear. Or like, blackmail you for money."

Each second passes like a needle poke to the heart. Finally, he asks, "Why'd you ask for that amount?"

He says it lightly, as if he's joking, but why ask if he doesn't care?

"I didn't want your money, I wanted to expose you as a cheater, but Tam approached me and said that you and Eliza should have the right to handle it privately. She threatened me, pressured me for a number, and anyway, I thought you were a liar and a cheater, so maybe you deserved to be punished, but I swear, I didn't plan any of it. Mischa keeps a pet camera by Attila's pen to check up on her and I completely forgot and—"

He laughs. "I know. What I meant is, you could've asked for a lot more than that. Just, you know, keep that in mind the next time you blackmail a celebrity. Know their net worth."

My guilt evaporates. He's not upset? "Tam started negotiations at *two thousand*."

"Ha! That's what I pay her for."

Two thousand. *Two*. I quickly google his net worth and see how many zeroes worth of an idiot I am. Too many. Though I know from my research that he throws a lot of his wealth into non-profits.

"What will you use it for?"

"The money?"

"Yeah. Tam said something about your own fashion line?"

"Yeah. That. But mostly my sister's tuition, my family's insurance. Rent." Even with a boatload of new cash, there's never enough. "We have a lot of bills to pay."

"What do your parents do for a living?"

"My mom is a seamstress and works at a laundry place. My dad left when I was young."

My dad is whatever—I don't give a shit about him. But the fog rolls in every time I think about my mom squinting down at her weathered hands, the mix of hard and delicate labor she puts them through every day. She didn't want me to move out to L.A. to become a fashion designer. Her understanding of the work comes from a lifetime of sewing, mending, altering, and washing clothes. She wants me to use my brain, not my hands.

But it's because of her that I learned to create my own clothes. She gave me this gift.

It'd be nice if I could pay her back.

"I figured it was something like that," says Darien softly. "You don't seem like the blackmailing type."

"Because I look like a nice person?" I say, remembering what he said to me that first time.

"Exactly."

"You were so full of shit."

"I really was."

We both chuckle, and I relax into the seat, breathing easy once more.

"That sounds tough, though. About the bills."

"It's okay. We make do. But it'd be nice if I could make this fashion thing work out."

He looks at me, but in the shadow of his hat and glasses, I can't quite read his expression. "It'll work out, I promise."

"Thanks." Weird thing to promise, as if he's the patron saint of fashion designers or something. But that title belongs to Saint Homobonus, whose name sounds like an extra discount you get for being gay, but is actually Latin for "good man." Because yes, I looked it up, and I might've prayed to Homobonus once. Didn't hurt to try.

We cruise in silence past bustling shops, restaurants, and neon-lit buildings, down through Los Feliz. I watch the way he scans the streets, gripping the steering wheel like it might fly out the window, adjusting and readjusting his hat and glasses whenever someone pulls up next to us. Eventually, he parks on a dark, empty street, and I can almost feel the air settle as he relaxes.

"Where are we?"

"Frogtown," he answers. "Have you been here before?"

"I don't think so."

"It's a good place to think." The car beeps as he locks it. "And it's pretty empty at night."

We walk up a short dirt path and encounter a long, paved bike path, dimly illuminated every twenty feet or so by high white street lamps. A metal railing separates the bike path from a sloped concrete bank, beyond which I make out a line of rocks and trees.

"What's that?"

"The L.A. River."

"Is it a river of rocks?"

He chuckles softly. "No, there's water. It gets fed by wastewater treatment plants."

When I listen again, there's a burble under the breeze, a meditation soundtrack on low. It's a beautiful night, slightly chilly, but clear, with a slim crescent moon that's high in the sky. My eyes quickly adjust to the lighting, and my steps grow sure on the smooth path.

As dark as it is, Darien's still wearing the baseball cap and glasses. It's mostly deserted, but we do pass a woman pleading with a tiny growling dog, and another person whips by us on a bike, close enough to clip the fabric of my hoodie.

Darien switches sides with me, guiding me to his right so that any cyclists will have to pass us on his left. It's a small thing, but my stomach does a little twirl. And he lets me set the pace. I fight my East Coast speed-walking urges and keep it moderate so that we can talk.

"So you have some questions for me?"

"Yeah, I do. Why do you always wear a black tux? Why don't you ever branch out?"

"Most guys go to the Met in a tux. Haven't you noticed? It's not about us, it's about the gowns."

"So? You really want to be like every other guy on this occasion?"

He shrugs. "I have an image to maintain."

"And what exactly is that image?"

He turns towards me and holds out his hands, inviting me to look. "Can't you tell?"

"I have an idea, but explain it to me in your own words."

"I guess you haven't seen *Pride and Parallax*? Or the *Moonlight Saga*? My fans call me Prince Charming for a reason."

"So you want to be handsome and boring?"

"No. Prince Charming is dependable. Strong. Gallant. Masculine. He's the ultimate female fantasy, and the classic look for a guy like that is a tux."

I hold back a snort, but as we pass under one of the lamps, he gives me a miffed look. "What, you disagree?"

"There's no *ultimate female fantasy*, and those aren't the adjectives I'd use to describe you." Though when a scooter whizzes by on his left side, I grudgingly admit that it *was* nice of him to switch positions with me.

"How would you describe the Darien you know?"

"Introspective. Sensitive. Weird." *Insecure.*

"Wow, very flattering, thank you," he says dryly.

"Well, I think those are better qualities than *strong* or *classic*. That just reeks of toxic masculine bullshit."

"I don't mean in the sense of not crying or acting macho. Women these days want a more nuanced kind of guy, one who's in touch with his emotions and knows when to be vulnerable. But they still want someone who can toss them around in bed and beat up creeps."

I cough and make barf noises from the back of my throat.

"You disagree?"

"Please don't say 'women these days' ever again. And yeah, maybe don't lump us together or make assumptions?"

"I'm not saying that all women are the same, obviously not, but my team has done a lot of market research and those are the types of fantasies that appeal to my fanbase, which consists primarily of cis-het women. They want a man who's witty and charming, one who will respect them, but also push them. And I know it sounds a bit outdated or old fashioned, but tossing them around in bed and protecting them from creeps are still top-tier fantasies."

"Whatever. Good for your fanbase, I guess. Personally, I'd rather have an earnest, noodle-armed goofball than an overprotective stud-muffin. As a society, we shouldn't value anyone's capacity to do violence. It's like the fallacy of a good guy with a gun, but it's the good guy with *guns*," I say, poking his bicep. "We should teach people to stop being creepy, not to beat each other up."

He nods. "That's true."

He gives in so easily that I hardly realize I'm still talking. "And as much as I enjoy being tossed around in bed, a good sense of humor is ten times sexier."

He turns and looks right into my eyeballs, his lips easing open to show those perfect rice-white teeth. The ones he faithfully flashes every time I crack a joke.

I know for a fact that he can toss me around in bed.

But that's not helpful. "Anyway, you haven't answered my question. Why the persona?"

He swings his gaze forward again, and I'm not sure how I feel about the sudden coolness on my skin. "It's what sells."

"What about celebrities who are popular because they're awkward and authentic?"

"They have carefully curated personas, too. They're not just being themselves."

"All of them?"

"Pretty much." He gives me a sideways glance. "In the age of social media, everyone has a public persona. Even you."

"I do not have a persona. What you see is what you get."

"Yeah? Then why do you look so pissed off all the time?"

"That's just my face. And I usually *am* pissed off about something."

He chuckles. "I don't know, I think you put on this mean, tough-girl act, but you're not like that at all."

"That's just because you're not used to seeing women like me."

"Women like what?"

"Women who aren't trying to please you all the time. I fucking hated that that's what was expected of me. My family used to push me to be more feminine and obedient, all that bullshit. But it's not me."

He chuckles. "Sure, those aren't the words I'd use to describe you. But I still think the tough-girl thing is an act."

"Oh yeah, then what am I like?"

"Conscientious. Sensitive. Stubborn."

"Is your hat cutting off circulation to your head? That's not me."

"You know I'm right," he says, laughing. "Especially the conscientious part. You pretend like you don't give a damn, but you *do* care about doing the right thing, and to some extent, about what people think. You don't want them to get the wrong impression of you. And you're trying to protect yourself, because you actually *are* a nice person."

"Hello? I half-blackmailed you."

"Yeah? And you feel guilty about it. You're judging yourself for taking the money, even now."

Part of me wants to pull my hood up even further and hide, but I harden my face until it feels like a bust of Clint Eastwood. "You don't know me at all."

"I spend a lot of time getting into other people's heads. I'm reading you right." He leans forward a little and stares even more closely at my face, and again, I wish my hood would swallow me up. "You wear that frown like it's a weapon. But it's because you're a sensitive person."

"Uh huh. The same way you wear that smile?"

He opens his mouth, and it stays open and silent like a dumb fish. Ha!

"Anyway, this isn't about me. My point is, you think this persona of yours is all that will sell. But to me, Prince Charming sounds like a snooze-fest."

"Maybe Prince Charming isn't your type, but he's a lot of people's type. And if the point of this conversation is to figure out what look best suits him, it's a classic tux. That's why I asked you for one."

"I don't think he's the *only* type that people would like. And I don't think a classic tux is it, either. Think of all the actors who wear avant-garde stuff and get praised for it."

"Yeah, well, they don't have hundreds of years of emasculating stereotypes to overcome."

I lightly slap his bicep like it's a thick cut of meat. Which it is. "I think you've overcome them pretty well."

"You'd be surprised." His hands slip into his pockets, the thumbs hooked into the belt loops of his pants. "Obviously, there've been Asian actors before me, but they weren't major sex symbols, not to the same extent. And even after getting to where I am, there are *still* assholes out there who think I'm unattractive, or who think I can't please a woman. I even get hate from other Asians for not repping them hard enough. Plenty of people want to see me fall."

His tone is light, but it's light the same way butane gas is, ready to burn at a hint of friction. As the most public face for Asian men in America, I can only imagine the pressure he must feel, but he's still a star. Sure, some of his movie reviews weren't stellar, but that's normal for actors, isn't it? And there *was* a racist #notmydarcy campaign for when he was cast in *Pride and Parallax*, but from what I could tell, it hadn't caught much steam.

"I think you might be blowing things out of proportion. You have a ton of fans! You're an icon now. And even if there are people who want to pull you down, they will always exist, they're in the minority, and you don't need to do anything to prove them wrong because they will never change their minds about you anyway. And you don't represent all of Asian America. Maybe you think you do because people ask you about it all the time in interviews, but that's not who you are. You're not just a representative."

Our steps are synchronized, left-right-left. "You've been watching my interviews?"

That's what he got out of my rant? "Yes. I've been researching you for the look. Obviously. But my point is, confidence in who you are is sexy. Hotness doesn't have one definition, and the more you feed into this macho-dude bullshit, the more that racist, sexist fucks win. Everyone is different, and we should celebrate *that*."

"Yeah. If only it were that simple." He gives me a grim smile. "Anyway, I don't mean to complain. I know that I should feel lucky to have my job and fame, and most of the time, I do. But when I say that I have an image to maintain, it's one that my team and I have thought about and carefully curated. So work with me, will you? I have enough people doubting me."

I bite back the urge to argue. He's wrong, and authentic Darien would do just as well or even better than Prince Charming. But I guess it's up to me to prove that with my design.

"Also," he says, "I'm only going as Eliza's guest. She's the one who's supposed to shine."

Eliza. That Z in her name, pointy as a needle, pops our happy little balloon. "*Supposed* to? According to whom?"

"Good question." He stares off into the distance, as if the answer is shimmering there in that swarm of gnats. "I think the design houses would agree, because they're the ones who invited her. And anyway, she's the bigger and brighter star. No matter what, I'm always going to be in her shadow."

He falls silent, but I can hear what he's not saying. Eliza's the one who wants the attention. And because Darien's so *gallant* or in love or whatever, he'd rather take a step back and fade into the darkness, all the better to let her sparkle.

Well, too fucking bad. He's my model, my canvas, and it's time for her to take the backseat for once.

I stop walking, and a half-step later, so does he.

"You're not just a backdrop to her, you know. You're a star in your own right."

"Yeah, well…" The rest of his reply is late, and quiet, as if to himself. "I guess we'll see."

Seriously? What does that mean? He's been nominated for awards, there's fan-fiction about him, and there are listicles ranking his top smiles. How can he think so little of himself when so many people love him?

Even I find myself…well…liking him. More than I would've thought.

He's still wearing the cap and glasses, but when he stares down at me with those starry, ink-drop eyes, those lips that twitch with laughter at the slightest whiff of a joke…it's easy to imagine how he's gotten as famous as he has. He's been selling this dream of Prince Charming, the one from the storybooks, but the real Darien is even better.

Something fizzes in the back of my head. There's something here, some hazy idea coalescing—

"Watch it!"

A group of teens on BMX bikes, coming fast in the dark. He turns his face and steps in as I grab him and pull him closer, and we collide against the handrail, his body pressing me into the metal, just in time for them to whip by in a rabid cluster of wheels.

I look up—my nose boops his. His heart pumps double-time against my own, the wall of him warm and hard against me, trapping me where I stand. Our lips are so close, the slightest gust of wind might bring them together, and then we'll be kissing, sweetly, madly, deeply, kicking off every fantasy that lurks in the shadows of my mind, daring me to set them free.

But the wind doesn't come. Darien, hardly breathing, doesn't move, except for his eyes, which click into place with mine. My hands grip his arms, clutching the fabric, itching to pull him closer—

I push him back. "Sorry."

"Thanks," he says at the same time, stepping away. "For getting me out of the way."

"No problem."

We stare at each other, but not directly on. Not at anywhere important.

"I think I have what I need," I say. "Thanks."

"So should we head back?"

"Yeah."

We turn around and retrace our steps in silence, two feet apart like someone's tied a stick between us. Which is well and good. But instead of being proud that I didn't hump him, I feel queasy and off balance, like I just failed a test.

Why can't I shut it down? I'm like a fluffy cat that's obsessed with a tiny, ill-fitting box. We don't fit, and yet I want to feel his hard surfaces all around me, squeezing me tight, holding me close.

But from everything I've seen and heard, it's clear that he loves Eliza. The man lives for her like some walking, talking Giving Tree.

From now on, she's the only one who gets to be in that box.

Which means that the faster we get this over with, the faster I can leave them behind.

"In a hurry to get home?"

I snap out of autopilot and slow to half speed, though my legs are warm and itch to go faster. "Sorry, it's a habit. East Coaster and all."

"I've lived in New York. You're faster than most. You'd make a champion race walker."

"Race walker?"

"You know, race walking? It's an Olympic sport where you walk as quickly as possible."

"Uh... You mean, *running?*"

"No. In race walking, you're not allowed to lose contact with the ground. Like this." He shoots forward, legs straight and hips bobbing side to side like a salsa dancer who's late to class. Laughing, delighted, I follow his lead and hurry along to catch up, enjoying both the visual of Darien power walking and the brisk stretching in my legs.

When I get even with him, I puff out, "Wanna race?"

Without replying, he leans forward and takes off like a two-legged rocket, his arms pumping front to back like windshield wipers at top speed. I huff and I puff until I've closed most of the distance, but when we see the car, I break into a sprint, cursing my heavy boots, and Darien race-walks even faster until we're scrambling to touch the car and get inside, laughing our asses off, gazes sparkling and tangling together like Christmas tinsel.

We're silent on the drive home, but it's the kind of silence that hums rather than screams.

Chapter 14

Darien

Darien,

Here's this week's pick for fan mail. LMK if you want me to respond for you.

Cady

Hi Darien (Mr. Lee? Idk how to address you),

I've never written a fan letter before, and anyway, you probably get a million of these a day, so I doubt you'd reply to mine, but after watching Agents of Icarus, I had to reach out. I'm a hardcore fan of the book series, and I hafta say, you were the best Agent that anyone could have picked. When you turned around and delivered that line: "Shoot, or shut up. My steak's getting cold." I swear my soul quivered. It was so so so good, even better than the book, because of you. I hope you win all the awards.

Anyway, just wanted to say, thanks for making my new favorite movie. I'm gonna dig into all your old films, and I'm looking forward to seeing what you do next!!

Anthony X., 19

P.S. You are an inspiration, and you and Eliza are too cute together. Here's hoping I find my Eliza someday, too.

"Morning."

I glance up from my email, surprised. "Morning," I say to Eliza, but remain seated at the kitchen island.

Dressed in gold silk pajamas, her hair loose about her shoulders, she takes a glass from the cupboard and fills it with filtered water from the fridge door. Which wouldn't be unusual except that there's a water filter in the kitchen downstairs, closer to her suite of rooms. What is she doing up here?

"How long are you back for?" I ask instead.

"A couple of days. I'll be off to London on Friday."

"I see."

Leaning against the counter, she holds the glass of water by her shoulder and doesn't drink. "Where were you last night?"

Ah. I give her a level look. "I went for a walk."

"By yourself? In public?"

"Why do you ask?"

Why do you care? What right do you have to know?

She holds my gaze for one miserable moment before shaking her head and looking away. "I hope you know what you're doing."

I go back to typing out a response to Cady, ignoring the unease floating between us like black smoke. I tell Cady not to bother with a reply. Anthony's only going to be disappointed in a couple of months, along with the rest of my fans. Except maybe the ones who keep trying to send me nude photos.

Leaning against the counter with the glass dangling from one hand, Eliza swivels her head around the kitchen, peering here and there. I'm not sure what she's looking for, but the kitchen is exactly the same as it was months ago. Back then.

With nothing left to say, she soon leaves.

An hour later, Tam confirms my suspicions.

Tam: I can't believe I have to tell you this

Tam: Stay away from Diana

Tam: She's just using you

Tam: If you get caught again, shit hits the fan

Darien: Nothing's happening between us

Tam: You sure about that?

Darien: Yes

Liar, says a voice, but it's true. Sure, I'd almost taken her against the railing last night. And yeah, she makes me laugh in undignified ways. But that type of openness and easy chemistry is something I've cultivated for a living. It comes from a lifetime of meeting strangers, of playing along with them, of embodying other lives. I meet lovely, charming women all the time, ones who are better suited for my career.

I like that Di is herself, always, with everyone. But that's exactly why we'd never work out.

Tam: Well, stay away from her, please

Tam: She's not going to help you or your career

Tam: She's only looking out for herself

Actually, she's looking out for her family, but that part of the story never matters, does it? We're all Jean Valjeans to ourselves and Javerts towards everyone else. Not that I don't care about the two hundred thousand dollars. She shouldn't have taken advantage like she did. But I do believe that she was acting more out of a misplaced sense of justice than purely selfish gain.

When the stakes are as high as they are, though, intentions don't signify.

The end result is what matters most.

* * *

"Took you long enough," says my sister as I step into her house. It's been a week since she gave birth, but only a day since she came home from the hospital.

"I know. I'm sorry I couldn't visit you at the hospital."

"Sure." Spat out like a watermelon seed.

"It's too public and crowded, and the paparazzi knew that I'd been there. You know that, right?"

"Right."

"You saw the media frenzy, the day that Eliot was born?"

"Yeah, I saw. Sucks to be you."

I'd known it was likely, but the sarcasm clinches it—I'm officially on Claire's shitlist.

Which means it's only a matter of time before she decides enough is enough and I lose her too.

I take off my shoes, and the drop of soles on ceramic fills the cavernous void. There's a cool, powdery smell in the air, and despite the open blinds, the foyer and living room are dim and gray. Might be all the neutral tones my sister likes, or maybe it's the Mexican fan palms outside blocking the light, but I've never liked how gloomy her house is.

"Mom around?"

"She's out right now. She'll be back this afternoon."

I carry a bag of Rainier cherries to her kitchen and leave it on the granite island before returning to the first floor master bedroom, where my sister perches on the edge of a king-size bed, ankles crossed and palms flat on the crumpled white comforter. Her black shoulder-length hair sits limp against her scalp, and her skin looks dull and heavy, as if resisting her every movement.

My older sister is finally starting to look older.

"Sorry, Je. You know I wanted to be there."

"Yeah, well...I'm used to it."

"There's no excuse. I should've been there for you. Is there any way that I can make it up to you?"

"Sure," she says wryly, a fleck of life back in her eyes. "Ten weekends of babysitting."

"Uh, ten? That's a lot. I told you I'd be willing to hire someone—"

Her right eyebrow climbs halfway up her scalp. It's always the right, never the left. I'm surprised her forehead doesn't have a six-pack on that side.

"I'll do it," I finish lamely. "Make it twelve." Though we both know that they'll have to be claimed over a glacial time scale.

"Good." She nods towards a bassinet by the side of the bed, where I find a tiny bundle of human with pinkish skin, pouty lips, and a dusting of wispy hairs, so fine as to barely register against my palm. The newest member of our little family. His bulbous eyes are closed, but his mouth and tongue move as if he's tasting something sweet and sticky, or maybe exploring the sensations of even *having* a mouth and tongue. Of being alive.

I smile at his patchy, puffy cheeks. He's more old man than cherub, but he shares our genes. He'll turn out alright.

Everyone used to say that Eliza and I would have gorgeous babies. We used to joke about giving them pretentious names—Descartes, Montgomery, or Billions Lee—but of course we wouldn't. We would've wanted them to have normal experiences, the way that we were able to as kids.

Now, if Eliza marries Ethan, they'll have to explain to their kids how Mommy and Uncle Darien have six years of photos together, and several movies where they've made out. A few where they've gotten married.

"He just went down," Claire whispers. "And if you weren't here, I'd be napping, too."

"Sorry. Should I leave?"

"No, let's talk outside."

She takes my arm and we shuffle our way out into the backyard, where she's been growing mangos, persimmons, figs, and oranges, an entire grove of fruit. She dug those holes and planted and watered those trees herself. I've offered to pay for professional landscaping, but Claire insists on being self-sufficient. To her, the process is what's important, the experience, not the end result. Why pay someone to do something when you can do it yourself, or have family do it? To her, that's what family is for.

Which again, is why I'm on her shitlist.

We sit down on a couple of ornate steel chairs, and from the matching patio table, Claire picks up a small glass snifter of something dark brown.

"Is that tea?"

She deflates on a sigh. "I wish. It's Mom's postpartum brew."

"What?"

"She swears that it helped her heal up faster when grandma made *her* drink it, but I think it's just an ancient Taiwanese hazing ritual for new moms." She takes a sip and makes a face. "Tastes like wood chips soaked in piss."

"Yum. Is it worse than that aloe vera and corn husk drink she used to make for us?"

"A thousand times worse. Clinical grade." She presses a hand to her chest as she sets the glass down. "Blech. Ugh. Anyway... How are you? Who's this woman you're in trouble over?"

"Just someone I met."

"Right." She gives me a tissue-thin smile. "I'm glad you're moving on."

"Really, she's just a friend."

"Uh huh." She picks up her glass again, swirling the contents like it's a favored vintage and not medicinal jungle juice. "The same way Eliza and Ethan are just friends?"

I shake my head, mildly regretting telling her the truth. Though not really. She was the only one I could talk to about it who was definitely on my side. At the time, at least. "How are you, Je?"

She sighs and adjusts herself in her seat with a wince. "I'm still bleeding. I smell bad. And I can hardly sleep at night, not because of Eliot, just because my body refuses to fall asleep. But my son is alive and so am I, so I guess I'm okay."

Claire's okay when she's "good." When she's "okay," though... "Just say the word and I'll buy you all the perfume and deodorant, whatever you need to mask your own scent."

She lets out a dry chuckle. "Yeah, well. You know I don't need you to buy me anything."

I hold back yet another apology. There's only one love language she trusts. "Then I'll come by often. Maybe I'll stay over some nights, give you and Mom a break? Besides my training sessions, I cleared my schedule for you. You know that."

She looks down at her lap, swirling the dregs of her drink. "I know how it is with you. Things come up. Mom and I will be fine."

How it is with me, like my flakiness is an immutable fact. "Je, I messed up, but it was one time—"

"I'm not blaming you." She looks directly at me, head tilted, lips thinned. "How were you supposed to know that I'd need an emergency C-section? No one suspected that. Even Ethan didn't respond right away. He was asleep, and you know how he sleeps—I had to call him so many times. But that's why I got so freaked out. I started to realize that it's not reasonable for me to expect you guys to always be there. You have your own lives and I'm the one who chose to have Eliot on my own."

"You're not on your own. I'm the one who let you down. I was supposed to be there for you—"

"No, you weren't. You asked for the weekend for yourself. Even though I'm still sore about it, you were completely in your rights to ignore me. And what am I supposed to do when you get busy again? I can't ask you to fly back from a shoot. I can't ask Mom to move in or drive over all the time from La Jolla, or ask Ethan to take care of us on top of trying to get tenure. I need to be able to do this on my own. This is what I signed up for. So I don't blame you, but—" She swallows, a sudden gasp that jerks her chest back, "—I didn't expect it to be so hard. Which is stupid, of course it was going to be hard, even with two people in the picture. But that night, it hit me that Atsuko made me choose, and I fucking *chose*, but it wasn't until then that I really understood what it meant to be on my own. Not just to physically take care of him, but mentally, emotionally. I was spiraling. But I'm the only person Eliot has, and I was always the angry, depressive one. Atsuko was the sunny one. Every time I look at Eliot, I think he's perfect, precious, he's mine and I want to die of love and wonder. But then I get so scared that I'm going to mess him up because Atsuko's not here to balance me out. I selfishly brought him into this world and I'm all he has and I'm not *good*."

I've never seen Claire so shaken, not even when our father died or Atsuko left. Anguish twists through every party of her body, distorting the strong, confident lines I've come to associate with her, and to rely on.

It's my turn to be there for her.

"What are you talking about? You're going to be an amazing mother. You're the one who looked out for me after Mom and Dad got divorced, and after Dad died." I exhale through my nose, trying to control my words rather than the other way around. "After Dad passed, it felt like Mom kind of moved on from us. She had Carl and Ethan. I had you. So I know for a fact that you'll be a wonderful mother. And if you get tired of being so awesome, you can foist him off on his cool uncle and go on vacation for a while. I'll babysit until you come back."

She lets out a cry-laugh. "You'd better mean it. It might happen."

"It might, but I doubt it. You're going to love that kid so much, you won't want to be apart, and vice versa. And I know that I've let you down in the past, but whenever you need me, I will be *here*, I promise. Fuck the job."

"You say that now, but—"

"I'm serious. My career doesn't come first. Loved ones do." And as soon as I say it, I know it's true, it's always been true. I'd just let the needs of one *specific* loved one come first, and for her, work was life. "I'm done being gone. I'll take less work if I have to, or maybe do something completely different. But please don't think that you can't rely on me. It kills me to think that you feel that way."

She looks at me with red, watery eyes. "Thanks, Darien. I'm lucky to have you and Ethan as my brothers."

I swallow my words about Ethan. "I'm lucky to have you, too." Not just because she looked out for me when I was a kid, but all along. It was her place that I crashed at while doing the L.A. shuffle, bussing tables, taking up odd jobs, landing gigs, getting over shitty reviews, finding my footing. She'd even braved the audience during those dark days of improv, and told it to me like it was after every show: "It really wasn't funny, Dare."

I owe her so very much.

She turns and stares out over the garden, wistfully scanning the fruit up on the trees. "I'm not sure if I'm imagining things, but I think he looks a bit like Dad."

I hear what she means: Dad should be here. "You'd know better than I would."

"I may have been older, but he spent more time with you. He loved his little boy more than his daughter."

"That's not true."

"Yes it is. I'd know better than you would." She tips the glass to her lips and swallows down the rest of the brown liquid with only a slight gag. "I don't even think I understood what I was missing until I became an adult and things got hard. Carl's great, but...he's not the same."

"I get it. But you know he'd still do anything for you."

"I know. And so would Ethan." She puts down the glass and gives me a sideways look. "Have you spoken to him at all?"

"No, I haven't."

She turns to face me full-on, and from the way she squares her shoulders, I already know what's coming. "You should forgive him, Darien."

There it is. "Not you, too."

"People do stupid things, they make mistakes."

"What he did wasn't stupid, it was wrong."

"He's been in love with her for years."

"So? That doesn't make it okay. If anything, that makes it worse. Instead of forcing himself to get over his feelings, he harbored them. What kind of brother would do that?"

"Is it possible to force yourself to stop loving someone? If so, you need to tell me the secret."

"It's possible if it can never happen. Like if that person is going to become your sister-in-law."

She sighs, rubbing her forehead. "All I'm saying is, it's complicated, he's sorry, he knows what he did was wrong and—"

"If he knows what he did was wrong, then why is he still with her?"

"Just hear him out. Regardless of what happened—"

"I don't care what he has to say, I just want him to fuck off."

I can't sit. I launch out of my seat and pace circles into the pavement.

"You don't mean that. I know you still love him, and he obviously still loves you. And I'm sorry for what happened to you, but he was here for *me*, Darien. We're family." Her lip trembles, not with sadness, but with censure. "If I hadn't called him after I'd tried calling you..."

That night, she'd left me message after message, minutes apart, calls, frantic, questioning whether or not she should go to the hospital, asking if I was free and could come by, certain that something was wrong. Mom and Carl live two-and-a-half hours away, too far to be of immediate help. How must she have felt when I didn't respond, when she had no one there to help her?

No one except Ethan.

"I fucked up. I should've been there for you. But their cheating didn't just *happen* to me. They chose to do this. I thought you understood."

"But he's our brother, Darien."

"He didn't care that I was his brother when he fucked my fiancée."

"He's sorry. And I know you don't like how things are, either. You both deserve to be happy, and life's too short to stay mad at each other."

She's too good to use it against me, but I know what she's trying to say. Dad died at 35, and of course my last memory of him was a shouting match because he wouldn't buy me some toy or other. My mom picked me up from his place, and he'd died that night, alone.

But I'm not a kid anymore, and what Ethan and Eliza did was infinitely worse. Why should I forgive them and let them go unpunished? Beyond saying sorry over and over, ad nauseam, they haven't tried to make amends at all. All they've done is sheepishly tip-toe around my misery while their happiness grows.

Why should I forgive, why should I hide their shame, why should I do anything to help them when all they've done is fuck me over?

The plug blows, my geyser erupts, and my hands curl with the effort of holding back the boiling froth. How could they have been so fucking selfish? And now, Claire—

"We're all family, all of us, and the longer...the longer you drag this on—" She begins to sob, face in hands.

I breathe and breathe, mentally grabbing, shoving, slamming back the anger, shutting it behind a door. My sister is innocent. My sister needs me. "I'm sorry, Je, I didn't mean to make you cry."

"I didn't mean to start crying like this. You know I usually wouldn't be. Postpartum sucks."

"It's fine, don't worry. Cry or complain all you want. I'm here." For once. "And I'll talk to him later. When I'm ready." *Never.*

After a few muffled moments, she lets out a shuddering breath and nods. "Thank you. I know it's hard, but I can't stand to see you both like this."

"I know." I smooth my hand down her back, the contact between us as much for me as for her. "I know."

The stirrings of a tiny monster come through the baby monitor, punctuating the silence. My sister sniffles and wipes away the last of her tears. "Want to hold your nephew? Possibly get pissed or puked on?"

A chuckle unlocks my chest, but Old Faithful's still churning beneath the surface. "Yeah. I'd like that."

As we walk back into the house, my phone buzzes multiple times. Later, as Claire breastfeeds Eliot in the privacy of her room, I check the messages.

Eliza: I'll need the upstairs kitchen tonight after 5pm.

Eliza: Ethan's coming for dinner.

Eliza: Join us if you'd like. We should talk.

Staring at her messages, my neck begins to heat again. When we were together, I never stayed mad for long. No matter what she did, a home-cooked dinner and an apology was all it took for me to forgive her. But if she thinks that'll work this time, she's out of her mind.

Darien: What are you doing tonight

Di: could you come over to my place? I'd like to discuss the look with you.

Perfect.

I send a message to Eliza.

Darien: Tell me when you're done.

Darien: I'll be out tonight.

She doesn't respond, but she knows exactly whom I'll be with.

Chapter 15

Di

My eyes do another lap across the spread of drawings: one alone at the top of the desk, four in a row underneath. Each one has its charms, but which would Darien prefer?

I let my hand drift over the designs. It lingers over one, the one at the top.

I gather the bottom four drawings and toss them into my portfolio. Just as I finish zipping it up, there's a knock. I leap towards the door and pull it open, trying not to stare at Darien as he enters the apartment, doused in expensive bear repellent, with perfectly tousled hair like he's just stepped off of a private jet.

Except that there's a small yellow stain on his ivory-white polo.

I close the door and point at the yellow splotch on his huge chest. "Hot dogs for dinner?"

He looks down at himself. "That's puke, not mustard. My nephew's."

"Ah. He smelled your cologne?"

"Funny. It's Clive Christian," he says, as if that means anything to me. "They're one of my sponsors."

He sweeps his gaze around the room before taking a seat on the orange futon and staring up at me. "Is this your bed?"

I cross my arms and secretly wipe my hands off on my shirt, but they're still sweaty. "Not recently."

One thick brow rises in question.

"I haven't slept much these past couple of days."

I grab the sketch from the desk and sit down next to him, ignoring the heat coming off of him, or the way his eyes beckon to mine. With a quick, quiet breath, I flip the page around and show him.

"The Met Gala theme this year is the Military Invasion of Fashion, so I created a look that weaves together elements of military uniforms, Prince Charming, Chinese formal dress, and my own darker, edgier aesthetic. I've heard that Eliza's wearing a pale pink dress with crystalline epaulets, so I wanted something that would emphasize your shoulders too, but with a different silhouette. So *this* is a jet-black, open topcoat, with mandarin collar and black trim. The shoulders are detailed with overlapping layers that will be lightly ruched to resemble pauldrons, which will give a nod to Eliza's outfit without making you look too similar. Inside, there's a black folded tunic shirt with a complementary low collar, as well as fitted, tapered pants with ribbed accents. Everything will be made of some mix of wool and organic cotton." Materials that I already have on hand, because shopping for new ones would take too much time.

I hand him the sketch and unlock my phone to show him some photos, wishing for the eightieth time that I had a more professional setup. "I wasn't sure if you were going to use Jill or someone else to style the look, but I took the liberty of putting together some options. We could pair it with these boots from Yin Yoto, some combination of these rings from John Wallace, and this triple-wrap leather bracelet and black ingot amulet from Karlotta Polnick."

He scans everything I show him with a small frown, and I can't tell what it means. But when he looks up, the light in his eyes dims so quickly, I'm not even sure it was there.

"Could we, um...do this another time?"

My breath grinds to a halt in my throat, but I refuse to analyze his response. "I'd rather do this now. I don't have much time left."

"I get it, but right now, I'm not in the right frame of mind to judge these things—"

"It's simple, Darien. Do you like it or not?"

He sighs, while my breath comes as if through a cocktail straw. "I mean... It's cool. Nice."

Spoken like a kid who got socks for Christmas. "Why don't you like it?"

"I didn't say that. I said it was cool. And nice."

I fist my hands in my lap to stop myself from grabbing his shirt and shaking him. "Tell me the truth."

It takes him a few lip-licks to gather his thoughts. "I really do like it. You've put an impressive amount of thought into it. I just, you know, worry that this will make me look like I'm trying too hard."

"As opposed to not trying at all with a tux?"

"I've gone three years in a row in a tux and nobody's cared. Some stuck-up fashion people commented, obviously, but for the most part, nobody minded that it wasn't on theme. I'd rather be safe than sorry."

"Okay, but... Pretend this isn't for the Met Gala. Pretend this is just for you. What do you think of the outfit?"

He searches for words among the lines of the sketch. "I mean, it's cool. I think it's badass."

"So why can't you believe that other people will think it's cool and badass, too?"

"If I could predict what people think is cool, I wouldn't be in so many poorly rated movies."

He snickers, and my brain struggles to process the change in him. What's going on?

"Okay, forget that. What would it take for you to feel comfortable wearing something like this? I mean, come on, you wore alien makeup in *Pride and Parallax*, this isn't even half as weird."

"Yeah, but I was playing a character in *Pride and Parallax*, and it turned out to be a hit. At the Met, I'll be playing myself. If I look lame or silly, it won't be anyone's fault but my own."

"No, it'll be *my* fault." I close my eyes and take a deep, shuddering breath, willing even a bit of life back into my heavy limbs. "So the bottom line is, you don't like it?"

"That's not what I said. I do like it, but I'm not sure what other people will think, and...I mean, whatever. Fuck it, I'll wear it."

Whatever? Fuck it?

Why is he acting like this? Like he suddenly couldn't care less about me or our agreement. Like all of this is a joke to him.

"You're really going to wear it?"

He gives me a limp smile, the facial equivalent of a shrug. "Sure."

My knuckles crack as I curl and uncurl my fingers. He's agreed, so I've won, haven't I?

But then why do I feel like screaming?

"Fine. I guess this is the look." I take the sketch back from him and stand. I have little more than two weeks left, hardly enough time to complete the look and the rest of my line, hardly enough time to sleep.

Is it even worth it at this point? Maybe I should just throw it away and go home. Call up my old boss and get my web design job back. Because at least I was good at that, and it made money. It was fine, safe. A smarter decision than throwing away months of time and effort for the chance to say I tried.

He stands, lifting his hand as if to touch me, but doesn't. "I really do like the design."

I don't respond. There's no point. He's not convincing anyone, least of all himself.

But this next part...

Just get it over with.

I pull out a soft tape measure from a drawer. "Let me get your measurements and we'll be done."

He stares at me for several seconds, and without my asking, begins to undo his belt.

"What are you doing?"

"You don't need me in my boxers for this?"

I glance at his slacks, letting my eyes slide away before they linger for too long. They're fitted well enough. "No."

He drops his hands. "Fine."

I don't want to think about him in his boxers, or how I'm going to be touching him, kneeling in front of him, inhaling the...um...

Well, actually, he smells terrible, like he's wearing Axe's sleazy older cousin, Shank. But even then, there's a rich, intoxicating undercurrent that I'm tempted to explore more deeply. To lean in and take a drag of and—

Nope nope nope. I focus on the stink.

And the fact that he has a fiancée, Sexiest Woman Alive.

She's the Prince, he's Cinderella, and I'm the mice with the sewing needles getting him ready for the ball, where the look is going to get ripped apart.

I shake myself a little and focus on the task at hand. He keeps still as I move about him, measuring from shoulder to wrist, but his eyes follow my every move.

"Lift your arms."

He does, and I briefly wrap my arms around him, just to get the tape around his waist.

"You're really talented."

I grunt.

"You clearly take pride in your work." He's said it quietly, dispassionately, but his eyes stick to me like they're playing defense. "Thanks for your effort."

"We signed a contract," I say. "It's the least I could do, literally."

After noting the trouser waist and jacket waist measurements, I bring the tape up to his chest. My hands flit and fly, barely landing, but everywhere I touch him is sun-warmed granite. The urge to press myself against him and soak him up hits me like a mob against a barred door, rattling me, but I note the measurement and step away. "You can put your arms down now."

He lowers his arms, and I step to his back to take the jacket length, pressing one thumb to his nape, holding the other down by the bottom of his ass. I barely brush him there, but again, it's warm rock, and my cold lizard brain wants me to lie down and sun myself all over him.

"You know that I'm going to do whatever I can to help you, right?"

I move the tape, measuring from armpit to spine for the half-back.

"No matter what happens the night of the Met Gala, I'm going to support your brand."

"You told me." So much for trying to make me feel better—he thinks the fashion writers are going to tear the look apart, too.

Well, let them, who cares. Not me, not when I'm so tired that I almost stabbed someone with my shears when they started a leaf blower at 9 a.m.

I can't keep going like this. I need rest. Maybe after this, when he's gone, I'll finally collapse into the futon and sleep like the dead, or just die.

God, that sounds nice.

I walk back around to face him—it's time for the legs. My eyes meet his before quickly sliding away. The weight of his gaze practically pushes me to my knees as I crouch and measure the outside leg, hip to heel.

"Lift your arms again." My hands are surprisingly steady as I wrap the tape around the widest part of his hips for the seat measurement. The tape meets the end by his hip, which brings my gaze—and hand—near his obvious erection.

I can't help it. Like Pavlov's dogs at the ring of a bell, my mouth waters, and I swallow, hard.

When I look up, the spark in his eyes has gone full inferno.

Shit.

I adjust my position for the final two measurements.

"Di."

I ignore him. I don't look up again, just focus on the in-seam measurement, balls to heel, balls to heel, balls to—

"Do you ever think about that night?"

I suck in a slow breath. My hand barely brushes against him before I move on to the ankle measurement.

Be like a Ford and Focus, Di. Don't look up. I look up, I lose.

"Do you ever think about me choking you?"

Don't. Not right now, not when I'm so tired and he's so close and I'm not thinking straight.

"Do you ever—"

"No, I don't," I lie, when even now, crouching at his feet, I want to take him so deep into my throat that his balls scratch the back of my tongue. "And I'm only kneeling in front of you because I have a job to do. So keep it fucking professional, will you?"

He falls silent, which only makes me want to look up even more. But I finish taking the measurement and stand, turning away, silently gulping down air like an angry frog.

"I'm sorry," he says quietly, and though I'm a poor judge of it, he sounds sincere. "You're right. I shouldn't have put you in this position."

"No, you shouldn't have." I close my notebook and toss away the measuring tape, but don't turn around. I can't.

He doesn't come closer, doesn't say a word, but I can hear him breathing, shifting, waiting.

"Are you trying to distract me? Trying to make me feel better about not liking my design?"

His laughter hits like nettles, until he explains. "No. I'm trying to make myself feel better about my shitty life decisions."

I spare him a look over my shoulder. "What decisions?"

"Nothing. Nothing new, anyway." He rubs his face and runs a clawed hand through his hair. "But I shouldn't have taken it out on you or said those things to you. I'm sorry."

Is that all that was? "Taking it out" on me? Not an admission that he fantasizes about me as much as I do him?

It's not fair. Working on this look, studying his form, spending every waking moment thinking about how to please him, means his image has been etched upon my eyeballs. He invades my thoughts in every form, clothed and naked, laughing and growling. I sleep so little that whenever I do nod off, my dreams are vivid and intense, so realistic that I wake up disoriented and gasping, vibrating with the need to be touched.

All because of this jerk who doesn't like my design, and who probably hardly thinks of me at all.

Well, you know what? Maybe it's time I teach him a lesson. Torture him the way he tortures me.

Make him remember my name, and curse it.

A floor creak. I turn around. He takes a small step backwards, gesturing towards the door with his thumb. His vaguely embarrassed expression reminds me of a special night, not long ago. "Anyway, if you're done with me, I guess I'll leave you in peace—"

"I do think about you," I whisper before I can think too hard about it. "And not just because I have to."

His lips part, sparking a dozen ready fantasies, all thighs and abs and sliding of flesh. He takes another step towards me, crowding my air, making it thick. "What do you think about?"

My heart is racing, but I calmly meet his gaze. "You. Here. With me."

His gaze burns right through me, down to my aching depths. "Doing what?"

"Everything." I hardly dare to breathe.

"Everything?" He steps, and steps again, and one more step and we collide, chest to chest, our eyes darting and daring each other to make the next move. His hands land on my hips, searing. We stand, frozen against each other despite the throbbing heat between my legs, the warmth emanating from where I can feel him getting harder, pressing into my belly. "Can you be specific?"

"I do mean *everything*," I whisper, sliding my hands up his rigid arms. Any second now, I'll push him away and send him packing. Any second now... "But mostly, I mean you, fucking me against the wall."

"The wall," he says finally, soft as a prayer against my lips. "Is that an invitation?"

"No." I press my hips into his and set off a delicate web of electric sparks. *Now*, says my brain, urging me to hit with a cutting remark, to send him home with the bluest of balls. But my mouth doesn't listen. "It's a dare."

One second, we're standing by the table; the next, my back is up against the wall, clawing at his as he kisses me back. His hand cups my breast over my shirt, his thumb teasing my nipple until I moan against his mouth. His other hand slides down my hip, pulls on my thigh until I lift and he holds my knee, pushing my legs open enough that he can shove his huge erection exactly where I want him most.

We kiss, we grind, we reacquaint ourselves with *us*, slowly melting together, our clothes rasping as we undulate deeper and harder. My hands slide across his shoulders, up into his hair. My skin fizzes, begging for his touch, and his hands move all over, setting fire to everything in their wake.

He drops my knee and flips me to face the wall, tosses my hair to one side, and greets my neck by sucking, nibbling, tasting me greedily, his hips bearing down against my ass. My breasts are pressed into the icy wall, bracketed by my hands, and my breath echoes and condenses along the eggshell paint as he reaches around my hip to undo the button on my jeans, slipping his hand under the waistband and along my ass to pull them down. He palms me, squeezes and slaps my ass—oh!—before sliding his finger—*fingers*—along the crest between my thighs.

I can't help it. I push against him, urging him inside, moaning for him. "Darien."

"Legs apart."

My breath practically echoes against the surface as I spread my legs as much as I can with my jeans still at mid-thigh, locking me in. Behind me, he fumbles with his belt.

"You're so fucking wet already." I arch into his fingers as he strokes me, tracing my edges, nudging me open little by little. "Been thinking about me, huh?"

"Yes," I whimper.

A second later, his hot, bare dick is slapping against my ass, his teeth tugging on my earlobe.

I clench. I need him. I've got an IUD, but, please, for the love of god, tell me that—

A jangle of metal against wood. His phone and keys are on the desk next to us. And yes!—the crinkle of foil.

"You brought a condom."

"Of course."

I almost laugh. "Aren't we supposed to be *friends?*" At least, according to our contract.

"Friends can have sex." His breath on my neck sends a shiver down my spine. "Friends can do whatever they want."

Is that what we are, though? Friends? The question hangs between us, but he brushes it aside as he closes the distance and thrusts into me, and all conscious thought dissolves in a sea of sparkling bliss. His hips work against my ass, grinding slow and smooth, in and out, driving me up the wall with mind-melting pleasure. My fingers curl into fists, my elbows bent and tucked against my sides as if to fortify the arch of my back. Which is at real risk of caving in, given how he's liquefied my insides.

Somewhere in the back of my head, there's a chorus of "we shouldn't"s, "we can't"s, and yet we are, and it's better than I remember, better than anything.

And god, *the sounds*, especially with the wall amplifying everything. I'd almost be embarrassed by how wet I am if it didn't feel so goddamn good, or if he wasn't thrusting into me like his life depended on it.

He steps backward, tugging my hips with him so that I'm bent forward, palms flat against the wall, legs still restrained by my pants around my knees. When he starts to move again, I have to fight to keep my arms and legs from buckling. His hands grip my waist so hard it almost hurts, but the pain is seasoning for the sweetness of each thrust.

Why the *fuck* weren't we doing this all along?

His warmth envelops me as his left hand interlaces with mine against the wall, the fingers of his right hand slipping knowingly between my legs. I shudder with pleasure as he begins to stroke my clit, and I bring my own right hand on top of his to show him exactly how I like it—down to up, rough to light. He's a fast learner, and soon I'm holding my breath, pinpointing my focus to the movement between us, the taut strings he plays with each stroke, in and out, in and—

Darkness swallows me, soft and wavering.

And a flash of brilliant sparks as he takes me over the edge, gasping, writhing against him, begging him to finish.

With a few bruising strokes, he mashes me into the wall and cries out. "Fuck!"

Blinding, blinding pleasure as he convulses deep within me, setting off a second cascade that takes long, rippling moments to recover from.

He catches his breath, panting into my left shoulder. I bring our interlaced hands to my chest, wrapping him around me like the warmest of blankets. And for a few long, blissful moments, there's nothing between us, nothing except the soft patter of our hearts.

But through the fog, a buzzing. To our right, on the desk, on the lockscreen of his phone, a message, hidden except for the sender's name: *Eliza.*

He reaches for the phone and silences it immediately, as if he doesn't want me to see.

It's like dreaming of falling: suddenly, I jerk awake, flooded with panic, and it takes me a moment to come to my senses, to remember that I was supposed to push him away and send him packing, *before* he'd made me come.

I push him away now and find a towel to wipe off, collecting myself all the while, rebuilding the defenses that I'd disabled in a moment of stupid stupid stupid—

"Di? Is something wrong?"

I want to throw the towel at him, but I'm not a child. I knew the situation, even if I don't understand it. "What's the deal between you and Eliza?"

He licks his lips, opens his mouth. Sighs like he knew this would happen. "Why do you need the details?"

"Doing this with you...I need to understand what I'm getting myself into."

I hold back a dozen other concerns, my back and shoulders stiff and shaking, preparing to sag with disappointment. Because I can already tell from his confused smile, I'm not going to like his answers.

"I'm sorry, but...I thought we already had this conversation. You know I can't tell you the details, but that everything is fine. Isn't that enough?"

"No, it's not." God, I'm such an idiot. I cross my arms, more self-hug than anything. "I've already agreed to keep my mouth shut or else bankrupt myself. *That's* not enough?"

"You don't get it. The stakes are too high for both of us. It's better if you don't know." He lets out a frustrated sigh. "You signed an NDA because information about me is valuable. It's a burden to carry. And I like you a lot, I enjoy spending time with you, but...I don't want you to get hurt. Do you understand?"

Information about him is *valuable?* What? Can't he see that I give zero shits about his fame? I'm not some groupie slobbering for the privilege of his dick. Maybe some women would take that attitude from him and keep messing with him when he's openly engaged to someone else, but not me.

Even if I am an idiot who fucked him *again,* and knowingly this time.

"You trust me enough to sneak over here to fuck, but not enough to answer a basic question. Do you know how hypocritical that is? Being famous doesn't give you the right to keep me in the dark about your current romantic and sexual relationships with other people. If you want to have any kind of physical relationship with me, then I deserve to know. Imagine if I were fucking other dudes on the side, would that bother you?"

His eyes flash. "Are you?"

"No! But if I were, I'd have the decency to tell you, because people should be able to make informed decisions, don't you think?"

His face softens, and he searches for words, grasping at air with his hands. "It's not that I don't trust you, I just don't think you understand what—"

"I understand enough," I say with as much cold steel as I can muster. Which is a surprising amount, given how ashen and crumbly I feel inside. "If you can't treat me as an equal, then I'm not interested. Get out."

He opens his mouth to say something, but I give him a withering look and he's smart enough to grab his keys and make his way to the door.

I follow in three strides, push him out the door, and slam it in his face.

Chapter 16

Darien

Darien: Can we talk? I'd like to apologize.

"Should I leave her alone?"

From her perch on the bed, Claire smooths her hand in circles on Eliot's back, like she's waxing a tiny car. "Probably. The messages were delivered, right? She didn't block you?"

"No, she didn't block me."

"Then she knows how you feel. She'll reach out if she's interested."

"But it's a good sign that she didn't block me, right? She's still willing to hear from me?"

Claire shakes her head, and Eliot lets out the littlest *uh*, then gurgles and smiles like he guessed today's Wordle first try. "She didn't block you, she hasn't told you to leave her alone, but frankly, unless a person says, 'Yes, please talk to me,' you should probably leave them alone. That's how consent works."

"Yeah? Tell that to the paparazzi."

"Trust me, I have, in no uncertain terms. But really, give her time. Based on what you've told me, she doesn't seem like the type to hide her feelings."

She's not, and yet it's been two days with no response. As much as I work out, change diapers, and scroll through my contact list looking for someone else to talk to, my finger drifts like the arm of a record player back to her name.

I can still feel her ass squirming against me, hear her sharp, tortured breaths as I took her from behind. The pleading looks over her shoulder, her fingers guiding mine on her slick, swollen clit.

But what haunts me most is that look of pure hurt, her lovely, sex-flushed face, wide eyed and wounded as she pushed me out of her apartment. Her words.

If you can't treat me as an equal, then I'm not interested.

It's not a matter of being equal—we *are* equal. And I'm fairly confident that she means well. But if I tell her every-thing, she'll have to balance that heavy book on her head. It'll tip and tilt as everyone pushes to know what's going on, friends, family, anyone who knows we're affiliated, itching to read that book, pulling her down to get to it, hoping she'll slip. They'll promise not to tell, to help her lighten the load, and she'll be tempted. But if I confide in her, they'll keep coming back and demanding more. She doesn't know how cruel and obsessive people can be, how many friends I've lost because they trusted the wrong person. She's not used to the lying, the attention, the pressure. And if word gets out, we'll both get hammered, but with the NDA, which Tam and Eliza will move to enforce, she'll be destroyed. That's why the stakes are high.

So no, I'd rather not give her that burden, not when there's no point in continuing our relationship beyond the first Monday of May. She won't want that kind of life.

Yet, I crave her, the silk of her hair trapped between her neck and my hands. The push of her body against me, the pull of her body around me. Like blood spreading through water, memories of her fill my senses and drive me to gnaw-ing distraction, and swimming in my cage does nothing to help.

Most of all, I miss her laughter, her voice in my ear, the way her words jostle with mine like old friends elbowing one another.

I miss her even when I'm not alone.

Like right now, on this pointless video call.

"...two sisters, both of them are way older than me, though, so I had a lot of attention growing up. Maybe that explains it?"

I let out a polite chuckle, my eyes focusing back on the screen. On Madison Lin, possible Mrs. Prince Charming number two...though I doubt it. "I wouldn't know. I was the middle child."

She runs her hands through her hair, bouncing and fluffing up the long, curled locks that drape down the front of either shoulder. Almost as long as Di's hair, but not quite, and much lighter in color. "Are you and your siblings close?"

Why did I let Tam talk me into this again? "Yes, especially my sister."

Madison half-winces and asks in her mild Valley Girl accent, "But like, what about your brother?"

It feels like a kick in the ribs, but I keep my face neutral, my voice steady. "My brother and I are fine."

She leans in towards her camera as if I'm actually inside the computer and whispers, "You don't have to lie to me. Tam told me what happened. So if you want to talk about it at all, you can talk to me. I'm here for you." She draws her fingers across her lips as if closing a zipper, which reminds me of one of my worst movies, *Zip It*. A wife, a wish, a literally zippered mouth, et cetera, et cetera a la *Liar Liar*. You can imagine the reviews.

Pretty sure that's not what Madison is referencing. "What exactly did Tam tell you?"

Because Tam told *me* that this was a friendly chat. That Madison wanted a video call to ask for career advice. But unless she's worried about the career implications of her sibling fucking her partner...?

"Oh, just like, your brother..." Her face freezes as she finally realizes why I'm asking. "Well, I guess I should ask you what happened instead of telling you what she said."

"No, I'd like to know what she told you," I say lightly, promising not to bite.

"Um. Okay. She said you and your brother had like a falling out over Eliza. She told me to pretend like I didn't know and to just talk to you about your career, to try to get to know you better. But I don't want to lie to you. I want you to know that I'm an honest person, and I'm here to support you if you want to talk about it. What they did to you was like, so terrible and wrong and I'm so sorry you had to go through that." She tilts her face forward, eyes widening from almond to raw walnut. "I've been through something similar. My college boyfriend..."

Ten percent of me wants to listen, to this innocent woman who's mostly earnest in her desire to connect. Twenty percent of me is *livid* that Tam would both lie to me *and* tell this stranger my private business. The rest of me is preoccupied with a certain hot, moody designer.

I want to tell her what Tam did to me. I want to tell her about this forced, farcical conversation with this person my manager completely misread. I want her to laugh and poke fun of me, to tell me how stupid my life is, and most of all, I want to tell her the truth so that she can stop looking at me like I've kicked a puppy. So that she'll smile that dark, mischievous smile and kiss me and fuck me and make me forget everything in that way she's so good at.

If there's anyone who deserves the truth, it's Di. And if my manager thinks that Madison is worthy of knowing, then why the hell is Di not?

"Madison knows what'll happen to both you and her if she blabs," says Tam, not at all flustered or confused about my call later that day. "She understands how this works, and as someone in the industry, her own neck is on the line, too. Your fashion designer, on the other hand, doesn't. She's an unknown, we can't trust her, and I've proven that she can be bought. Which is why I hope you've followed my advice and left her alone."

I rub circles into my forehead as if I can massage in some sense, but there is none, it makes no sense. Knowing Tam, she made Madison sign an NDA, but then she's no better or worse than Di. She might "get it" a little bit more, but when it comes to leaks, a hole is a hole, no matter its shape. Now, if word gets out, it'll be harder than ever to determine where it came from—which means that Di might be a bit safer.

"You told me that the fewer people who know, the better, and yet you're telling people at your own discretion without asking me, or even Eliza?"

She sighs like I'm the densest chunk of concrete on the block. "Darien, you know I would never do something to jeopardize your career. I want nothing more than for you to succeed. But you refuse to listen to me. You're not taking steps to prepare for the next phase. I made a call to push you in the right direction because frankly, you're not think-ing clearly right now. You're hurting, and I get it, it sucks, but I'm not going to let you fail because of it."

Let me fail, as if my natural tendencies are pushing me in that direction. And they probably are. If success were a downhill sprint, everyone would be a star.

In the past, that thought might've galvanized me, but the gap between the client she wants and the client I am is too big, and I don't have what it takes to bridge it anymore. Nor do I want to. Because like Claire reminded me, life is too short to stay unhappy. Not when I know exactly what I need to be happier in this moment, assuming she'll have me.

"Please, Darien. Look at the scripts. Talk to Madison. Move on—"

"Tam, stop. Please don't do anything else on my behalf. And when I say *please don't*, I mean I'm grateful you're my manager, but really, seriously, *stop*. I'll call you when I'm ready to work again."

A pause. "Okay, fine, forget about Madison. But the scripts—"

It's rude and uncalled for, but I hang up, and it feels like clocking out early on a Friday afternoon. But as I've been telling her for months, I need a break. Like with dieting and working out, everyone needs a cheat day every so often, and right now, there's only one thing I crave.

Chapter 17

Di

I have never been one for violence, but if those birds outside don't shut the hell up, there's going to be an avian massacre.

I groan into the futon and drag a pillow over my head. It's been a day—two days?—since Darien left, and despite sleeping as much as mortally possible, my thoughts cling together like a tangle of loose necklaces. I have to tease them apart, sort which ones are real or imaginary.

Darien, standing in my kitchenette, slowly eating strawberries? Not real.

Darien, driving me up the wall, curling my body from toes to fingertips? *Too* real.

Darien, stroking my hair as I lie next to him, his body dressed in a shadowy black outfit that I can never quite focus on? I wish.

Each time I dream of *that* Darien, the look feels within reach. Like if I turned my head a little further or squinted just a bit harder, I'd see exactly what he should wear.

But the birds have decided that I've slept for long enough, and when I check the date, I guess they're right. Time's up.

Sighing, I force myself to get up, get dressed, and go to the Asian grocery store. I buy a box of Pocky—chocolate, obviously—some shrimp tom-yum-flavored Mama ramen, a lime, some eggs, a jar of sambal, and one rubberbanded bunch each of green onion and cilantro, because vegetables are an important part of a balanced meal. When I get home, I make myself the most delicious, comforting bowl of ramen in the world, and pair it with an overpriced sour beer from the store down the street.

After that warm, flavorful meal, I almost feel human again. It wasn't anything fancy (except the beer), but it never had to be. My mother's best meals were her simplest ones: rice with eggs and fried Chinese sausage, congee with strips of chicken and cilantro, a plain bowl of pho with chewy tendon-filled beef balls. As a kid, they were all the balm I'd ever needed. Because for all her harsh words, my mother never let us miss a meal, no matter how many hours she'd worked that day. It was her way of saying, *I may be tough on you, but it's out of love.*

Nostalgia blankets me from head to toe, and suddenly, the silence is suffocating. But when I pick up the phone and call my mother, she's not the one who answers.

"Hi, Je."

"Hey, Hana. How's it going?"

"Gooooood. We have over a month until school's out, but some of my teachers are already showing movies in class. Like, we watched *Gattaca* in AP Bio today."

"Haven't seen that one."

"It's good, you should watch it. The actors are sososo hot. And speaking of hot actors, how's Darien doing?"

My last memory of him floats back to the surface. The doubt and quiet yearning warring on his face before I'd slammed the door shut.

Hmph. I hope it hit his dick, too.

"That was the worst segue ever. And I'm not going to tell you anything, so don't ask."

"Ugh, *fine*. Then why are you calling?"

"Is Mom around?"

"She went for a walk. You want me to give her a message?"

"No, it's fine. Just wanted to see how she's doing."

"She's good. But I think she's concerned with how *you're* doing. What's going on over there?"

Ha. It's the question on everyone's mind, including my own.

"Not too much. Just figuring out what's next." She's my kid sister, not my mom, yet the next words cling to the back of my throat and take some coughing to dislodge. "I'm thinking about coming back home."

"Like, for my graduation?"

"Yes? But then staying on after, too. Like, for a while." Mostly likely until I die a bitter death and haunt our tiny rowhome.

"O...h."

It's a single, slow-cracking syllable that hits like a seam ripper, plucking out the stitches of my chest. I hold it together and keep my voice light. "It makes sense, right? I mean, at my age, it was kind of ridiculous to try something new."

"How can you say that? It's not even true! Vera Wang didn't design her first dress until she was forty."

"How do you know that?"

"Because I just googled 'never too old to become a fashion designer' and that's what came up."

"How did you do it so quickly?"

"Because I'm young and spry. Keep up."

I let out the groan of someone twice my age. She laughs and continues, "Je, I know you're worried about us, but we're fine. And I have some news: I just found out that I got a full ride to Stevens! We don't have to worry about my tuition anymore!"

"Wait, really?"

"Yes!"

"Oh. That's great." A full ride. Free college. Something *I* never accomplished. "But you said you wanted to go to Bryn Mawr, right?"

Our voices are similar, so I know that she's putting on the same "light" tone that I just did. "It doesn't matter. College is college. I'll be fine."

"College is not *college*, and besides, I have the money to cover your tuition." I Robin-Hooded Darien for *you*.

"College is, like, *literally* college. And if you have the money, then why are you trying to leave L.A.? Why not put it towards your business?"

"Because the money's for you! And besides, I told you, I'm too old for this. I don't have what it takes to hustle out here. So I'm going to use the money for more practical things, like your education."

The light tone is gone. She puts on our mom's *You're Being Stubborn* voice, which makes me feel like the roof is slowly coming down. "I have a *free ride*. Four years of *room*, *board*, and *tuition* for *zero* dollars and *zero* cents at a *good school*. I'm not turning it down, so just keep the money and invest it in yourself! I mean, you're designing a look for the *Met Gala!* How cool is that? My friends are so jealous and curious and totally *obsessed!* Which, by the way, can you *please* tell me what the look is like? Please please please?"

I consider forcing us back to the original topic, but let it slide. She's like a Chinese finger trap—the harder I pull, the harder she'll pinch, and the more groany-grumbly we'll both get. "Fine. I'm making him a tux."

"Oh. Really? But, like, that's so not you."

Even my sister knows that. "Exactly. But it's what he asked for." And now that Darien's seen my best effort and shown me his reaction, it's lost its sparkle for me, too. I'm not going to pour my heart into a look just to have him and everyone else take a steaming dump on it. Better to make a simple tux, fulfill the contract, and fade into obscurity back in New Jersey, where I can eat all the subs and pork roll that I could ever want.

"Je, if you're quitting fashion, shouldn't you go out on a bang? Do something amazing as a big eff-you to all the haters? I thought that was your style."

That's not how life works, I want to tell her. Not everyone gets a chance to do something amazing or say eff-you. Some people are destined for nine-to-fives, and for scrolling on their phones to admire other people's acts of hopeful rebellion.

But she's 18 and just getting started. She should hold on to her shine for as long as possible. "You're right, I'm not making a tux, but I can't tell you the truth. It's a secret."

"I knew it! It's going to be so awesome! I can't wait to see what you come up with. Especially because—" She pauses and clears her throat. "I know you were worried about moving out there to do something so risky, but I'm really proud of you for taking the chance. And Mom's proud, too. She brags about you to everyone who will listen, says she has a daughter who's going to become a famous fashion designer."

I close my eyes against the sudden flood. "That's surprising. You know how unhappy she was when I left."

And with every other decision in my life. The tattoos, the clothes, my close friendship with Mischa...every choice has been a battle between what's important to me and what's important to her. But the older I get—the older *she* gets—the easier it is to simply agree. Which is why coming out to L.A. has felt like the last stand, and I'm on the verge of surrender.

"That's just because Mom was nervous about not having you around. But we've adjusted, we've gotten by just fine. You deserve this time for you."

I don't deserve anything. I've spent almost a year in L.A. already, and while I've learned a lot, I still don't have much to show for it. It's only because of Darien, of what I took from him, that I was able to find my footing. Before him, I was juggling shards of glass, and everything was either ready to cut me or crack at the slightest misstep. Now that I've had a few weeks of not worrying about rent, insurance, food, and so on, I've been able to take a step back and see what's important. Reprioritize.

As much as it feels like closing the book, I'd rather have stability than excitement and meaning. I'll leave that to the youths, like Hana.

Though it'd be nice to go out with a bang, wouldn't it.

Oh, god, speaking of banging... "Hey, you never told me about Mom's boyfriend." And my mother hasn't been picking up my calls. Almost like she knows what I'm going to say.

"Oh yeah, sorry! But unless you tell me about your boyfriend, I'm not telling you about Mom's."

"He's not my boyfriend," I grumble, tapping back over to his messages. "I'd hesitate to even call him a friend." Unless even his friends don't know about his relationship status. But if that's the case, how sad.

"Are you *suuure?* I swear I won't tell anyone."

"Yeah, right." If I tell her anything, it'll be all over JibJab in a second, and I'll be posting on Craigslist about selling my eggs, hair, and blood with bulk discounts.

Durian: Can we talk? I'd like to apologize.

It's funny when people say "I'd like to apologize" instead of just apologizing. It makes me wonder if he's got some sort of act planned for me. But even if I let him do a full song and dance, what's the point? It won't change anything about our situation.

When she's positive I won't tell her a damn thing, Hana heads off to ultimate practice and I get on with my day. I poke around my apartment, hunting for the bolt of black satin I bought forever ago, but while searching under my futon, I find something else: a recycled black wool-cotton blend that's softer than Attila and way less aggressive. I let my hands wander over its length, let their threads whisper against my thumbs.

Don't waste us, they tell me. *Use us.*

I could sell the entire bolt for a fraction of what I paid for it. Or I could donate it to a more promising twenty-something, one who doesn't have a lump of coal in her chest.

Or...I can stop making excuses and start making clothes.

I ditch the satin and pick up my shears and pins, letting my hands *go*, flowing over the gorgeous fabric like a ship with no sails on a winter sea. It feels like dancing alone in my room to the trashiest, guiltiest, pleasure-iest music, enjoying the experience of *me* and what I like. Not anyone else.

I let myself simply play.

After a long night, I emerge from the trees, taking a step back to see what can be salvaged. Most of it, actually. It feels like deja vu, like this dark, daring outfit was waiting to step out of my subconscious, my own personal Galatea.

But just the clothes. There's no face or flesh beneath the cloth.

My Prince Charming doesn't exist.

Anyway, the look. It's dramatic. It has flair. It's got that *Ho factor* that Mischa was asking about. And I have his measurements. I'll make it fit. He's going to wear what I want him to wear or not at all...and in any case, the look is for *me*.

I cut, I sew, I stitch, I press. I fiddle around while the sun sends shadows dancing across my walls to the sounds of modern synthwave, blasting from my laptop.

Which is why it takes me several seconds to realize that someone's knocking, and it's not Mischa's knock.

I almost drop my shears in my rush to the door. But when I look through the peephole, it's not anyone I know. "Who are you, what do you want?"

The skinny young man looks straight back into the peephole, blocking the light from outside. "I have a gift basket for a Dee Ho? Die Ho? Oh damn, I hope that's not a threat."

Hmmm...a gift basket, or a murder basket? What if a deranged fan of Darien's or Eliza's has found my address?

Or what if... "Leave it there."

"I need you to sign for it."

"*You* sign for it. And leave."

He frowns, but does as I ask. When he's good and gone, I bring the basket inside to my desk and untie the gauzy pink silk that's wrapped around it.

The fabric falls away, and I gape.

Pink, so much pink. Strawberry Pocky, strawberry Chocorooms, pandas, koalas, Yan Yan, wafers...strawberry everything, even fresh strawberry-yogurt-dipped strawberries. And nestled among them, a card. It's an image of Gravedigger Barbie with pink heels on, smiling her plastic smile and holding a shovel with a skull on it, with a word bubble that says "I REALLY DIG YOU."

Inside the card, a simple message.

Let me change your mind?

Please.

-D

I drop onto my futon, heart flapping like a bat in a cave, screeching into the dark.

I stare at his words, at that one little *Please*, and my cat-in-a-box feelings come roaring back.

During the one episode of *FBOY Island* that I'd watched with Mischa and her friends, I'd shaken my head at those poor gullible women, falling for all those slimy smiles. And yet, here I am, quivery and buttered up like piping-hot popcorn, with no idea of what kind of man I've got on my hands: a fuckboy, a nice guy, or something else entirely.

His past words and actions should speak louder than a basket of sugar, but they don't change the fact that I *am* quivery and buttered up, or that it beats feeling dead and dull and completely hopeless, like the story is over before the climax. So I know it's stupid, and I guess I never learn, but...I want to keep playing the game. Because even if I'll probably lose, it's fun, right?

And at the very least, we've already agreed on an end date.

Di: are you trying to give me ants?

Di: who's going to eat all this

Durian: I'll help you. Just say the word

Di: it's fine. the raccoons have been looking hungry

Durian: Okay. If that's what you want to do with it

Durian: And I'm sorry for what I said, or how I made you feel

Durian: I'll make it up to you, I promise

Di: I'm kidding about the raccoons

Di: thank you. very sweet of you

Di: literally, so much sugar

Di: and I already bought a box of chocolate pocky yesterday, but I'll save it

Di: we can do a taste test together next time you're here

Di: and you can see the error of your ways

Durian: When?

Good question. I glance at the half-formed outfit on the mannequin, tabulating the remaining work.

Di: give me a couple of days
Durian: Okay. I'll wait
Durian: In the meantime, I'll be playing Unhunter
Durian: If you need a break
Di: I'll let you know if I have time

I don't, not really, not if I'm actually going to make this look for him. But I use it as a dangling carrot to go even faster and snort a few boxes of strawberry-covered snacks as fuel. So by the time it's dark out again, I've got most of the foundation for the look complete: the overcoat, the cowl, the pants underneath, all sewn and fitted and ready for detailing. Of course, it's the detailing that's going to take forever to do, especially now that I care about his opinion again and I'm second-guessing all the changes I've made. I mean, I like it better and I think it's my favorite thing ever, but that's what makes it even scarier now. I'm not sure I'm ready to share a bigger piece of my heart only to watch him shrug and kick it down the road with a "Could we maybe do this another time?"

But it's too late to go back, too late to back down. If he doesn't like the look, I'll just have to sell it to someone else.

Even if his name is stitched into every seam.

Chapter 18

Darien

Di: 9pm. my UH handle is sesamecake22

I'm online by 8:30, practicing. I wait until a respectable 9:02, however, to give her a call.

"Hey."

Spoken like a PA on a weekend shift, and yet I grin like an idiot. "Hey. Thanks for getting back to me. I—"

"Did you want to do co-op or High Moon?"

Right. I swallow the full apology for later. "You talked so much smack about being able to hold your own against me, we'd better do High Moon. Best of five."

It takes her a second to respond, and I hope it's because she's recalling the night she said that to me. When we were lying in bed, me between her legs, on the verge of the most intense sexual experience of my life...with the exception of last time, when I fucked her against that wall.

God, I miss that wall.

"Fine. But if I win, you have to tell me what's going on between you and Eliza."

"I'm going to tell you anyway, so you might as well ask for something else." When she doesn't reply, I add, "Sky's the limit, really." And while I don't really think she'll ask for another two hundred thousand dollars, my stomach is tight and prepared for a punch. She was pretty mad the last time I saw her.

When she finally speaks, her tone is softer. "Could I get a tablet computer for my design work?"

"Sure." My stomach relaxes. "But if I win, I get to come over."

"Tonight?"

"Yeah. We won't do anything you don't want to. We can just hang out. Eat a snack. *Talk*. I just...I want to see you."

Again, she's slow to answer, but I have this feeling that it's because her mouth is too busy trying not to smile. I hope. "Fine."

"Then it's a deal. Okay?"

"Deal."

I press start, and the match countdown begins as the level loads. It's a map I've played many times before, a bleak and foggy cliffside jungle setting with a beach and caves, trees and treehouses, densely crammed together like a haunted Donkey Kong Island.

"I hope you're ready to stay up all night. *Talking*, that is."

There it is, a tiny exhalation, a definite smile in her voice. "And I hope your wallet is ready to pay for my tablet."

When the match starts, I pick my poison—heart—and dash up to the high point of the map, a tree on a hill, to find her. At the top of my screen, off in the distance, a she-wolf appears, complete with Popeye-level biceps and tattered peasant attire. She's carrying a slingshot and jumping up and down as she moves.

My he-vamp doesn't have the best range, but he's still capable of sniping. When she gets close enough, I load a silver coin into my crossbow and take my time, aiming carefully, carefully...

My first shot pops harmlessly off to the side, and the she-wolf slides and jumps to avoid another shot, but I quickly aim and reload. Once, twice, first with a heart, then with a garlic bulb.

The bulb sticks.

"Boom! Headshot!" I hurry over and teabag her molding corpse several times.

"Nice," says Di, tone flat.

"That's it? I took you out in like fifteen seconds."

"Yeah, well, it took you a couple of tries. And it's best of five, so..."

"Sure, whatever."

The next match starts, but this time, I take off in a different direction. If she's any good, she won't fall for the same trick twice. I make my way down instead of up, towards where I think she's spawned. But I march around the map, and she's not there. Maybe she's in the cave—

My vamp is smacked with a heart. Somehow, Di's gotten behind me, close enough to hit me by hand.

"Lucky."

She cackles. "Luck had nothing to do with it." And she teabags my ashes a half-dozen times before they float away.

The next round, I pick heart as my poison again. Her Medusa and my golem leave traps for each other on the map. She sets off one of mine, but gets away because it's the wrong poison. But I know where she is, and as I run towards her, she jumps out at me from the side. I aim for the face, but she strafes around me, trying to shank me first with a coin. She misses—wrong poison.

"Do you only melee? No shooting?" In first-person shooters, melee attacks are only meant for unexpected close-quarters combat. Maybe she's trying to melee because she's a terrible shot...which means that I have this match in the bag.

But she sounds strangely smug when she says, "I'm not telling you."

She circles past and runs off, and when I turn to use my character's special rolling ability, she reappears and slaps me in the face with a heart.

I growl and flex my fingers, shake out my hands.

"Getting annoyed yet?"

"No," I lie. "Getting ready to finish you off."

"I don't think so." She laughs, taunting me, but I find myself relaxing into the sound.

Next, I select vamp again and spot her banshee dodging between trees. I line it up, but can't quite pull off a headshot. But the next shot—a bulb—gets her, and she melts into a puddle.

"I hope you're wearing something sexy. To talk to me in."

"I'll be wearing whatever you want me to...in your dreams."

I chuckle at her confidence, but then curse when the last level loads before I've cleared a too-detailed image of her from my mind.

I choose heart again and decide to play it her way—slow, careful, creeping around the map and looking around. I head to the center of the map, near the treehouse. The way she plays will require her to—

A pop, and my character is hit with a heart.

"Woo! Headshot!"

I stare, dumbfounded. "Seriously?" The screen zooms out and her ghoul is far off on the other side of the map, up on a hill behind a rock. A tough shot. If she'd been capable of that all along, then why has she been melee—

Wow.

Wow.

She's been messing with me.

And I'm not sure if I'm impressed, annoyed, or turned on.

All of the above.

The screen goes grayscale, and the words "YOU DIED" appear. Shit.

"Way to be predictable with the hearts."

"It wasn't predictable. You got it wrong a few times."

"Uh huh. Well, I know exactly which tablet model I want. I'll send you the info later, when we're done. Do you want to keep playing?"

"What, so you can keep murdering me?"

"Hey, don't you believe in yourself? Can't you rise to the challenge?" She laughs, and it's so nice to hear the sound again that I find myself smiling, too, even though she's rubbing my face in it. "If you want, I'll give you a chance to redeem yourself. Beat me in a Creation Contest and I'll let you off the hook."

"Fine, you're on." Though I'll happily send her a tablet anyway.

We keep playing and we keep talking. And *Unhunter* won Game of the Year for a reason, so soon I'm lost in the jungles with her, side by side, turning as many human chimeras into vamps or werewolves as possible.

She tells me that her friend Mischa is the one who introduced her to video games. They used to play in the basement of Mischa's mom's house and challenge guys to matches for money.

I tell her about Claire and her once-upon-a-time love for role-playing games. I briefly mention Ethan, but only to emphasize how bad he was at video games because he's always been more into sports.

Di's sister Hana plays frisbee, but I already knew that from her social media accounts. Hana only wears sweats and listens to top-40 music, but Di loves her anyway, like a second mom.

And it turns out that neither of us have our dads in our lives.

"What happened to yours?" I ask. "You said he left?"

"He said he was going to Vietnam to visit and then he never came back. We found out from some of my mom's cousins that he's got another family over there."

"Fuck. I'm sorry."

"I'm not. It was hard on my mom, but things were stressful for a different reason when he was around. We've been better off without him." In the game, she corners a creepy ostrich-man and turns him into a howling wolf. "What happened to yours?"

"Stroke. He was 35."

"That's awful. I'm sorry."

"Yeah. My mom and dad got divorced way before that, though, and my mom had custody of us, so he'd already felt like less a part of our lives. And she seems pretty happy with her new husband."

Without my father around, she'd turned into a completely different person. Before, she was strict and anxious, unable to make a move without butting heads with him. With Carl, she's confident, happy, and relatively independent. Ethan got the upgraded version of her.

"Are you close to him? Your step-dad?"

"He treats me well and he loves my mom. I wouldn't say we're close, though. He's got his own son."

"You mean your half-brother?"

"Yeah."

"And how's your relationship with *him*?"

My laugh is brittle and wilted, and I'm glad when the level finally starts and I can go shoot things. "Fucked."

She disarms a coin bomb and we do a sweep of the cave, both of us shooting hearts and bulbs at the three snarling possum-men who jump out. "Why? If you don't mind my asking."

I open my mouth to answer, but shame clogs my throat. I agreed to tell her, but I know how it's going to go. Like that kid's book, *If You Give A Mouse A Cookie*: if you tell a person you were cheated on, they'll ask about what happened and why and this and that until you've gone full circle and nothing has changed except that you're annoyed at both yourself and the mouse for asking for so much.

But I have to get used to talking about it. This is what it is from now on.

"We used to get along well," I say finally. "I'd even go so far as to say that he was a close friend, especially when I went away to college. I think the space helped us be a little more honest with each other." I rapidly tap on the trigger and take a boar-lady. "But that all went away when he and Eliza had an affair."

He and Eliza had an affair. It's a short sentence, but I've had to endure its violent echo for months.

Di takes a while to process it, too. "Your fiancée...cheated on you with your half-brother?"

"Yep."

I wait for the questions. The disbelief. The sympathetic anger. I prepare to admit my own guilt in the situation, the things I could've done, my own wild speculation. Meanwhile, a slimy moth-man takes my character out with a baseball bat, and I have to wait a full twenty seconds to respawn. They crawl past like ants through sap.

"That sucks." Di's voice is firm, yet gentle, a caress to the cheek.

"It does." I take a sip of my bubbly water and wish that it burned going down. "But now you know who cheated on whom."

Her character gets boiled to death, and she waits to respawn, too. "But then why are you still faking your relationship?"

"We're waiting for the premiere of her upcoming movie, and to see if they're going to stay together. If they don't work out long-term, there's no point in creating a scandal out of it."

"So you're covering for her?"

"It's not just for her. The scandal will affect both of our careers. The four months gives me time to prepare for the announcement, too."

We're going to pretend like it was a joint decision, but I already know what people will say. Even if she stays with Ethan, they'll say that I'm the one who fucked it up somehow. That I was never good enough for her. That she was with me out of pity. She was always the bigger star, and I'm the one that people speculated about. Of all the men she could've picked, why me?

"So what's the best case scenario? She stops seeing your brother and you both pretend things ended on good terms? Or like...are you hoping she'll come back to you?"

Her question gets quieter with each word.

"We're done. There's no coming back from this. And the two of them can do whatever they want." It surprises me how much I mean those words, and how little it hurts. Like I've yanked out an abscessed tooth and now all that's left is the odd, empty sensation of the hole closing. "Anyway, you mentioned how much people have been prying into your life because of me. I didn't want to make it even harder for you. And if this does get out somehow, even by accident, Tam and Eliza will be looking at *you*. I wanted to be able to protect you and say that you had absolutely no idea."

"Are you saying that no one else knows?"

"I can count the number of people who know on two hands, I think." Unless Tam's been giving out NDAs like free samples.

"I see." Her character narrowly avoids falling into a pit, but now it's two against one, and there's a lobster-woman with a chainsaw hot on her tail. "So what happens when four months is up?"

"Nothing," I say after a moment. "We announce our split. We move on." I pick up another dumb movie and kick off the official decline of my career. After years of growing alongside her, we'll see how well I stand on my own, like a vine that's been stripped of its trellis.

My character jumps up, alive once more, but there's an immediate spray of fire that comes my way. I can't focus. I'm killed again, and when the final count appears, Di's beaten me 28 to 13.

I toss the controller onto the couch. "Sorry. I think I'm done with this game for tonight."

"Yeah. Me too."

I get up to turn off the console. "I'll admit it—you're better than me at *Unhunter.*" I stand and stretch, yawning. "Thanks for playing. This was fun."

"You're going to bed?"

"Yeah." I turn off the TV with the remote. "I have an early morning training session tomorrow."

"But...didn't you want to come over?"

Her words are a shot of adrenaline. "You're inviting me over?"

"Or maybe, you know, I've been cooped up all day so I kind of want to get out. Should I meet you somewhere?" There's a desperation in her voice, a quickness to her words that feels like a limited time offer.

I grab my keys. "I'll swing by and we can decide there."

"Okay. See you in twenty."

She ends the call, and I rush to grab my jacket and head out, ready to make it ten instead of twenty.

But when I open the door to the garage, I come face to face with Eliza.

She's crying.

Chapter 19

Di

I fly around the apartment, a fluttery mass, shoving things away and getting ready to go out. I even throw open the door to my closet and take it out—*the dress*, the only dress I own. It's not black, but midnight blue, and the soft mushroom-leather fabric hugs my curves like matte paint. I remove my pajamas and slip on the teeny shoulder straps, tugging the skirt down to my knees, making sure that the slit at the back doesn't reveal my bare ass, or the wide v-neckline doesn't pop my nips out. A combo choker-and-titanium-bar-pendant hangs between my breasts, with matching chain earrings on my ears, and I leave my hair down, mostly tame but on the edge of wild, the tips just barely kissing the top of my ass. My cherry red Docs will finish the look.

But when I stop to study my reflection, the gust that sped my movements dies, and swirling petals fall to the ground.

What am I, a horny virgin? He's done nothing to deserve this dress. I shouldn't show him my hottest look before he's earned it.

And worse, why did I agree to let him come over again, and at this hour? It's like I'm begging to go bankrupt.

As I reach for the zipper to undo this mistake, there's a knock at the front door. I press my body against it, peering into the peephole. He's here, dressed in a plain black tee and joggers, leaning and looking around like he's about to pee against the wall. "Di?"

"Could you give me a few minutes?"

"Still?" He frowns, turning his ear in to better listen at the door. "Everything okay?"

"Yeah, I just…I need to change."

"Why?" He looks at his watch. "I'm sure whatever you've got on is fine."

"No, I need to change." But I stay rooted on the spot, unable to move.

He rests his hand against the door and leans in to whisper, "Then can I help you get out of your clothes?"

My heart crumbles, imagining the things we could get up to, the way his hands would caress my body like warm rain. But rushing into things hasn't been working out for us, and I somehow doubt that third time's a charm. "Not happening."

He blinks straight at me through the door. "Is something wrong?"

I step away from the hole, unable to look. "Just give me a few minutes, okay? I'll be quick."

"Then let me in. Don't make me wait out here. Someone might walk by. Di, please—"

"Fine!" I throw the door open.

He sucks in a breath, and his eyes go all intense like a lion spotting an antelope. And it's sad to say, but this antelope's first instinct is to spread its legs and stick its ass out.

"Why do you need to change again?"

With him there, real, blanketing me with his gaze, I have to ask myself the same question. "I don't want you to get the wrong idea."

He takes a slow breath, and when his words come out, low and husky, I feel each one like a brush between my legs. "I don't know, you look like the right idea to me."

Heat scalds my cheeks. "Just hurry up and come in."

My skin feels like I've left a chemical peel on for too long, and his hands are the only balm. But I gather the will to shake my head and step aside to let him in. He brushes past me in a cloud of spicy musk that I both hate and want to linger in, but I force myself to stillness and let him in before closing the door.

The softness on his face is unbearable. "Di, you look—"

"Shut up, Darien. Don't say anything. I'm going to change."

But he catches my shoulder as I leap away. "Wait, why, what's wrong? What did I do?"

"Nothing! But we're just friends. Don't make this weird."

He frowns at my dress, then up at my face. "It's fine if you invited me over as a friend." His eyes go dark. "Friends can do whatever they want, remember?"

"See? Wrong idea." I sigh and rub the back of my neck. "Look, this thing between us? We can't act on it. Neither one of us can afford to get caught together. You can't keep sneaking over here, and I'm not sneaking out to your place."

"Why not? The paparazzi haven't caught on yet, right? Your place is safe. As long as we don't go anywhere too public, we should be fine."

He says it so casually, like it's not a big deal for a mega-celebrity to sneak over to my tiny WeHo apartment. Like he doesn't care about the risks.

Or like maybe he thinks...I'm worth it?

I peer into his face, searching. "You want to keep seeing me that much?"

"I do." He smiles so beautifully, my sewing mannequin sighs. "I'm sorry about how I've treated you. I thought I was protecting you, but I've finally come to realize that it's up to you to decide if I'm worth the risk. And honestly, after spending these past few days without you, I've realized that you're worth it to *me*."

I pat my cheeks, surprised that they're not on fire after my brain just short-circuited. "Oh."

He steps closer. "May I?"

"May you what…"

I trail off as his fingers lift my chin. His face looms closer, and panic erupts, a swirling maelstrom of doubt whipping about in my head. It vanishes when his lips touch mine, soft and dreamy—the eye of the storm, where dozens of dew-kissed flowers drift on warm wafts, falling and rising sweetly with our tongues.

As soon as his lips are off, the storm is back, leaving me spinning and on the verge of being swept away. But Darien's eyes lock onto mine, pinning me.

His fingers caress an earlobe, tracing down my jaw. "I know things are kind of weird right now. But that felt good, didn't it?"

My lips still tingle from his kiss, and my head craves that meditative calm. That rightness.

I nod.

"Then let's just enjoy ourselves. See where this goes."

Dingdingding! screams my FBOY-dar. *That's what a fuckboy would say!* And yet, when he smiles and lowers his head again, this time, I rise up on my toes to meet him, eager to leave my tangled doubts behind, at least for a little while.

His fingers thread through my hair, combing, lifting, lightly tugging. I moan and tuck myself further into him, my hands cupping the corded muscle of his lats, sliding down the twin ridges on either side to his waist. God, he's ripped.

We kiss, and we kiss, and it's wonderful, sweet and rich, better than my aunt's special dessert of warm tapioca pudding with coconut milk and bananas.

But that's precisely why this thing between us won't last. With hunger this exquisite, we'll gorge ourselves silly and get sick after. It's a pattern I've repeated over and over, which is why none of my non-cheater relationships have lasted longer than six months.

But the intensity of my craving for him, his full-bodied kisses... I've never wanted someone as much as this.

And it's going to hurt that much more when we're done.

There's a sound that's eerily similar to one of those plastic groan-tube noisemaker sticks from my childhood, but deeper and longer lasting. We stop kissing, and it takes a moment for my hazy brain to realize that it was my gut.

His lips twitch, but he has the decency not to laugh. "Have you eaten yet?"

I have to pause and think about it. "No, actually. I haven't eaten all day." Oops.

"Nothing, not at all?"

I shake my head. "I was busy."

He takes out his phone and begins swiping through delivery options. "What would you like?"

"Um..." The restaurant menus he's looking at seem healthy and overpriced. If I'm being honest... "Could we maybe get some In-n-Out? I've been craving it all week."

He considers, and for a moment I worry that he'll judge me for wanting fast food. But all he says is, "I guess so, but they don't deliver so you'll have to run in and get it. I'd rather not pull up to the drive-thru, in case I get recognized."

I hook my fingers in his belt and pull him close again, gazing up into his eyes. My antelope urges are back. "You're willing to go out for me? In public?"

He blinks at that, examining the question more closely. After a moment, his eyebrows rise, as if surprised at his own conclusion. "I'm willing. But only if you have a better disguise for me."

I take a step back and assess him, standing there all big and muscled. Disgustingly hot. "Okay, I can find you something. I'll change into something else, too—"

He grabs my hand. "Don't. Please."

He spears me with a look, and suddenly it feels like a greenhouse in July.

"Okay, I won't. But let me find you something."

I go into my closet and find an old jacket that I made, an oversized hooded techwear jacket with a large collar, patchwork pockets, and metal studs on the sleeves. "Here. For you."

He eyes it skeptically before accepting and slipping it on. It's a bit snug around the shoulders, but it fits well enough, and I can't help but admire the way it looks on him. Paired with his black tee and joggers, he's halfway ready for Berghain.

He smooths his hands along the cloth. "I love whatever this fabric is. It's so comfortable."

"It's hemp. I get it from a sustainable manufacturer here in L.A."

He pulls up the wide hood to cover his face, and stuffs his hands into the pockets. "Do I look creepy?"

"Less creepy than when you wear a baseball cap and sunglasses at night."

But then he puts on this pervy, flat-eyed grin. All that's missing is a thin 'stache. "How about now?"

I mirror it back to him, and we laugh like kids hopped up on candy.

We get into his car and drive to the closest In-n-Out, the one on Sunset. He parks and slouches into the seat, hiding, while I walk into the building, order, and wait. It's packed with customers with whom I carefully avoid eye contact, just in case they recognize me, or in case they like my dress a little too much. I don't start breathing normally again until I'm headed back to the car, my grilled cheese with onions, animal-style fries, and chocolate milkshake neatly arranged on a cardboard tray for easy eating.

As I walk out the door, a group of three guys in jeans and tight tees approaches. One of them whistles, unsteady on his feet, and comes a bit too close. I step aside.

"Hey sweetheart, where's the party at?" he shouts, as if I'm not right next to him.

I look him dead in the eyes and say, "Your mom's house."

His friends laugh as they walk away, but not before one of them calls me a slur.

I freeze. Whip around. "Wanna say that to my face, squirrel dick?"

They keep walking, but one of them calls out, "Shut up and eat your food, you fat slut."

Oh good, just what I needed tonight. I look for a place to put the tray down, heart pounding, rapidly composing the most gruesome takedown of these human lice, when the car door swings open and a huge figure in black steps out. Hood on, collar zipped, sunglasses in place, he gestures menacingly towards them. "Did you say something to her? Huh? Do you think it's okay to—"

"Hey, you!" I push him back towards the car. "Back inside."

But he's still barking at the three rats, who hurry into the restaurant. "Get back out here. Come say what you said to *me*—"

I slap his chest.

"Ow. Hey, what are you hitting me for?"

"You're not listening to me! Back into the car, now."

Still fuming, he shakes his head and gets back into the car. I slide into the passenger seat and put the tray down on my lap before clicking in my seatbelt. "Let's get out of here."

But he doesn't start the car. He sits there, staring out the driver side window, his hands gripping the door handle so hard I'm surprised the car isn't honking in protest.

"Darien, it's fine. Let's go."

His jaw flexes. "Someone should teach them a lesson."

"That person isn't you," I say, shifting the tray on my lap, "and none of them are going to learn the right lesson from your fists. Or probably ever, from anything."

He watches for several moments longer before turning his glare forward. Still, he doesn't start the car.

I unbuckle my seatbelt, put the tray on the console between us, and adjust my legs so that I'm mostly facing him. Comfortably settled, I open the box of animal-style fries and begin to eat. In seconds, the entire car smells of fried, cheesy heaven.

He takes off the sunglasses and turns to watch as I munch. "You don't care about what just happened?"

The fries are thin and overcooked, but after not eating all day, they're the best I've ever had. "Of course I care. I was ready to throw down and punch them all in the dick. Verbally, at least. But then you came along and almost blew your cover."

"I couldn't just sit there while they did that to you." Darien squeezes his hands on his lap as if wringing their tiny necks. "That one guy called you an ugly chink."

"Yeah, I heard him." I use two fries as a platform for a glob of delicious Thousand Island sauce. "And I had it handled. You shouldn't have gotten out of the car." If he'd been recognized, our 'see where this goes' would've ended after less than an hour, and I'd be on my hands and knees at the dump, searching for old crypto wallets.

He scoffs. "Handled? Three against one?"

"You really think they were going to do something to me in a busy parking lot? All I was going to do was give them an earful." But now, instead of remembering that I stood up to them, all they're going to remember is the physical threat of another guy.

"You don't know how people will react. Especially when they're drunk."

"Yeah, well, as soon as you stepped out of the car, things were headed in a bad direction. And as much fun as *Unhunter* is, I'm not actually a fan of violence."

I pick up a well-coated fry and hold it up to his lips. He starts to shake his head, but then opens his mouth and lets me slide it in. "Does this happen to you a lot?"

"Not to me, no. I'm usually too scary looking. But the things that men say to women *like* me, or my mom, my sister, my aunts? God, there's so much that I wish these guys could experience from the other side."

I want them to understand what it feels like to be treated as less than human, as an object for pleasure and entertainment. I want them to experience powerlessness, victimhood, for them to be defined by the things they've endured rather than who they are. I've seen the dark spaces in the internet where men like that think they can hide, where they fester and infect each other into believing that women are the reason why they're lonely and can't get laid, as if their lack of nutting is a reason to hurt us. Where they accuse us of rigging an impossible game against them, instead of examining their own selfish assumptions. I want them to be exposed and reviled, punished for the crimes they induce each other to commit.

But most of all, I want them to leave me and people like me alone so that we can live our fucking lives.

I've been shoving fries into my own mouth, but I pick up another fully loaded fry and hold it to his lips again. He opens up, and I insert the fry, but this time, his warm lips close on my thumb, sucking away the animal sauce, sending heat straight from his mouth to my core. And when he looks at me with those dark, dangerous eyes...

Ugh. It's unfair.

As much as I hate to admit it, I love how big he is, how physical. And knowing that he was willing to use that in service of my safety and dignity...

I squeeze my thighs together and wipe my fingers off on a napkin. "Let's get out of here. Please?"

Finally, he starts the car and we zip out of the parking lot. I move the tray back into my lap so that it doesn't go flying.

We drive in silence for a few minutes, but I can tell it's still on his mind. He's not angry anymore, but there's a shadow hovering over his brow, and it's not from the jacket hood.

He notices me glancing his way. "It feels like we let them get away with it."

"You scared them, and that's good enough. They didn't strike me as people who'd be open to having a heart-to-heart."

"Yeah, but—"

"And beating them up wasn't going to change how they felt about me or you or anyone who looks like us. That requires actual empathy and effort on their part, a desire to change their minds, and heading into an In-n-Out while drunk is not the time to change hearts and minds. Anyway, my mom believes in karma, so I assume they'll get food poisoning or speeding tickets tonight. Maybe syphilis."

"You're eating from the same place, so you'd better hope it's not food poisoning."

"I have the raccoon of a stomach. Wait. Other way around."

He doesn't smile. I pick up his right hand and straighten out his fingers, massaging them. "I just want to enjoy my night with you. And I know you talk and think about it a lot, but it's not your job to undo all of racism or asshole-dom. That just sounds exhausting."

He doesn't respond, but his fingers tighten around mine. So thick and callused. So strong.

The car slows to a stop at a fresh red light. Safely putting the tray on the dash, I unbuckle my seatbelt and swoop over to his side, grasping his cheeks in my hands, molding my mouth to his. My ass must've bumped a button, because the car radio comes on and *Lovefool* by The Cardigans blasts all around us.

It started as a thank you, but with the music spurring us on, I kiss him with everything I've got. Everything, every unspoken hope and midnight longing, every soft-glowing fairy tale fantasy that even I've had once upon a time.

When I pull away, his eyes blaze so hot the air is almost shimmering between us.

I trace his jaw with my fingers. "Thanks for wanting to stick up for me. That's sweet of you. But I'm not one of your princesses. I don't need rescuing."

His thumbs caress my hips, burning through my dress. "You might not need rescuing, but you deserve respect."

His gaze is earnest, steady with promise, asking me to believe.

It almost hurts, how much I want to.

For so long, I've been the pillar. I've been Hana's pillar, my mom's pillar, and my own damn pillar, too. I've had Mischa to help me along the way, but with John, her lifestyle, and her other friends, she's not as reliable as she once was.

To think that I can lean on someone else...

I shouldn't get used to it, but it's a nice thought.

He gives me a teasing smile. "Aren't you named after a princess?"

"Darien—"

The car behind us honks. The light's green again.

I sit back into my seat and click the seatbelt on before replacing the tray on my lap. Once I'm settled, he starts driving, but reaches over and steals some of my fries before I can swat his hand away. "Hey!"

"It's a driver tax." He licks a bit of sauce from his lips. "These taste better than I remember."

"Fine, but keep your eyes on the road."

On the radio, the 90s hits play on.

With one long, folded fry, I swipe up some cheesy sauce and feed it to him as he drives, his eyes dutifully trained on the road. I give myself one, then him another. He tries to lick my finger with each one, both of us laughing when he drives over a bump in the road and I accidentally shove one up his nose.

Even after the fries are gone, my smile is slow to fade, like it's been stamped into clay. This is what it could be like, this simmering pot of laughter and lust, the most delicious, hearty, healing stew.

He looks my way and gives me the tiniest of smiles, an apostrophe at the end of his lip. That's all it takes to set my skin aflame, my heart to pumping double-time, so hard and fast that it makes me think of something Mischa's boyfriend told me once, that there's a correlation between heart-rate and life expectancy. Small animals have quick pulses and short lifespans.

If I don't do something, this thing between us is going to die faster than a chain-smoking hamster.

I pick up the grilled cheese and begin to eat, coating my mouth in cheesy onion essence. And when we get back to my place, I tell him not to stop the engine. "I'll just get out. Thanks for tonight."

His disappointed expression almost undoes me, but I have to hold steady. If I want this to last, we have to fuck like sloths, not dolphins.

Besides, my breath is unforgivable.

"You don't want me to come inside?"

Fuck yes, I do! All the way inside! But I swallow down my response. "Not tonight. I have some things I need to finish. And you said you have an early morning session, right?"

"Yeah, I do."

I give him a quick peck on the cheek and escape from the car. "Then goodnight."

"Goodnight, Di."

I hurry into my apartment and force myself not to look back.

Chapter 20

Darien

"FRENCHING AND FRENCH FRIES: DARIEN LEE CAUGHT CHEATING ON FIANCÉE AND DI-ET"

That's the headline I look for as I scroll through my phone at 6 a.m., but there's nothing at all about me threatening guys or eating fries or kissing women at traffic lights. Instead, there's an old photo of me and Eliza, and all of a sudden the mess comes tumbling out of the closet again: her, last night, eyes rimmed with runny mascara. She'd been standing in the stale-aired garage, shivering and clutching her elbows in nothing but a sheer peach-colored cocktail dress.

I'd placed my jacket around her shoulders and left her there, eager to get to Di, telling myself that she's not my problem anymore, that she's a grown woman who can take care of herself. But as I brush my teeth and cleanse my face, I can't wash away the image of her messy eyes, angry splatters of black across a bleak canvas.

Before I can overthink it, I shoot her a text.

Darien: Are you okay?

Eliza: Better today, thanks.

I type out a response, but it takes me a full minute before I hit send.

Darien: I'm here if you need to talk.

I half expect an "It's nothing," or maybe actually nothing at all, but ten minutes later, she trudges up the stairs, still in her silk pajamas, and slides into a chair at the kitchen island.

I fill her a glass of water and slide it across the island countertop.

"Thank you." She clutches the glass with both hands and stares down into the water, studiously avoiding my gaze. "Where did you go last night?"

I entertain a non-reply, but let it go. "I went to see Di."

She looks up, but there's no pointed accusation or anger there. Just dull acceptance. "Are you hanging out with her to punish me?"

Immediately, I regret inviting her to talk. "No. Not everything I do is about you." Though I guess it used to feel that way, didn't it.

She flinches as if slapped. But then she averts her gaze back to the water, her knuckles whitening on the glass. "I guess I deserve that. But I still don't understand why you'd want to hang out with someone who did that to you."

Funny how she says that, and yet she continues to try to get me to hang out with her and Ethan.

She must have the same thought, because she sighs and continues, "I know the world doesn't revolve around me, especially now. You remember Ethan's favorite phrase? 'There's nothing like outer space to make you realize how small and insignificant you are.'" She smiles, but there's no warmth or humor in it. "He's got this whole spiel about how silly it is that celebrities are compared to stars. Something about how there are an infinite number of them, and none of them matter on their own. They only matter to the objects that are closest to them." She closes her eyes, and her smile crumbles. Despite her healthy diet and skin treatments, she looks older. Tired. Drawn.

"Is that why you came up here? To tell me about his observational humor?"

"No," she says softly. "I'm just rambling. Because I miss him."

I miss him.

Her words hang in the air between us, ringing like a tuning fork. "Did you two—"

"Not yet, not officially, but we will soon. Because you mean too much to him."

It takes me a second to parse her meaning, during which I nudge over a box of tissues. She pulls them out like magic scarves and covers her face with a huge wad.

It's strange to watch her cry without wanting to do anything about it. Like being in a scene where the script doesn't make sense. A quivery lip or a sheen in her eyes used to make me drop everything, but now I analyze rather than feel her performance. What's her purpose? How do I respond?

Eliza dabs at her eyes and the tip of her nose. "Can't you forgive him already? Like, fine, stay mad at me, hate me, I get it. Figure out a way to punish me, if you have to. But I'm the one who messed it all up, not him. Ethan would do anything for you, and right now, he hates himself for what happened and he's starting to hate me, too. So what can we do, Darien? How can we make it right?"

I stare at her dewy lashes, her puffy eyes. For some reason, what comes to mind are Di's words from last night: it's not my job to fix all of asshole-dom. It takes empathy and effort on the part of the offender.

"I don't know. It's not really my job to help you apologize. But if you want, you can start by promising not to ruin my career to save your own." I straighten and rinse my cup, preparing to head back to my room.

"You really think I would do that to you?"

"You've threatened to more than once." I wipe my hands on a drying cloth and walk towards the hall, but her quiet words stop me short.

"I only did that because I've been scared about what you could do to me. Because deep down, I know, I deserve to be punished."

I turn to look at her again. There's something new in her expression. Yes, there's fear, and maybe some remorse. But there's a tension in her gaze, a dawning desperation, the look of someone watching a glass slip from their fingers on the way to the floor.

It's not my problem anymore.

"Take care of yourself, E."

I walk back to my room and get on with my day, but not without several stops and starts.

* * *

"What are you doing here?"

Later that night, Di frowns and pulls me into her apartment. Things are even more cluttered than yesterday, with scraps of black fabric scattered over every surface, as if a murder of crows had flown into a hurricane. The sewing mannequin in the corner is covered with a plain black cloth, like she's hiding something under there. I can guess what.

"I brought you dinner. Because apparently whenever you're busy, you don't eat."

She's wearing a simple black tee, loose wide-leg pants, and no makeup. I love getting a glimpse behind the scenes.

"You shouldn't sneak around here too often."

"I won't. But if you get a random food delivery from someone else this week, you'll know who it's from."

She gives me the same kind of look my mom does whenever I buy her the pastries that she loves but doesn't want. "I don't need you to take care of me."

"Did you eat today?"

"Yes."

"What did you eat?"

"Enough."

"What did you eat?"

She sighs. "Half a bag of baby carrots and some strawberry koalas."

"Uh huh. And are you hungry?" I tear open the brown paper bag and begin to unpack the contents. She stares at the containers of dan dan mian like Sleeping Beauty seeing a spindle, wide-eyed and inching forward.

But the glow in her eyes dims. "Yes, but—"

"Then accept the food. I know you're busy, it'll make your life easier. Just let me know if you have any requests or anything you're allergic to."

I open the containers, and the scent of rich, peppery sauce fills the tiny room. After clearing away some of the largest garment pieces, she plops down next to me in awe.

"Are these mushrooms?"

"Yep. You're vegetarian, right?"

"I'm pescatarian. But how did you know?"

"Your burger last night looked like it was missing something."

"It was a grilled cheese," she whispers with a smile. "Thank you."

"You're welcome."

I hand her a pair of wooden chopsticks, and she picks up one of two huge platters of noodles, tentatively tasting one before sliding a pile of it down her gullet. I imagine those noodles—my favorite in all of SoCal—gently breaking between my teeth and sliding down my own throat, and my mouth waters, and my dick might've twitched, just once.

After a long moan, her eyes snap open, and she watches me over the mound of mian. "Not eating?"

"Nope, it's all for you. Keep the leftovers for lunch."

Her eating slows, and her jaw moves up and down, chewing after all. "Still dieting?"

"Yeah. It's for my next project." Project *Single and Hotter Than Ever*.

"Oh. Are you playing a bag of rocks? Because if so, spot on."

Annoyance heats my neck. My mom and sister nag me about my dieting all the time. They're offended that I won't eat their cooking, even when they scoop out the fatty bits and call it *healthy*. But it's for my job. "You like how it looks, right? Admit it."

"Sure, I guess it's impressive, but I'd like you just as much if you allowed yourself to eat." She takes another huge, saucy mouthful of noodles. "Trust me, I get it. Mischa's a model and she used to go on a liquid diet a few days before every show. I'm not judging her or you for whatever choices you make, but it'd be cool if we could move away from celebrating the same old limited preferences. There's not just one kind of hot."

"I agree, I think there's beauty in diversity." I give her a meaningful look, eyeing those soft curves that are so wonderful to sink into—and she chokes on a noodle, coughing. I rub her back until she waves me off and steals my bubbly water. "But you said it yourself, it's impressive. It's distinct. Not many people can say that they have *this* kind of body."

Her lips are shiny with chili oil after massacring half the noodles, but she delicately dabs at her chin with a napkin. "Why does that matter to you?"

"You've clearly never gone to a casting call. Imagine walking into a room full of people who look exactly like you, vying for a single role. Every advantage counts."

"Yeah, but you're famous now. You don't need to fight for roles."

"You'd be surprised. I rarely win roles that are non-race-specific. And for the Asian roles, there are newer, hotter Asian actors coming up all the time. If I don't stand out from them, I'll be replaced. They're hungrier, they want it more, they'll do what it takes."

Already, I've lost roles to younger, more eager, less demanding guys. Even in this day and age, there aren't enough roles for all of us, and sometimes a director would rather take a chance on newer talent than on someone more expensive whose career has already played out. If I want to stay relevant, I have to work at it on all fronts.

"Why does it even matter to you, being on top? You've already accomplished so much."

I taste the answer on my tongue, analyzing how best to describe it today. It used to be about keeping up with Eliza, but now... "Don't you ever wonder how far you could go, if you really pushed it?"

"Not really? Getting big isn't my goal. I just want to earn enough for me and my family to live in moderate comfort, ideally through a job I don't hate." She purses her lips, and the crease between her brows is back. "Why, is that what you're trying to do? See how far you can take it?"

"Yeah, kind of. I'm in a position to do it. I'm the first Asian sex symbol since Sessue Hayakawa, back in the silent film era. He covered all the bases of leading manhood, and I want to do the same."

It sounds like bragging, but it's true. Before me, the only roles that guys like me got were of nerds, doctors, martial artists, or punch lines. Early in my career, even when I was a romantic interest, it was only as a foil to the guy—usually white or Black—who eventually got the girl. Before getting into shape and building up my image to what it is today, I was interchangeable with every other Yang, Choi, Kim, Duong, and so on, and it didn't matter if we could speak the right language or do the right accent. All that mattered was looks, or who you knew. Once I starred in my first major profitable film, I started getting other types of roles, too. I've starred as love interests, a president, a spy, even a cowboy. And now—

She sighs and does a slow, fluttering eye roll, as if she tried to fight it but couldn't stop herself.

"What, what is it?"

"Is that your main motivation?"

"What do you mean?"

"Like, I guess it's cool that an Asian American person has gotten to your level of stardom? And like, yes, duh, Asian men *are* hot, and I'm glad that people have finally figured that out. But all I've seen is how anxious this job makes you. You're always dieting, hiding, lying, or stressing about what people will say. You paid me fifty bucks for a bag of chips because you felt like you couldn't go out. You basically told me that you feel powerless at times in the face of your fame. And I don't think you've ever actually said that you *enjoy* acting. Do you?"

"I do enjoy it. The craft of it, living many lives, making people feel things...I love working with a team on such a big goal, and seeing it all come together at the end. But yeah, it's the fame that I'm not so into. I don't mind the attention when things are going well, but it never goes away, and if anything, the scrutiny gets worse when things are bad. So of course you'd think I hate it. You've caught me at a low point."

She picks up the tray again and slurps up a noodle, which leaves a trail of red across her lower cheek. "As much as I hate most people, I don't think I could handle not being able to go out in public."

"Yeah, it's true. Even when I'm doing well, it's kind of depressing that I can't be myself in public. I haven't been anonymous in a crowd in years. These days, I'm basically trapped in my house, my sister's house, and...well, here."

I know that I'm not literally trapped. I could go anywhere in the world, do anything with my money and fame. But not when Eliza was always with me. Not when I'd have to go alone now and pretend that I'm okay.

"Is that something you miss? Being anonymous in a crowd?"

"Yeah, for sure. But it is what it is."

She gives me a thoughtful look, holding her chopsticks pointed like she's about to pick me up and dip me in sauce. "I see."

"Anyway, I want to clarify that things would've gone very differently if I'd had a career separate from Eliza's. Being with Eliza pushed me in a more mainstream direction. I'm hoping to pick up more indie films in the future."

She shrugs. "I'm not judging you for any of it, just trying to understand."

"That eye roll you gave me earlier says otherwise."

"Fine, I take back my eye roll."

I look her up and down, the simple clothes she's wearing. So unlike her designs. "Why do *you* want to be a fashion designer?"

She wipes her cheek and finishes chewing before answering. "I love working with my hands. I love having complete control of what I wear. I love giving birth to items that only used to exist in my imagination. Do you have any idea how heady it is to *create* something, something you love? And when people feel like my garments speak to them, that they can express something with them, it makes me feel proud and not alone. So I could work a more straightforward job like designing websites, which is what I used to do, but if I can make this work, I'd be happier, I think." She blinks down at the carpet, unseeing. "But I'm also aware of the fact that I'm getting my start late. There's still so much to learn. And so many other designers. A lot of young ones with new ideas. I know it's a stretch for me."

It's so familiar. The fight to stay relevant against a tide of fresh-faced kids. The heavy words which have the qualities of a sigh, like hope seeping from her body, each breath an exhausted step as she plods into the unknown.

"It's a stretch, but it helps that you're incredibly talented and have the work ethic of a bullet train. In my experience, it's the hardest working ones who have the most luck."

She gives me a dry look. "Sorry if I don't believe you when your reaction to my design was so lackluster."

"That wasn't because I didn't like it. I think it's perfect." Perfect might be a strong word, but from her expression, she needs extra-strength encouragement.

"Then why did you sound so down about it?"

"Because I was worried about *me*. When the news about me and Eliza breaks, I don't want there to be any speculation around what happened, or about my mental state. If I start behaving differently or wearing clothes I've never worn before, I might give off the impression that I'm going through a crisis."

"So? Isn't it warranted? You were together for years and she cheated on you. And anyway, why does change have to mean crisis? If you really like the outfit, then just wear it." She blinks and looks away, pursing her lips. "Unless you're just saying that to be nice."

"No, I'm not just saying that." I take her hand in mine, stroking her long, callused fingers. "I really do admire your work, but no matter what my intentions are, people are going to have their own interpretations, and I don't want to go down in history as some sort of meme about a loser with a broken heart embracing the dark."

"Well, if you did, that would make you a goth icon. What's so bad about that?"

"Eh…I'm not sure that I'm goth enough for that."

She smiles softly, and it's a gentle breeze that lifts my sails. "You're only going to be a loser with a broken heart if you act like one. Wearing an outfit that you *actually* like, in part to support *me*, is not a broken-hearted-loser move. It's just you being a good friend."

Friend. There's that word again, falling flat between us. But I'm not ready to ask her what she thinks might fit better.

She's probably right, though. The possibility of me going down in history as a sad meme is unlikely. I mean, it kind of happened with Victor "The Loser" Lu's wedgie scene, but that was ages ago, back when I was a completely different person. And as for my brand or image, why can't I believe that Di *will* make something incredible? Even if she doesn't, whatever impact her outfit has on my career will be nothing compared to the scandal with Eliza. Why worry about a scratch when there's a bullet hole in my gut?

All of my doubts come from Tam, who's just doing her job, filling my head with the worst case scenarios. But honestly, what does it matter? It's one night, one look, and it'll help Di. She deserves a fair chance.

I squeeze her hand. She squeezes mine. Her smile brightens, heats, and when she leans in to kiss me, I kiss her back, light and light-headed after coming to a decision. The obvious decision.

I *will* wear the outfit, no matter what.

For her.

Chapter 21

Di

DI HO'S EX CHARGED WITH MUR-DER...SHOULD DARIEN BE WORRIED?

Durian: Care to explain?

Durian: Am I next?

Di: wtf *skull emoji*

Di: no, you're not next

Di: i hooked up with this guy twice. both mistakes.

Di: i didn't even know he put that photo of us on his socials

Di: i guess they just mentioned you to get clicks???

Di: i don't plan on murdering you

Di: any time soon

According to the "article," a guy I sloppy hand-jobbed last year got dumped by his most recent girlfriend, and he's been accused of killing her ex in a seriously graphic way—think dicks getting shoved into places—that's caught the attention of the media. The tabloids went digging, and there was one single photo of us together that he'd posted long ago, so according to them, I might be involved in this murder polygon, and Darien, as a known associate, needs a bigger security detail. They pulled an old photo of me from social media, scowling at the camera and looking like I'd totally date a murderer, and put it next to a photo of Darien looking very unmurderer-like, all tailored pants and fitted shirt and shiny, swoopy hair. Very different from *Zip Kragus,* my "murderous ex," with whom I've long seriously regretted hooking up, and not just because his name is Zip Kragus.

But the longer I stare at the article, the less funny it seems. How many people have seen this photo of me? How many people now associate me with this disgusting excuse for a human being?

I scroll down to the bottom of the article, my stomach folding over itself tighter and tighter, the sensation of eyes crawling over me intensifying with every swipe of my thumb...but I lose my nerve and close out of it before reaching the comments.

Instead, I tap Darien's name—Durian—and wait for the call to connect, hammering my foot like a sewing machine needle.

He picks up. "Hey, are you okay? Are the paps after you?"

The concern in his voice hits like a morphine drip. "Oh. No, I'm not calling about the article—which, again, I don't have a thing for murderers. Just a wild idea." But now that he mentions it, I get up and peek through my window shades. Outside, there's an elderly neighbor and their derpy chihuahua, squatting on a nearby lawn in the last golden rays of light. The chihuahua, not the neighbor.

"A wild idea about the look?"

I step back from the window. "No, it's...you know how you said...wait, do you like surprises?"

There's a wary, ticking silence. "Why, what's going on?"

"Okay, I realize now that you probably don't like surprises. But I wanted to do something nice for you because you've been so nice to me."

"You're right, I don't like surprises. So what's the idea?"

I plop down onto the futon and cross my legs to stop them from shaking. "Do you want to go to a costume party with me tonight? It's at this club, they do it every year. The event is called Aprilween, you can look it up. I thought you might want to go because you said you haven't been anonymous in a crowd in a long time, and I thought it might be fun for you to, I don't know...experience that."

Because when I say he's been nice to me, I mean that through the long hours and mounting pressure, he's kept the meat from falling off my bones. After taking two days off last week, I've fallen behind on everything. I've had to haul all the ass to catch up, and because of him, I haven't yet turned into Jack Nicholson from *The Shining*.

I wake up to his texts in the morning and fall asleep to them at night. Some nights, we hang out, but not for long because I'm always busy and tired. Those times, he'll pull me onto his lap and put his big hands on me, whispering stupid jokes against my neck between kisses until I dissolve into foam.

Not once has he pressured me for sex, even when we make out and his hands find their way to within inches of my prime real estate. Every time I'm tempted to ask him—or beg him—to fuck me, I leap up and yell, "Gotta pee!" and hide in the bathroom until I've calmed down.

Only once did he give me a strange look and say, "Are you okay? Do you want some cranberry juice or something?"

"Cranberry juice?"

"Uh...I've heard it's good for UTIs."

I'd cackled it off, but also stored that away as a good possible excuse. It'd be easier to pretend that I've got an infection than to tell him how scared I am that things are too good to be true. That I'm afraid that as soon as we fuck again, we won't be able to stop until my heart or vagina's broken, probably both.

Even when he's not around, I feel giddy and lightheaded, like I've reached a cold peak with a beautiful view. I can't stop gulping in lungfuls of fresh air.

I want him to get a little fresh air, too.

"A costume party? Tonight?"

"Yes. And I can run out to the closest costume store and pick up some stuff right now. I'll make sure no one recognizes you. Just say the word."

Despite my mile-a-minute speech—or perhaps because of it—he takes his time responding. "Isn't this kind of sudden?"

"Yeah, well I only started looking ten minutes ago and it happens to be tonight, so...now or never?"

Obviously, he doesn't like surprises. We've gone out walking once more, but only to Frogtown again because he likes knowing what to expect. Crowded places are kind of the opposite of that. And does anyone *really* enjoy squirming among the masses, soaking in the scents of butt sweat and cheap cologne?

But whenever I ask him about his day, he smiles and tells me about Claire and Eliot and working out, maybe gaming and...that's it. And then he gets this sad, almost panicky look in his eyes, like he's worried that this is all he has. This is what his life has come to.

I know that feeling too well. "So...party?"

"That does sound kind of nice," he says slowly. "But I don't have a costume."

"Don't worry about it. I'll run and get you a costume before the stores close. Is that okay?"

"Uh...I guess so. But can you make sure it covers me completely from head to toe and doesn't really show my physique? And I can pay you back—"

"Don't worry, I got it. See you soon, okay? Byeeeee!"

I hang up before he can change his mind. Before I can change *my* mind. It irks me that, as both a goth and a designer, I'm not taking the time to make us some truly epic costumes, but the iron is hot and I am striking.

I speed through the closest costume shop, and after an anxious round-trip scuttle across the store, spot the perfect costume, then hop in the car and drive back home, where we've agreed to meet later tonight. Soon. I have an hour to get my own costume assembled.

By the time I'm done drawing the last of the lines on my pants, there's a knock on my door, and when I unlock it, Darien steps inside, dressed in black joggers and a plain black tee again. My heart does a little Wednesday dance—we match, and she likes him in all black. Especially when he smiles and leans in for a quick peck that very soon turns into a toe-curling kiss, one that leaves me moaning and swaying when his fingers delicately land on the base of my throat.

I break away and force myself to focus, grabbing and holding up the option I got for him. "You cool with this?"

"Where's that from again? *Ghostbusters?*"

I stare. I judge. "No, it's Oogie Boogie from *The Nightmare Before Christmas*, though the costume isn't licensed so the official name was *Worm-filled Sack Man*. Try it on."

He opens the plastic packaging and pulls out the rough brown fabric. "What are you dressing up as?"

"Jack Skellington." Sally would've been more fitting, but Jack's faster to put together and that's good enough for me. I hold up my black backless leotard, wide-leg pants, and makeshift bat-tie, all of which I've pinstriped with white fabric marker. "I'll hop into the bathroom to change. You can just put your costume on over your clothes."

In the bathroom, I change, draw some exaggerated black lines and circles on my face, and pin my hair up into a bun. I step out to show the final result. "What do you think?"

Darien's got the mask on and everything, so he looks like a burlap sea star with fake plastic worms sticking out of his nasty, grinning mouth. Now *that's* a smile.

"I can't see very well, but I think you look great."

"How's yours? Comfortable?"

"Surprisingly, yes."

"Then are you ready?"

He's slow to nod. "Yes."

"Cool." I douse my face in setting spray, and we hop into my little old car for maximum stealth.

After parking, we join the throngs of costumed partiers on their way to the venue, walking between a swarm of Sexy Bumble Bees and a Neurotypical Clown Posse. "Ready to party?"

Darien—or Oogie Boogie—turns his face to look at me. "You sure you can't tell it's me?"

"You're covered from head to toe. No one will be able to tell."

"Not even from my voice?"

"Do you want to try a different voice? Maybe one that's more Oogie-Boogie-like?"

He clears his throat. "Like *this?*"

Spoken like a drunk jazz singer. "Yes, perfect. You'll be fine, I promise."

We approach, and his words are swallowed by the muffled bass of early-2000s pop coming from inside.

"What did you say?"

"It's kind of hard to see out of this," he says more loudly.

"Don't worry, I've got you." I take the corner of sack that serves as his arm and squeeze his hand.

We join the short line that's formed, and Darien looks around a bit too much for it to be just nerves. "Is this a line for the cover?"

"Yeah, and for—"

Our gazes snap together just as we arrive at the front of the line. The person at the door is dressed as a Sexy Minion.

"ID?"

I almost, *almost* facepalm, but catch myself before smearing my makeup. "Yeah, sorry, one sec." Leaning into Darien, I whisper, "Do you have yours?"

"I have it," he whispers back, "but it has my name and face on it."

Shit shit shit. "Then maybe...do you have cash?" I've never done the handshake-wink-wink before, but I imagine that if my palm were, um, *greasy* enough, then anyone would look the other way?

Except me. I know I wouldn't.

Patting around with his pointed fabric hands, he looks like if a zombie Patrick Star were trying to get out of paying for lunch. He tries to reach inside a couple of side slits for his pockets, but can't seem to get a hold of anything.

"If you don't have your IDs ready, could you step aside?" The bouncer blows a gum bubble and pops it, the same way she's popped my brilliant plan for the evening.

"Sorry, yeah, one sec." We move out of line and I unzip the back of Darien's costume in order to reach into his pockets, patting around the hardness of him, those warm thighs, for his wallet. For the briefest of moments, my hand slips under his shirt and brushes his soft, heated skin, and a fevered pulse starts beating between my legs. When my fingers close around the thick leather bulge of his wallet, I'm breathing way too hard. "Got it."

I pull it out and check the ID. It's him, alright. But instead of sliding out the ID, I pull out a hundred dollar bill, fold it up so that it fits in my palm, and step back into the line, holding out my ID to the bouncer. "Here's mine. And his."

The bouncer takes the ID-plus-money wad and frowns, snaps her head up to look. She gives me an unimpressed look that I find quite impressive, and holds up the hundred dollar bill. "This isn't an ID."

"No, it's...I mean..." *Damn you, bouncer, just take it!* Though in other circumstances, I'd be proud of her.

The bouncer sighs and hands my ID and the bill back. "Please leave."

"Wait, but—"

"Don't make me call Big Bob over." And she points towards a huge, towering Pikachu, smoking a cigarette.

It feels like the whole line is staring as we hurry away. "Shit. Sorry, Darien."

"It's not your fault. I forgot about my ID, too. Usually, when I'm going out, my security guys would handle it."

"Fuck. I'm a terrible security guy."

Oogie Boogie perma-smiles, but I can feel Darien smiling in there, too. "It's fine. I'm not much of a night club person anyway. This was a fun little adventure."

It was meant to be a full adventure, not a thirty minute drive for nothing. And as we walk back to the car, I study his mask, that creepy, worm-filled smile, sadness and frustration mixing in layers inside me like a rancid Rita's gelati. The poor guy is always smiling in public, but I imagine him hiding in his home, sneaking out to empty spaces, never going anywhere there might be a crowd. Despite the open space and cool air around us, it makes me feel hot and tight. Closed in.

"Do you want to go back home?"

He waves his fabric hands in a don't worry gesture. "We're already out and in costume. Why don't we keep walking around?"

The world opens up again. "You sure you won't mind attracting some attention?"

"This kind of attention is fine."

Thank goodness.

We stroll around near Echo Park and get a ton of stares and compliments.

"Love your costumes!"

"So cute together!"

Each time someone looks our way, Darien stiffens, but after a minute, he starts wiggling his V-hands at everyone who walks by. Within five minutes, he's positively strutting.

"You make a very convincing Oogie Boogie."

"What can I say? I'm actually a creep."

"Uh huh. Well, it's nice to see you letting loose and having fun. It just sucks that you have to wear a costume to do it."

"If I did walk around without a costume, it'd probably be okay for a bit, even without a body guard. Most people mean well, and they try to be respectful."

"But...?"

He pushes his mask back a little, probably realigning the eye holes. "But when *everyone* wants to say hi or try to be your friend, it gets to be too much."

Everyone. Like he's a character in *The Last of Us*, and everyone within sight is infected and rushing to take a bite out of him. The tight, closed-off itchy feeling is back.

Sitting alone at home is lonely. Going out among others and not being able to connect must feel a thousand times worse, especially when it's because *everyone* thinks they could be his special friend. Most of us have the opposite problem—it's hard to make new friends as an adult because we hardly engage outside of work. The only people who seem to act on their "friendly" impulses are—

"Creepy dudes."

"Creepy dudes?"

"They're my teeny tiny version of what you experience. All you want is to go out in peace, but then creepy dudes say shit to you because they think you want their attention. That you should be grateful for it. I'm not saying that your fans are creepy exactly, but like, there are respectful ways to engage with strangers in public. I think it's pretty clear when someone's not looking to talk to you, yet so many people disregard those cues. What do they expect?"

"Yeah," he says softly. "People don't think of me as a stranger. They think they know me because they've seen me, they've read about me, and so on."

"But they don't *really* know you. They just assume they do."

"Yep. And that's why I've got my disguises and you've got your Willem DaFoe face."

He's right. I have my scowls—though "Willem DaFoe face" seems a bit strong—he's got his security and costumes and hats and glasses. There's always going to be a barrier between him and the rest of the world. I'm flattered that I get to be on the right side of the barrier, but god, how sad it must be to be a Bubble Boy. If only there were a way for him to interact with the good ones a few at a time. But how would you—

"Stop for a sec." I walk a few yards away, pull out my phone, and call Mischa. "Hey."

"Hey, Di, what's up?"

"Where are you right now and what are you up to?"

"I'm at Ella's with John and the crew. Why, want to come over?"

No? I'd wanted her to come hang out with us, just her, because she's already in on the secret. But now that I think about it, this isn't about what I want, it's about what Darien wants, and he'd wanted a crowd. And Mischa's friends, they're nice. They're all intimidatingly hot, they know famous people, and they're fun and they love L.A. Maybe they'd be better friends for Darien than they are for me.

But can we trust them?

I lower my voice to a mouse whisper. "Do you think I could bring, you know, *him*? And the crew would be able to keep it a secret?"

She gasps. "Um, yeah?"

"You really trust them all?" *Do I?* "Because if word gets out and it's my fault—"

"Di, we've already assigned tasks for the apocalypse and decided who's getting eaten in which order. Bring him."

Damn. I'm vaguely offended that I'm not in their prepper plans, but also kind of relieved that I'm not on the menu. And if Mischa trusts them that much...

I offer Darien a questioning smile. "Want to meet some new friends?"

And that's how we end up walking towards an apartment building on the other side of town, off Centinela.

"I'm not sure if this is a good idea," says Darien, when we're almost there.

"It's too late, they know we're coming." They don't, actually. I asked Mischa not to tell them who I was bringing in case Darien really wanted to bail. But I can tell from his tone that it's regular jitters.

And here, I used to think he was the cockiest musclehead who ever cockied.

I catch his arm and stop him from walking out into the street just as a car zooms by. And when we cross the street, we're holding hands again, and it's not weird. No, it's just warm and tingly, and my heart is thumping like a soil compactor, like it's trying to lay the foundation for something.

"I don't know, maybe I should just go. They haven't signed NDAs—"

"Darien, they're Mischa's friends, and Mischa's my best friend. I trust her, she trusts them. Do you trust me?"

The briefest hesitation. "I do."

"Then it'll be fine, really." I say it like I mean it, and soon we're buzzed up and knocking on the door to an apartment on the fourth floor.

Darien drops my hand, and though I kind of expected it, it feels like my plug's been yanked from an outlet. He—or his mask—stares straight ahead, not noticing my glance.

I know, I know, it's not personal, but it still stings.

"Hey!" Ella says, pulling me into a hug. She's as tall as me, maybe taller, hourglass-y, effortlessly gorgeous in an olive green frock and her hair in knots against her scalp. "You guys look so fucking cute! What's the occasion?"

"Oh, we just came from a costume party."

"And who's this with you?" She looks expectantly at Oogie Boogie. So do I.

He freezes for two beats and then whips off his mask, revealing, somehow, a perfect head of hair, like it's been gelled with epoxy. He holds out his sack-hand, his charming work smile on. "Hi, I'm Darien."

Ella's eyes go wide, and she lets out a half-moan that makes me want to shake her. But then she collects herself. "Oh my god, it's soooo nice to meet you. I'm Ella. Come on in!"

We do, pulling off our shoes to match Ella's bare-footed example and then following her into the living room.

"Look who it is," sings Ella as we approach. They all look up, and it's like walking into a glittering penguin pit with a bucket full of fish. More than one mouth falls open.

I point to each person in turn. "Alan, Carina, Opal, Donny, my best friend Mischa, and her boyfriend John. Everyone, this is Darien."

Darien puts on That Smile and shakes each of their hands in turn, repeating their names like he's at an MBA networking event.

"I love your costume, Di," says Alan Nguyen, who is by far the most famous influencer of the bunch. "Where were you?"

"Um, this random event. It's kind of a long story," I say. "What are you guys up to?"

"We were about to start playing *Overcooked*," says Opal, and they hold up a few controllers. "Wanna play?"

"Have you played this before?" I ask Darien. He shakes his head, and everyone shoves their controllers under our noses. We each take one and sit down on the couches between the others, while Ella offers us a selection of drinks. We each accept a glass of orange wine.

"This isn't the Met Gala look that Di's making for you, is it?" asks Carina, eyeing Darien up and down. I know she's joking, but I'm doing whatever the opposite of laughing is.

But Darien laughs. "If I wore this, Lana Winter would never let me come again."

"Do you know Lana Winter?"

"Sure, but not well."

"Oh god." Donny rubs his temple. "I once walked a Fashion Week show and the shoe squeaked when I walked past her and I swear to god, she was wearing her sunglasses but she jerked upright like she'd just woken up."

"No fucking way. Lana Winter would never fall asleep at a show."

"Actually," says Darien, "Eliza swears she's seen Lana fall asleep, too. I've heard she wakes up every morning at five, so the later shows are hard for her. Thus, the sunglasses."

"I've heard that, too!" says Opal. "And Eliza? Oh my god, I met her once and she is *so* sweet. How is she these days? And *where* is she?"

When Darien smiles to himself in that wistful, soulmated way of his, there's a collective sigh from everyone in the room, except for me. He tells us about Eliza, her new movie, their relationship, as if it's his favorite topic in the world. His face glows with such warmth that everyone around me starts melting into their seats as they witness the depths of his love for his fiancée.

I know it's just a cover, but hearing him gush about her so convincingly leaves a tight, sour feeling in my throat. It comes too easily for him to be purely acting. Does he still have feelings for her? I mean, even with the cheating, they were together for six years, and you don't move on from six years that quickly, even when you have a rebound.

I chug my orange wine and stare at the wall clock, wondering how much longer he's going to go on about her.

"Should we play?" he finally asks, trying to catch my eye. I don't let him. "I've heard this game's a lot of fun."

Everyone leaps into the conversation to explain how it works, while I stretch my legs and yawn.

He stretches his legs, too, and I break my yawn off when his sock-covered pinky toe touches mine underneath the coffee table. And we don't just touch. He strokes my toes with his, and when I finally look his way, he flashes me a different kind of smile. One that's goofy and mischievous, and just for me.

I smile back.

He keeps his pinky toe next to mine throughout the night. I feel it with my whole self, like we're two ponds connected by a strait at our feet, sharing every rumbling laugh or secret smile.

And when we leave at the end of the night, thumbs raw and cheeks sore from laughing, his kiss burns away any lingering doubts.

He whispers the softest, "Thank you" against my cheek.

It scares me how much those words mean to me.

Chapter 22

Darien

After staying out late, I expect a slow morning with heavy eyes, but I wake up before my alarm. The sunlight seems more golden this morning, and the coffee richer and more fragrant. There's a warm buzzy wakefulness that lingers on through my morning workout and lunch spent with Claire and Eliot.

It finally fades in the afternoon, when Tam calls.

"You saw the headline right? Diana's ex is a murderer?"

I almost laugh. How are we seriously talking about this? "She hooked up with him twice. Also, that has nothing to do with me."

"Did you see her response to it?"

"No?"

My phone buzzes. I click on the link that Tam sent to Di's social media. It's a screenshot of the headline with the caption, "Secret's out: I love murderers. The weirder the name, the wetter I get. *droplets emoji*"

I chuckle. "She's obviously joking."

"Look at the comments."

Ehhh. "No, I'm good."

"Just look."

"Fine."

It's an odd mix of laughing emojis, gross men saying things like, "i'll murder you, babby," and others saying, "Prince Charming would never date this HO *barf emoji*"...or just plain old insults. They send my temperature soaring.

But there are several responses to the comments that make me laugh. They're all from a user named mischmasch666.

Shut up and eat your frozen TV dinner, you limp lettuce.

The only time you ever touched a p$$y was when you were born, ass juice.

Anyone would rather date her than you and your lumpy coconut tits.

She gained my respect with her *Overcooked* skills, but now I'm in pure awe.

I wish I had friends as loyal as Di's. Hopefully, they're gullible, too. My performance last night as Eliza's fiancé was mediocre, at best, because it's hard not to look at Di whenever she's in the room. Even now, I linger on these tabloid photos of her, silly as they are. She's a beauty, an original, and she's mine.

"Okay, I looked. What's your point?"

"She doesn't moderate her social media, her modest fan base is completely orthogonal to yours, and none of this is good press for you. I know you're on a work break right now, but please don't undo all of our hard work. Don't associate with her."

"Tam, I told you, I'll call you when I'm ready to work again. Everything is fine."

"What about the Met Gala look? Is it done?"

"It's almost done." I think.

"Do you need me to arrange a backup look for you?"

I cup the back of my head, staring up at the ceiling. "Tam, please. I'll be in touch when I need you."

She lets out a labored sigh. "I just…I worry. It's my job to worry."

"I know. But I don't need you to worry right now. I need time to myself, to think. Okay? So why don't you stop worrying and take a break, too?"

"I have a bad feeling about this. Take however much time you need, but I'll be ready for you when everything goes to shit. And I won't say I told you so, but you'll know. I did."

On that cheery note, she hangs up.

* * *

Di greets me in a sheer black rhomboid-patchwork tank top and wide, dark-gray pants that are rolled up at the cuffs. She's fresh-faced and bare, her hair thrown up into a large, messy bun that's secured in place with what looks like a knitting needle. I resist the urge to pluck it out and let her long hair loose. She's too tempting to touch as it is.

"Hey."

"Hey." I step inside, breathing in the now-familiar scent of her apartment. It's warm and sweet and slightly dusty, like books with coffee and crème brûlée, which I know from snooping around is from her various candles, soaps, and lotions. The main room is much tidier this time, with no scraps of fabric and fewer piles of things, but now there are a couple of large boxes and a full-length mirror by the wall.

"Was that here before?"

"It used to live in the corner. But we're going to need it out tonight." She's biting her lip, her movements jittery with more than coffee.

I pull her to me, wrapping my arms around her waist without needing to bend. The perfect height for me. "For tonight?" I nuzzle her temple and whisper, "You like watching yourself in the mirror?"

"Yeah, I love watching myself get stuffed," she says, walking her fingers along my chest before flicking my nose and laughing. But I don't find it funny at all, and when she sees my face, she clears her throat and steps back, reaching for something behind her.

"Um, can you put this on?"

She hands me what looks like a sash for a robe.

"Where's the rest of it?"

"No, turn around. Close your eyes."

Does she mean... I do as she asks, and she places the fabric over my eyes, tying a knot behind my head.

"You can't see, right? No peeking?"

"Right. What are you doing?"

She tugs on my shirt, pulling the hem from my pants.

"Whoa, hey." I capture her soft curves with my hands. "So it *is* time for games?"

"Not quite," she whispers, moving my hands away. "Just trust me."

I swallow and wait with shallow breaths, every inch of me buzzing, jostling to be where she'll touch me next. She unbuttons my shirt one button at a time, top to bottom, then peels the shirt from my shoulders, off my arms. Cool fingers trail down my chest, tracing a line from my throat to my navel before slipping into my waistband. She nimbly un-does my belt and pulls it, tosses it to the side.

I reach for her again, but she steps back. "Stop moving."

"But I want to touch you."

"Not yet." Her words are deep and rumbling with promise.

Once more, she positions herself in front of me and un-does the button on my pants, the zipper, and pushes them down to my ankles. My boxers, unfortunately, are still on.

"Step through."

I do. And from the sounds and pressure of her hands on my legs, she's kneeling directly in front of me.

My hands don't move, but my body reaches for her nonetheless, especially when her breath warms my front—

"Lift your leg," she says softly. "I'm going to dress you."

Ah, shit. "You sure you wouldn't rather have me naked?"

"I do want you naked. Very naked." She grips an ankle and guides it into what I assume is a pair of pants. "But later. Work first, fun after."

With cool efficiency, she tugs a pair of pants over my hips, slips a shirt onto my arms and over my shoulders, tucks and buttons it all up. Something stiff and heavy goes over my shoulders. Her hands caress my arms, my legs, tugging, smoothing, aligning each piece to her satisfaction, every brush sending a jolt of yearning through me.

Until her hands fall away, all goes silent, and suddenly, I'm dressed, completely dressed.

In clothes. *Her* clothes.

My smile vanishes.

She's going to show me the look, a look that she's been working on for days on end.

And I'm probably going to hate it.

"I'm going to take off the blindfold, but don't look at yourself, okay? Just look at me."

I take a deep breath. *Don't hate it.* "Sure."

She removes the blindfold and studies me from head to toe, every frown and careful squint setting off new waves of panic. Against every instinct, I keep my head up and try on a smile.

"How do I look?"

It takes her several pounding heartbeats to respond. "Is it okay if I mess with your hair and put a bit of makeup on you?"

Shit. "Do you think it's necessary?"

"Yes."

"Then, okay. Sure."

"Okay, then sit down and don't peek at yourself. Don't look."

I sit and close my eyes, happy to delay for as long as she wants. "I won't."

After a moment of loud rummaging, her fingers sweep some citrus-scented product through my hair, then a comb, then a hot curling iron?

"Are you curling my hair?"

"A bit. I'm mostly adding volume."

The number of cracks in my composure doubles, but holds as she swipes something across my eyelids and under my eyes. Something else on my lips. I open and close my eyes as she asks, but I can't make out what colors or how glittery the products are. But I already know—I'm going to look like a clown, a panda, a vampire doll. A stupid fucking joke.

I reach for recent memories of when I was pleased. *When my agent called me about landing the lead in Icarus. The last time my mom made pan-fried chive cakes for me on Lunar New Year. The time I won a People's Choice award.*

Yes, that! I think about that, and only that, filling myself with stale joy until she stops touching me and stares down into my face, lightly tilting my chin to study each angle.

It's her eyes, deeply focused and softly tender, that pull me furthest out of my pit. They're the look of a professional, a competent artist who's proud of what she sees. It's the look directors give you when they know they've got a blockbuster on their hands.

"You ready?"

"I'm ready."

"Close your eyes."

I do. She helps me stand and walks me forward a few steps, my heartbeats paving the silence.

"Okay. Open."

I stare at myself in the mirror. I'm neither an animal nor a flamboyant prince of darkness. The hair reminds me of a classic 1950s textured side part, soft waves swept back and to the side with some strands wandering flirtatiously towards the front. The eyes are penetrating, darker, but shadowy, not solid; dramatic, but not emo. The lips are barely tinted, the briefest kiss of a popsicle. Yet these few subtle changes scream sensuality, a shocking complement to the rest of me.

Because *the clothing*. The fabric is black, thick, heavy, impenetrable, yet comfortable. I'm wearing a knee-length jacket with a high, unbuttoned mandarin collar and stiff, structured shoulders that make me look massive and imposing. The shirt underneath leaves my neck and the top of my collarbone bare, but a half-exposed belt cinches the jacket to accentuate the shape of my chest, my narrow hips. A few cleverly placed slits reveal a forested, silken lining down my sides whenever I move. My tall boots shine like oil, large and heavy, as if every step is a declaration. There's black and silver trim on the sleeves, fine needlework connecting the buttons of the shirt, silver chains and detailing on the pants that hug my hips yet give me total freedom of movement. Long, swirling lines of subtle black and gold embroidery, like serpents weaving through clouds.

But what I love most about what I see is how I look next to Di. Standing beside me, her eyes flit everywhere around the mirror except to my own. But dressed as she is in her usual black and gray, tendrils of hair framing her beautiful face, I see an obvious match. Two people whose stories are intertwined.

I can't stop staring.

"The jewelry pieces haven't arrived yet, but they should be here tomorrow or the next day. But so far, without them...what do you think?"

Finally, she meets my gaze in the mirror, waiting for my response, a web of concern etched across her features.

"Di." I turn to grip her shoulders. She made this herself, with her own two hands. "I love it."

The clouds on her face evaporate in an instant. "Really?"

"Yes! The sketch was cool, but this...this is incredible."

She smooths a hand down my chest, brushing away invisible lint. "I made some changes since the sketch. I hope you don't mind."

"No, I don't mind." I look at myself from the side, from behind. A large hood of softer material drapes down the back like a small cape. "I'll need to find more excuses to wear this."

Her eyes light up. "So you like it? You'll wear it?"

"Of course I'll wear it." And I've never been happier to tell her the truth, because her teary-eyed smile is the sweetest thing I've seen all week.

I step into her space and lift her chin until our noses are hairbreadths apart. "Thank you."

"You're welcome."

My lips sink onto hers, and her hands come up to my shoulders, massaging the nape of my neck. I clamp her waist, my thumbs teasing the lower edges of her breasts, desperate to touch her everywhere and make her mine...

But after so many days of holding back, of her shrinking away, I need a definite go-ahead.

"So are you taking this off of me or am I?"

She takes a step back, a rueful smile on her face. "We're not done working yet. I need to check for adjustments, then I'll show you how to properly pack and handle it."

After noting some minor alterations that need to be made, piece by piece, she unbuckles, unbuttons, removes, folds, and places each garment and accessory into a tissue-lined box, talking me through each part until I'm back in my boxers.

As she replaces the lid on the box, I come from behind and wrap myself around her, loving the way she spills over my arms and fits against my chest. "Hi."

"Hey there."

I kiss the side of her head. "You're wonderfully talented."

She melts into me and whispers a trembling, "Thank you," towards the wall.

The rest of her is trembling, too.

"Are you okay?" I turn her around. Plump tears roll down her cheeks. I wipe them away. "What's wrong?"

"Nothing. I'm just exhausted. I've been working on this, my line, everything non-stop trying to hit this deadline..."

"You made it, okay? It's done."

"Almost. Just a few alterations left, and the website, too. But I'm so tired." She buries her face in my bare chest. "And I was worried about what you would say. That you wouldn't like it. I don't think I could've handled it if...if—"

"Shhh, hey, I love it, okay? You did a great job. And anyway, what happened to the woman who doesn't give a fuck about what people think?"

"Of course I care what people think. You can't have a career unless you have customers. And I've been rejected so many times. So many people have told me that I'm good, but not good enough. I was scared that you would feel the same way."

I'd been afraid of that, too. I'd been prepared to lie to her about the look, because I know all too well the sting of criticism, especially from the ones you...well, respect.

My arms band around her tighter. "You did an amazing job, and everyone else is going to love it, too."

"How do you deal with it?" she mumbles into my chest. "All the scrutiny and people saying mean things?"

"Poorly," I say, chuckling. "Why do you think I was hiding next door to you that first time we met?"

She pulls back to look up at me. "You were hiding?"

"Yeah. The reviews for *Icarus* were awful. And in general, I hate reading reviews of my movies."

"But you do it anyway."

"I can't help it. I want to know what other people are saying about me, the good and the bad."

"But then...before you got big, before you knew that things would work out...how did you take it and keep going?"

"I focused on why I was doing what I was doing. And I sought out the people who understood, my superfans, and kept their comments at heart."

She sniffs. "Yeah, well I don't have many superfans yet."

"Are you kidding me? Have you seen your social media posts? You have hundreds of people commenting about how they can't wait for your new line."

She rolls her eyes. "Yeah, but there are also comments from people saying that my designs are basic or derivative."

"There will always be haters. The best way to get back at them is to keep going and to get better."

She nods, unconvinced. "I know. But there are so many designers out there, so many clothes already. And on the rare days when I'm excited and confident, it feels so tenuous, like I'm not really sure I can handle another big failure. Not after everything I've already experienced. Like how many times do you need people to say no before you get the hint, you know?"

"No matter how successful you get, you never lose those doubts. Your sense of scale shifts, that's all. Successful people are the ones who just continue to work through it. They squeeze as much as they can out of those moments of wild, stupid optimism."

She scoffs. "I don't get those."

"Really? You aren't even a little bit hopeful about the Met?"

"I mean, a little. But I can't help thinking that I should just give up and go home already. Get my old job back. Because staying here for much longer isn't going to change anything. The only reason why I'm still able to stay is *you*. If I hadn't met you, I'd have nothing. This is hopeless."

"What are you talking about? Every success you've had is because you fought for it. I know I gave you crap for taking money from Tam, but you're right—she came to you, the situation called for it, and you did what you thought was best. And anyway, no one succeeds in a vacuum. Everyone needs help sometimes." Gripping her hands, I take a deep breath and look her straight in the eyes. "Honestly? I was skeptical about the look. Two minutes ago, I was psyching myself out because I was worried about what I would say, about hurting your feelings. But you did a fucking incredible job, and you did it in just a few weeks, on top of everything else you've been working on for your launch. You are one of the most talented and hardest working people I've ever met, so if anyone can make this work, you can. And you have my support every step of the way."

Somewhere during the course of my words, the current of tears slowed to a stop. She presses a kiss to my chest, her face open and soft like a new blooming flower.

"Thank you, Darien. Thank you for everything. It means a lot."

I search for the words to thank her, too.

For defibrillating me these past few weeks and making me feel alive again.

For putting up with my bullshit lifestyle.

For everything.

But I don't have the words. I'm an actor, not a poet. I take action.

I lower my mouth and kiss her with aching slowness, and she melts into me, her lips sweet and desperate, her hands gently squeezing my muscles, making biscuits like a cat. I laugh and press her into the wall, and our bodies mold and move in the kind of heady dance that leaves you lost and swaying for hours after.

But when our eyes open, I'm confronted with red rims and dark circles. They're curved with happiness, but they're there nonetheless.

"Should we go to sleep?"

She blinks up at me, lips parted. "You mean you'll stay?"

"If you'll have me. I should head back early, though."

"Oh. But then, shouldn't we use our time more...productively?"

She turns to look at the mirror, the blindfold draped over one corner. I let my gaze linger there, too, a dozen of the filthiest fantasies from the past two weeks flash-flooding through me...

But she's exhausted to the point of crying, and after two weeks of holding off, it feels like we've been building it up into something more. Something special.

Something that can wait for the right moment, which I'm beginning to suspect—and hope—will be after May 1st.

"Next time," I promise into her ear. "For now, how does snuggling in bed until you fall asleep sound?"

Her slow smile is everything. "Like heaven."

She falls asleep almost as soon as she closes her eyes, but not before pressing her lips to my neck and murmuring a few syllables that sink warmly into my skin, like a poem in a language I can't quite understand.

I sweep my lips across her hair and murmur a few syllables of my own.

Chapter 23

Di

A loud thump, and I'm 0 to 1 in an instant.

I'm tangled up in my blankets on my lumptastic futon. It's dark, but slivers of golden light line the window curtain, and though the birds aren't warming up an orchestra this morning, there are still a few unrelenting soloists.

Last night—warm, safe, lovely—drifts back to me like a lazy bumblebee, and I lift my head and turn around. Darien is gone. Only the bold, persuasive scent of him lingers on my sheets.

I press them to my face and smile. He really is a Durian: a hard shell hiding a surprising number of sweet, creamy fruits. Also, an acquired taste.

But when I sit up and glance at the door, I do a double take. His shoes are still here.

"Uh, Dari—"

"Shhh! Are you awake?" comes the quietest whisper.

"Yes?" I rub my eyes and look again, as if he's hidden in plain sight like Waldo. "Where are you?

"I'm under the futon. Can you check the window and make sure it's nothing?"

Under the futon? But I treat that space like magical storage.

"Please?"

There. Outside. A rustle. "On it."

I sit up, slip my fingers between the curtains and split them open to peek outsi—

A pair of eyes stare back at me, and I leap backward, almost rolling off the futon.

"It's her," says a muffled voice. "This is it."

Wrangling my heart back from its gallop, I leap up, throw on a robe, and pull the curtain back a baby hair, but the person on the other side holds up a camera. I drop the curtain, stumble backwards to grab my phone, and scurry to look through the peephole of the door.

Three people, standing around, all carrying cameras.

"It's them, isn't it." Even muffled, I hear his stale resignation. The voice of a man who's been called back to the front.

"Yeah. It's them."

He makes what sounds like a muffled "Fuck," and I couldn't agree more. I sink to the ground and check my phone. "Are they here for you?"

"Unclear. Apparently, you're trending."

He's right. On my phone, there's a text from Hana. I click on the article she's sent—*Who Is Di Ho and What's Her Deal?*—and am greeted with a giant up-nose shot of my face that looks like Gru from *Despicable Me*. The other photo is even better: it's me and Mischa, with her looking as hot as ever, while I've got a wild-eyed Nick Cage rictus going on. Clearly a joke photo, but the "article" treats me like I'm seriously deranged, with random information about me from the internet, more about the most disappointing lay of my life, Zip Kragus, and speculation around when Darien and I could've met. Most of it, of course, is wrong.

It'd almost be funny if it weren't so terribly malicious.

Next time, I should Peter Parker myself and sell my own photos to them. Because apparently, my photos are worth enough for three guys to spend the morning camped outside my apartment building.

"Should I go out and yell at them? Tell them to get off my lawn?"

"No." Darien's words are a mouse whisper. "Make sure every single line of sight is blocked, no matter how small."

Even as quiet as he is, there's something *abrupt* about his tone that rubs me the wrong way. But I do as he says, plugging up every hole as if we're vampires. My apartment has never felt more crypt-like.

Is this how Darien feels every minute of every day, like a trapped animal?

Is this what I have to look forward to, if we stay together?

I take a deep breath and shoo the thoughts away.

"Okay, done." I crouch down and seek his hiding spot. He's crammed against my crap and only half under the futon, an oversized sausage in a tiny bun. The blanket covers the rest of him.

"What's the plan?"

"You need to leave and draw them away. And when they've all left, text me to let me know and I'll sneak out. Okay?"

Again, he says it in a very matter-of-fact way, like I'm his assistant and not the woman he snuggled with all night.

It's fine. I feel the annoyance, I acknowledge it, and I let it go. Nothing a cup of coffee can't wash down. "How do you know they're after me? What if they know you're in here?"

"Di, can you please just go? Don't engage with them, just get them to follow you. I need to get out of here."

Nope, it's not my lack of coffee that's the problem. It's him. "You know what? No. I'm not going to leave. I'm busy, I'm behind on my work, and I don't need to go anywhere today, so solve this escape room on your own. You're welcome to stay under my futon for as long as you need."

I drop the blanket in his face.

He lets out a quiet cough, and I start to feel a twinge of guilt that he's probably breathing in months of dirt and lint because I haven't vacuumed under there in a while. But also, he's the one who chose to hide down there, so it serves him right.

"I'm sorry, Di," he says softly, "I'm just annoyed at myself. I wish I'd left earlier so that we weren't in this situation, but I didn't. So I apologize for dragging you into this, but please, help me. I know it's inconvenient for you, but the sooner you get them to go away, the sooner we can both get back to our own lives. I can't be seen with you here, not yet."

Not yet. That weak little promise, and his apology, soften my shoulders, but they don't change the fact that I'm behind on work and have zero experience with paparazzi. "There's nothing *you* can do about them?"

"No. If they're on public property, like the sidewalk, there's technically nothing we can do to make them leave."

"Okay... And you can't just stick around until they go away on their own?"

"No. They could be out there for hours, and I'll be stuck down here the entire time. And later today, I have to take Claire to an appointment."

"You can't just get someone else to take her—"

"Di, please. I know what the options are. Can you just help me deal with them?"

Okay, so not only am I now his employee, I can't even give my opinion. And to think, last night I'd half hoped to still find him here, unlike the first time.

But we're here now, and if this is what it takes to get rid of him, then... "Fine."

I put on some clothes and enough concealer and foundation so that I don't look like I just got out of the hospital, but my eyeliner goes on lopsided. Cursing quietly to myself, I wipe it off and try again, slowly this time. Like a toddler's sketch of a bird in flight, the left is still higher than the right, and I'm ready to scrub it all off and go back to bed. Why am I even doing this again? I'm on a tight schedule and I had an entire day of work planned, but now we're dropping everything in order to hide from a few dudes with cameras, all to preserve some fake story to protect *Eliza*, the cheater?

But in the mirror, my eyes catch on the remnants of the Pepto-Bismol-pink basket that Darien sent, and my internal whining quiets. If it's important to Darien, it's important to me.

I shake it off and finish putting on my makeup.

"How long do you think this'll take?"

"A few hours, maybe?"

"Seriously?" I tie my hair into a high, tight ponytail, wincing when I pull a bit too brusquely. "Is this how it's always going to be?"

"What do you mean?"

"I mean, will the public always be a third wheel in your relationships?"

He doesn't answer until I finish getting ready and sit down on the floor by his hiding place.

"Going forward, I'd want my relationships to be as private as possible. We're just being extra careful now because of the circumstances."

The circumstances. Right. Hiding that they've broken up. Hiding that she cheated on him. Hiding the fact that he's with *me* now, and literally, hiding.

"Why do you insist on protecting her so much, after what she did to you?"

"Di. Why are you still here?"

If he thinks that's going to get me to move, then he is sorely mistaken.

He lets out a quiet sigh. "Eliza and I agreed on a course of action and I'm sticking to it. And no matter what she did to me, she doesn't deserve to be publicly humiliated, even if you disagree."

"Okay, fine, if you want to hide that she cheated on you, then whatever. But I don't understand why you're still hiding the fact that you've broken up. Because frankly, it's kind of worrying me."

"Why does that worry you?"

"Because you're being super shady about it? And why wouldn't I be worried when I have no proof of your breakup, only your word?"

He lifts a corner of the blanket and dares to look surprised. Which is ridiculous because he's under a futon and there are dust bunnies in his hair. "You think I would lie to you about something like that?"

He wouldn't be the first. "I think that a few weeks isn't long enough to know. Especially when, like I said, I have no proof, and I still don't understand why you're hiding it. Who cares about her premiere? Will people really boycott her movie because you guys broke up? No. And anyway, it's just a movie, and movies flop all the time. It's not the end of the world."

He turns away, dropping the blanket back into place so that I can't see him anymore. "You would think that."

"And what's that supposed to mean?"

"You don't get it. It's not just her movie. Thousands of people have worked on this film, and it's her responsibility to sell it and to make sure it's a success. They're relying on her to keep the media focused on the right news, because unfortunately, people are shallow, and they react to things in unpredictable ways." He goes even quieter. "So could you just go? Please? We can talk about this later, when we're not at risk of being caught."

I open my mouth to ask more, but honestly, what's the point? Clearly, he's the expert, and I know nothing. Clearly, *his* time and *his* privacy are more important than mine.

I get up and get ready to go waste my morning, so that his ex-girlfriend's movie premiere sucks a little bit less. Or maybe it's his girlfriend's movie premiere, because he still hasn't given me any proof that they've broken up. To the rest of the world, they're still engaged, and I'm nobody.

I feel like I'm looking at a holographic image, two men from different angles. There's the Darien I'm falling for, the one who likes video games and animal fries and who peeks at your face when he's kissing...and the one who's hiding under a futon, who's engaged to another woman, who's lied to both me and the public.

As much as I like him, I need to remember: none of this is normal. None of this is necessary.

He's one guy in a city of millions.

A loud knock jolts me out of my thoughts. When I peep through the peephole, it's a stranger with a mic and a camera. They're going active.

I pull on my shoes. "I'll keep you posted. When they're gone, take the look and leave."

He doesn't reply.

I grab a light jacket, take a deep breath, and walk out into the light.

Chapter 24

Di

As soon as I'm outside, I turn to lock the door and go, looking straight ahead, all the way to my car.

"Di, look over here! Hey, hey! Where's Darien?"

"Are your tits fake?"

"Are you and Darien involved in a sexual relationship?"

A fourth person has joined the group, and they continue trying to provoke me with their stupid questions. For answers, I've got a huge list of items that they can sit and spin on, but I ignore them and keep going, pausing only to frown at my elderly neighbor and their chihuahua, who look on like we're the Macy's Thanksgiving Day parade.

"Hey Di, how old is your sister?"

I hit a mime wall, and my fists curl into rock-crushing knots.

They really want some action this morning, don't they?

But you know what? I'm not going to give them the story that they want. I get into my car and get the hell out of there.

I'm sure the image of me hate-driving my rusty Honda Civic is going to sell like hot dogs at the ballpark. The paparazzi must think so, too, because they follow along on foot and then get into their cars and come after me, even taking photos of me at a red light. I'm so tempted to floor it and lose them on the highway, but I don't want to rile them up even more. And when I remember how my namesake died trying to evade the paparazzi, I apply light, even pressure on the gas and brake pedals instead of stomping either one.

But somewhere along the way, they must spot fresher meat, because I find myself driving down La Brea on my own.

I circle back and drive past my place again. As far as I can tell, they're gone. I pull over to text Darien to tell him he can leave, but I don't get out of the car. Nothing good can come of me seeing him right now, not after what just happened.

Instead, I drive and drive, and I don't stop the car until I'm parked on the hill in front of Mischa's house.

But when I ring the bell, she's not the one who opens the door.

"Di!" It's Ella, and if she's here, then there's a good chance that—

"Who is it?" Donny's voice echoes down the central staircase.

"It's Di," says Ella, frowning my way. "Girl, what's wrong?"

I shake my head too quickly and back away. "N-nothing. Never mind."

But she grabs my arm. "Wait. Come in. Mischa's upstairs, and we've got bagels and mimosas." She brushes her thumb along my wrist, a small, sympathetic smile on her face. "Whatever's wrong, we've got you."

A clatter of footsteps, and Mischa's down the stairs and at the door before I can break away. "Hey, I was just about to call you. We finished shooting the website photos and..." Seeing my face, she trails off. One glance is all it takes for her to put her arms around my shoulders and pull me inside. "You're coming up and telling us what's wrong."

I give her a desperate look, but my footsteps don't slow as she whisks me to the living room and deposits me on a bean bag chair, surrounded by everyone, and I do mean everyone. "Talk," she demands.

I glance at each of their faces. All of them stare at me like I'm a mangy, three-legged dog who's been caught in a trap. I wonder how messed up I must've looked to the paparazzi.

I can't bear their expressions. Instead, I look up, around, out the window and—

On the TV behind them, there's a photo that Mischa must've been showing them. It's a photo of half a dozen fierce, beautiful people, each one a unique shade, shape, and vibe. Half a dozen models with unmistakable love for one another, dressed in a variety of looks from my new line.

It's exactly what I was hoping for for my marketing campaign.

And they refused to accept a penny from me, even when I insisted that artists should be paid for their work.

Pay us when you've made it, said one of them in an email thread, and the rest had agreed with a "when, not if."

My eyes drift back down to their sympathetic smiles, their encouraging looks. When I think about it, they've been kind all along. Whenever I'm around, it's not like they exclude me. They always make a point to include me in their conversations, or ask about how my line's been coming. I'm the one who's pushed them away, too afraid to admit that my career's been a stagnant pool for mosquito larvae, unwilling to risk letting them see what a mess my life is when *their* lives seem so charmed.

But I know they're not. They all have their own trials that they're going through, and I'd know more about them if I only stuck around to ask.

If I only trusted them the way that Mischa does.

But like a flickering overhead light, it's Darien's suspicions that have me feeling anxious about them. From what I've seen, he hardly trusts anyone. To him, trust is brokered through incentives or coercion. He's forgotten how to believe that people know right from wrong, and that they could genuinely have your best interests at heart.

Staring at that photo of *my* friends in *my* clothes—at their warm, caring faces all around me—I relax into the bean bag's fuzzy girth. "I had a terrible morning."

"Like, you rolled over and read the news and remembered that the world is going to shit?"

"Or you had too much spicy soondubu last night and couldn't sleep?"

"No," I say, quietly. "Man problems."

They blink as one, like NPCs in a glitchy video game. And the way their eyes widen, I know which man they're thinking of.

"Do you need us to go fuck him up?" says Alan, cracking his knuckles.

"Or do you need some tea, or coffee?" adds Opal. "Bagels?"

"Coffee, yes. And a bagel. And maybe...some advice...?"

Their ears perk up like someone said the word *treat*.

"Go on," says Donny. "We're listening."

And they are, all of them, watching as still as trees.

I make eye contact with every one of them, pausing at each person like we're playing a mental game of Russian Roulette. I end on Mischa, and she nods reassuringly.

"Does each of you swear on all that you hold dear that you won't tell a single soul what I'm about to say? Because if word gets out, then I'm dead, and I *will* come back to haunt you."

"Same," adds Mischa, crossing her arms. "You breathe a word of this and you are out of the bunker."

The bunker? What bunker? But they must understand what she means, because there's a collective intake of breath.

"We swear," say a few of them in unison.

"—on my Louboutins—"

"—my grandma's grave—"

"—my Frenchies, Cory and Topanga—"

"—cross my heart and hope to fucking die," finishes the last.

Mischa closes her laptop. "Go on, Di. Give us the details."

As soon as I begin to talk, it comes tumbling out, loosening the thick band of tension I've had around my gut all morning. I tell them about "this guy" and his constant need for discretion, and how that affects me. The doubts, the anxiety, the questions about what's real or not. They ask me if they think he's worth it, and at the end of the day, I don't know. If this is going somewhere, then...maybe? But not if he's lying. Not if I'm going to end up like a piece of litter tossed out onto the fast lane.

"In my experience," says Mischa, "discount sushi is never worth it."

"Um, what?" asks Ella. My question, too.

"Like, if it seems too good to be true, it probably is. Plus, he's got such a weirdly convoluted explanation for why he needs to keep things secret. You have no proof that Eliza cheated on him or that they're really broken up."

"And he's an actor," says Donny, no longer trying to tip-toe around "this guy's" identity. "I know it's a stereotype, but a lot of them do have issues. Fame messes with you."

"Please," says Carina. "Lots of people have issues, not just actors."

Opal frowns. "But the way you describe it, it sounds like he's being pretty transparent. He's just trying to make the best of a tough situation."

"I agree," says Alan. "I think the best you can do is decide what you need from him and to spell it out. Because if you're important to him, then so are your needs, and he'll have to decide how he's going to compromise for *you*."

Nods all around: the Glamor Council has spoken. And they're right. It can't just be me catering to his needs and accepting what he tells me. I need to take a stand and see how he reacts, even if he reacts badly. Because at least then, I'll know where I stand.

Hearing their advice, it feels like something I'd already known, but their confirmation makes it easier to bear. And the sudden lightness in my chest is a huge surprise.

"Thanks, everyone, for the advice, and for the photos. Could I see them?"

Their warm enthusiasm is a much better balm than Mischa's instant coffee, which Opal didn't add enough water to and so it tastes like wet sand. And the photos are everything I could've wanted for my website, a diverse array of real, powerful people wearing my looks, shot by my oldest friend.

When we group-hug goodbye at the end, I feel like a piece of pull-apart monkey bread, still warm and sticky-sweet.

I get back to my apartment in the early afternoon. The paparazzi are still gone, but I slip in and close the door like there's a demon chasing me—

"Di."

I whip around. "Darien? What are you still doing here?"

He comes to me, lifting his hands but not quite touching me. "I didn't want to leave things between us like they were."

Oh. I have the urge to launch myself and boa-constrict him, but I don't. "Why didn't you call and tell me?"

"I don't know. I kept thinking you'd come back when you were ready. I didn't want you to feel like I was taking up your entire day with my problems."

His words leave me both hot and cold. Right on the money. "What happened to the appointment with Claire?"

He stares down at the carpet, toes curling and flexing. "I asked Ethan to take care of it."

He'd asked his brother—*that* brother—for a favor so that he could stick around and talk to me? What must that have cost him?

I approach, and so does he. Our hands move in an awkward shall-we-shan't-we dance before we sit down on the futon together.

"I'm sorry about this morning," he says in a rush. "I'm sorry for being curt, and for bringing you into this mess."

"Same," I say, and mean it. "I was probably pretty annoying this morning. But I was stressed about losing my most productive hours when there's still so much to do...and to be honest, I really can't afford for this to happen again."

"It won't," he says softly. "I'll make sure of it." He pulls out his phone, unlocks it, and hands it to me. "If you want to check my messages with Eliza and Ethan, you'll see. We're really broken up, and it was their fault."

The phone in his hand is open, unlocked, as easily read as his eyes. I should've known from the very beginning; he's a terrible liar, and it's not an act. If only I'd believed what I'd seen instead of hunting for similarities between him and the men who've lied to me before. He's nothing like them.

I bridge the distance and pull him into a crushing hug, sagging with relief when his arms band around me, too.

"I don't need to look. I'm sorry for doubting you. I was just feeling vulnerable this morning. And confused."

His hands smooth down my back. "Do you want to talk about it?"

I let my arms fall, but leave my head in the crook of his neck. "Like I said, I don't really get why you feel the need to protect someone who's hurt you so badly. All I know is that she cheated on you with your brother, and you being who you are, it feels like she's taking advantage of you. But it's your choice, and obviously I'm going to respect that. It's just...I'm not interested in letting her take advantage of me, too. I don't want to have to lie or perform for the public."

His hand finds my head, and his fingers stroke through my hair, calming, comforting. "I get it. And like I said, I'm sorry for putting you in this situation. I'll do my best to shield you from this in the future." His hands fall still. "Now that they've started coming here, though, I might have to stay away for a while."

I'd known, but to hear him say it... I pull away. "Yeah. Makes sense."

He takes my hands and waits until I meet his gaze again. His eyes are wide, his pupils dilated, as if he's trying to let me see the contents of his brain. "We'll get through this period, and then things will be better after, I promise."

I squeeze his hands, so big and warm, and I try to beam my feelings back at him. "Thank you."

This next part feels like acknowledging the moldy leftovers at the back of the fridge. Pulling it out, dealing with it before it poisons everything else. "I also want you to know that I worry about what it will be like once the public knows about us. Like, if they end up hating me or our relationship, whether or not that'll mess things up between us."

"I get it. But right now, let's focus on us. We'll worry about the public when we get there." He gives me a smile, but it's lukewarm and quickly dims and fades out of existence. He pulls his hands away to run them through his hair. "Anyway, it was stupid of me to spend the night."

I wrap my arms around myself. No more nights snuggled up against him, for now. "But it was nice to have you here."

"It was nice to be here. But once we're in the clear, I'm buying you a new bed. One that I can actually hide under."

He says it in a joke-y manner, but I don't feel any urge to laugh. "I thought you said we won't have to hide anymore."

"I'm kidding, but you never know. Could be good to have, just in case."

Despite his teasing tone, his words aren't very reassuring.

Chapter 25

Darien

Like rain on cold mud, it takes a while for the headline to sink in.

"OVER FOR MONTHS": DARIEN AND ELIZA HAVE CALLED IT QUITS

...source familiar with the situation...

...French cafe outing was staged...

...recently linked to designer Di Ho, 32, fueling rumors of infidelity...

Already, there's a wave of vitriol directed her way, everyone piling on to give both me and her their opinion about what kind of people we are. I ignore the things they say about me. Their words are no worse than what I'd told myself these past few months. But the things they say about Di, when she's completely innocent? They're what make the news finally dig in, like the cold, bloody spikes of an Iron Maiden.

Karen texts me multiple times with a warning not to talk to anyone, as well as a video conference link. There's nothing to do besides get dressed, wash my face, and join. Tam, Eliza, and Karen are already on the call.

"Thanks for joining, Darien," says Karen. Her messy hair and lack of makeup say she's been up early in the war room, strategizing. "There are three things we need to discuss. One, where the leak came from; two, what it means; and three, what to do about it."

Eliza is quiet, her face shadowed and dimly lit. From the bookshelf behind her, I can tell she's in her office downstairs.

"It's likely going to take a while to pinpoint the source, so please don't say *anything* to *anyone* for the time being, unless I've cleared it first. We need to figure out where the leak came from, or whether or not someone's been hacked, and right now, no one is safe. But first thing's first. Now that it's out there, we'll have to move the timeline up on the announcement. We need to respond simply and swiftly. We're going with, yes, you two've split, but only recently, and no, there's been no infidelity. Can we agree?"

Nobody moves.

"Eliza, are you with me?"

She looks up at the camera, doll-like, her eyes glassy and dull. "Yes."

"Do you agree? Split, but no infidelity?"

"Sure."

"And what about your relationship with Ethan?"

Like a flower that's been dripped on, she gently shakes her head.

"Darien?"

I scroll through the comments on Di's photos. She hasn't responded to any of them, nor has she messaged me. I envision her anxious, annoyed, trapped in her apartment with a dozen paps outside, because of me.

Hopefully, I'm wrong. Hopefully, she's asleep and oblivious.

But no. My phone buzzes. She's calling me, but I don't dare pick up while on the video call with Karen and Tam.

They'd see the call as an immediate liability and possibly take action against her even sooner.

"How will Di be affected?"

"It depends," says Karen. "If the leak came from her, then there are legal consequences. But as for how she'll be treated by the media, if we deny that there was any infidelity, then she'll likely be out of the tabloid cycle soon." She clicks her teeth together in a half-grimace. "Unless you want to announce that you two are romantically involved? If so, the tabloids may continue to speculate that you were unfaithful despite the joint statement, and she'll likely be hounded further."

I doubt that Di was the leaker—not deliberately, at least—but the rest of what Karen said makes sense. If we continue seeing each other, our romantic relationship *will* come out eventually, which will only stoke suspicions about the timing. We'll try to keep things private, but how much harassment will she face? Will her business suffer because of me? Will she have to move or change her lifestyle?

Alone, Di and I are great together, but we're not an island. I imagine us out on a date, and how she'd react to fans coming up to our table, asking for autographs, trying to talk to me. I imagine how she'd handle the paparazzi getting into her face, yelling things to get her to look their way, intruding on her everyday life. The way she'd feel among my colleagues at red carpet events, or if she'd even want to go to them with me.

In every one of those situations, she's not happy. She doesn't fit.

"Looks like she's already posted about it on social media." Karen opens a link and shares it in the video call.

Minutes ago, Di posted a screenshot of the article with the caption, "Um, hello? I only date murderers. Please get your facts straight. #murderbae."

I can't help it. I laugh, but it's just me.

"This is good," says Karen. "She's making light of the situation and insinuating that you're not together. This will strengthen our statement, especially if we move right away."

"Can I talk to her before we decide anything? Or can we bring her into this meeting?"

"No," says Tam. "I know you think she's not the one who leaked it, but you don't know for sure."

"And even if it wasn't her," adds Karen, "it could be someone within her circle of friends. Stories like this could easily go for two to three hundred K."

I squash it immediately, but the thought does cross my mind: would Di or one of her model friends sell me out for that much?

"We need to decide now," says Karen. "Do you want to deny that anything is happening with Ms. Ho or not? She's already laid the foundation for what I would consider our best response."

She has. She's already gone ahead and made a statement, jokingly denying the fact that we're together. And if we deny it now, that doesn't prevent us from changing our minds later. We'll keep our relationship secret until things calm down, until we're ready to come clean on our own terms.

Slowly, I nod. "Go ahead. We're split, there's been no cheating, and Di and I are just friends."

Tam and Karen visibly release their breaths. "We'll draft that up and send it out as soon as possible. And like I said, close off communications with everyone. Our assistants will reach out to our contacts, comb through the tabloids, messages, and information that we have to see if they can figure out where the leak came from. In the meantime, please don't make our lives harder."

My phone quakes with messages.

Di: i didn't do it, i don't know how this happened

Di: i'm so sorry (not an admission of guilt, just sad for u)

Di: if there's anything i can do to help, pls lmk

Di: the paps are outside, so don't come

Di didn't do it, I know. But from the way Tam looks right now, she's sure of the opposite.

"I need to go," says Eliza suddenly, eyes shining in the darkness.

"But we're not finished—"

"Just do whatever Darien says," she says, and leaves the call. From downstairs, I hear her slippers slapping onto the marble.

"I also need to go, so just do as we discussed," I say, and leave the call. "Eliza!"

I rush down the stairs after her, struggling to compose the right thing to say, but all that comes to mind, body, and spirit is a single feeling: pure relief, that our months-long race is almost at an end. The finish line is in sight, and as tired as I am, it's time to end this thing with my head held high.

I hurry down the hall to the door of her suite and knock twice.

"Hey," comes her watery voice.

"Eliza? Can we talk?"

Her response comes two seconds late. "That's not why I'm calling."

A sigh, a bit rough in sound, and a familiar voice. "I have three minutes until my next class."

I turn my foot, ready to head off, but close my eyes and press my ear to the door.

"It's over. We're announcing the split."

A pause. "And?"

"And it's going to be okay. We're not mentioning the cheating. Maybe in a month or two, we can—"

"No. It's not right."

Her voice grows desperate. "I'll find a way to make it up to him, I promise. I know he has no reason to forgive us yet, but we'll find a way."

"It's not right—"

"No one will understand," she says, voice cracking. "No one cares if you cheat because you loved the wrong brother. No one cares about love when it's not clean and neat. They don't like to remember that sometimes being with someone means clawing your way through mud and rocks to reach the right time and place. They'll hate me, they'll hate you, and I can't...I don't want them to hate you. They won't under-stand."

He doesn't respond, and it takes me as long as it takes her to realize that he's not going to.

"I know you're there," she says, her voice louder, pointed in my direction. "Talk to him, please. Or else none of us gets anything out of this."

As if anyone should. "Can I come in?"

Her voice is barely a whisper. "Not right now, please. I need some time alone."

I drop my hand from the doorknob. "Alright."

I step away and return to my own room, where I pace around for a few minutes before finally calling Di.

"Help," she whispers in greeting. "The paparazzi are swarming. Also, I'm dangerously—"

"We need to talk."

"—low on toilet paper—" She stops. "I didn't leak anything."

"I know. But we need to talk about what this means."

"Okay. What is it?"

Her voice, that low buzz of a smooth zipper. It loosens my throat. "I'm just calling to let you know that we're announcing our split soon, me and Eliza. But we won't mention anything about you or Ethan. So for now, we're going to continue pretending that you and I aren't together. Can you do that?"

The barest pause. "Sure, of course."

"And you haven't told anyone right, not any of your friends?"

She's silent, and the longer her silence goes, the tighter my stomach clenches. "Di?"

"So...Mischa knows."

The news doesn't surprise me, but my neck prickles, like the feeling of being watched too closely by a stranger. "You told her?"

"She already knew. She owns the house and the rabbit and the camera, remember? How do you think I got the footage?"

How did Tam miss that? "Okay, so one of your friends knows. Is there any chance that she was the one who leaked the news—"

"No. She would never sell anyone out like that..."

Her silence feels heavy, like there's something big at the end of the line.

"But?"

She sighs, and the seconds drag me further into a deep well of wrongness. "Her friends all kind of know that we're together."

I take a deep breath and count to five. "Explain."

"I saw them yesterday and I talked to them a little bit. About us. But Darien, I trust them—"

"Why would you tell them anything? And do you mean *all* of them? All of those people—"

"Yes, okay? But they already knew something was up. The night we dressed up in matching costumes and went out alone together? They knew something was going on."

"What? No. I went there as your friend. I talked about Eliza. We weren't acting like a couple." But bits and pieces of that night return in strobes. Pressing my leg against hers. Hinting at past intimate conversations. Sharing smiles that I never show to anyone but her. Could her friends have seen past my words?

My biggest mistake? Going over there in the first place, with her, alone. I could've talked their ears off about Eliza and it wouldn't have done anything to lessen the strangeness of our situation, or the obvious chemistry I share with Di.

Di confirms my rising suspicions. "I didn't mention you by name, but they guessed. But I'm telling you, they didn't leak the news, either."

Yet from the flatness of her statement, she doesn't fully believe it.

And yesterday? After complaining about how much work she had to do, she took so long to get back home because she was out gossiping with her friends, breaking the NDA?

Tam told me this would happen. She told me not to become complacent. Di made me feel normal, when my life is anything but normal, and now I've broken my word to Eliza and jeopardized my career, and for what? Someone who'd never be able to deal with my lifestyle anyway.

"Yesterday, you told me that you don't want to deal with this kind of thing. The publicity, the lies. Do you still feel that way?"

"Yeah? Of course. Why would I have changed my mind?"

I imagine her now, standing in her tiny apartment, glaring out at the photographers as they lie in wait like wolves at the mouth of her den. She's been clear throughout: all she wants is to live her life without outside interference, and with me, that would be impossible.

And all I wanted to do was protect her, but look how that turned out.

"I'm so sorry, Darien. I shouldn't have suggested going out that night—"

"I don't think this is going to work between us."

Seconds pass by, and the possibility of taking back those words slips further away. My brain knows they're true, even if the rest of me struggles to accept that the cozy future I'd started painting for us was nothing but a lie.

"Look, Darien, I said I'm sorry—"

"I know you're sorry. But that doesn't change the fact that this *isn't going to work out.*"

"What do you mean?" The silence speaks for me, and I know she understands. "You told me the media circus is temporary."

"I did. But maybe I was being too optimistic. Because even after things settle down, if we say we're together, your life is going to change and I don't think that's what you want."

After *Pride & Parallax*, my life changed, too. I thought I wanted fame, that I was ready for it, but it was as if the public eye suddenly metastasized, and there was nothing I could do to control it or get rid of it. It was simply there, taking up too much room in my life.

"Of course it's not what I want," she says finally. "Is it what *you* want?"

"It's not about what I want. It's about what's real. Take a look outside. Think about those people and cameras, watching your every move, prying, commenting on everything. How do you feel about it? Can you handle it?"

Am I worth it to you?

"But you said that it's not what you want, either."

"It's not what I want, but it's what I've got. I can't undo being famous."

"No, I guess you can't, but…" She trails off. Falls silent for far too long.

Finally, "Are you still going to the Met with her?"

"I don't know. Maybe. Most likely, yes, to show that there are no hard feelings." It won't stop everyone from coming up with their own theories, though.

She lets out a cocoa powder laugh, dry and bitter. "Will you wear the look?"

I'd promised to. But when I think about how this has turned out—the sneaking around, the secret sharing, how reckless we've been in the face of Tam's advice or common sense—my promise feels so naive, like everything we've done. Like it was my secret existence with Di that was the lie, not the world where image *is* actually everything.

And her tear-filled eyes the night that she showed me the look? If the public rips her look apart, what then? I truly believed that wearing the look would be the best way to help her, but she doesn't know what it's like, the way the words of strangers can burrow inside of you and infect your mind, making you doubt every success and good thing you've ever done. Making you want to give up and disappear.

I can't let that happen to her.

"I'll find some other way to help you."

"Don't bother," she says quietly. "Just forget it. This was doomed from the start."

Her words slip like worms into my gut. Like I'm back in Oogie Boogie's skin, but for real this time.

"You're right. I'm sorry—"

"You know what the sad part is? For a while there, I really believed there was a future for us."

There could be, I want to say. But she's not done.

"My fault, I guess, for forgetting how fragile your ego is." She huffs as if amused. "I should've gotten the hint from day one."

Red, blistering heat rushes from my head down to my toes, but I don't let it color my thoughts. "Not everything revolves around you or me. There are other people involved in this."

"But what does that tell you about what *I* mean to you? Or your promises to me?"

"Just because I care about you, doesn't mean I get to drop my responsibilities to everyone else."

"Sure, whatever. You do what you need to do. But I'm not going to let you drag me around while you do your best to make everyone else happy. It literally feels like everyone else's opinion, even random people's opinions, matter more than mine. So if that's what it means to be with you, then no thanks, enjoy your life."

She hangs up, and suddenly the air around me is half as thin.

My fingers hover over her name for a long time, but even if she picks up, what can I say that will change our circumstances? What can I do to change who she is, or who I am, or what I have to offer?

Eventually, my fingers drift lower and tap on someone else's name.

Someone who will understand.

* * *

"Why do you think I always tried to stay away? Every time she invited me to something, I made my excuses."

We both take a drink and rest our glasses on the cool metal dining table. It's a new table, different from the dark wooden one that was here the last time I'd visited months before. It matches his modern apartment better, as well as the new 70-inch TV and powder blue mid-century modern sofa set. The room feels brighter now, less dreary, more adult. Eliza's touch has brought order from bachelor chaos. His mussed-up hair and disheveled clothing are the only things that look out of place.

"I thought you were just too busy for me."

"I'm never too busy for you or Claire," he says sighing, as if annoyed that I still haven't gotten that through my head. "I just wanted to stay away from *her*. I didn't want to disrespect you or put us in this situation. Christmas at your house, or that New Year's Eve two years ago—"

"Yeah, I remember. You didn't show up."

"Right. I was avoiding her. But for your birthday, Eliza specifically reached out to me and said that you'd mentioned how much you missed having me around. She told me that you weren't sure what you'd done to drive this wedge between us. So I came to the get-together she was hosting because I wanted to apologize to you and clear the air somehow."

"You were going to tell me how you felt about her?"

"No, I was going to...I don't know. Just tell you we should hang out one-on-one more often. I was never going to tell anyone how I felt. I was so ashamed. But when you didn't show up, Eliza was crushed. Everyone else left, but I stayed to help her clean up, and she told me about all the relationship issues you two had been having. I had no idea. I know, I should've left, but I stayed like an idiot. I tried to understand her side of things, but I also tried to defend you. Our argument got heated, one thing led to another, and then...you *did* show up."

I close my eyes, listening as if it's not our story but someone else's. Guy loves girl who's off limits, tries to stay away, but can't. They fall in love—have *been* in love all along—and their relationship makes all the sense in the world.

It makes sense, but it still sucks.

From the look on his face, Ethan feels the same. But instead of running away from me, ashamed of himself, he's been standing tall and trying to be there for me and Claire as a brother. Always trying to do the right thing, even when he's messed up.

"You don't have to break up with her, you know."

He swirls the ice in his glass. "I appreciate you saying that, but I don't think my conscience can handle it. She says she'll take the fall, but I know how much her career means to her, and I can't ask her to give it up. And anyway, we've been so happy together, while you..." He looks at me, the same way he used to look at me when asking to play ball or chess together. He respected Claire, but he preferred playing with me, and anyway, Claire used to cheat and make up rules. "I know you're sick of hearing it, but I *am* sorry."

"I know—"

We both jump out of our seats at the sudden pounding knock at the door. The plaintive voice. "Ethan? Please. Hurry, there are photographers."

He looks to me. I nod, and he quickly opens the door to let her inside. She rushes inside in a flurry of pale green fabric, and her eyes land on me and widen. "What are you doing here?"

"Same thing you are. Figuring out what to do next."

She looks between me and Ethan, mouth drifting wider with each pass. But she doesn't speak, as if worried about breaking the delicate peace between us.

"And I'm here to listen, if there's anything you need to say to me."

That cracks the ice. She stumbles out of her sandals and rushes towards me, sinking onto the chair across the table from mine. Ethan follows and takes the seat next to her. She looks to him once more, her eyes lingering on his like a warm caress, before turning back to me and splaying her hands on the table. "I'm willing to accept responsibility for what we did."

I blink, waiting for her to continue. There are too many ways to interpret that statement, too many excuses that could follow, as well.

She takes a deep breath and, holding my gaze, continues. "If the only way to fix things between you and Ethan is for us to take responsibility, then I'll take the blame. And if that means making a formal announcement about it, I'll do it."

Ethan's lips part, but he doesn't speak.

I search her face. Aside from the slight redness around her eyes, it's her industry face, the one she wears before every negotiation. The one that makes her most resemble her father, a tenacious barrister.

"Why?"

"Why what?"

"Why would you give up your career for him?" For as long as I've known her, her career has been her only priority. Everything we ever did was in service to her image, her fan base, her mark on the world. And now she's throwing it away?

"I'm not giving it up. Despite what Tam likes to think, it's not all or nothing." She turns and takes Ethan's hand, and her expression melts into something softer and more unsure. Faintly hopeful, but unmistakable. "I don't know how badly this will affect my career, but I made a mistake and I need to own it. And I'd rather spend the next decade rebuilding my brand with Ethan by my side, than alone with my guilt."

It's impossible to unsee, now that they're in front of me, together. The way his fingers tighten over hers so longingly. The way he looks at her like he can't breathe, like to look away for even one second would be too much.

It hurts to see, but not for the reasons I would've thought.

I'm not going to lie. I'd seen this look in his eyes before, a long time ago, directed at Eliza. But with how he is—intuitive, kind, *good*—I'd trusted him to make it go away, or turn it towards someone else, without my needing to confront him and make things awkward.

That was my mistake. You can't just make these types of feelings go away, even when you know it's never going to work. I know that now.

But Eliza's right. It's not all or nothing.

"Date if you want to. But you don't have to go public with the cheating. They'll eat you alive."

Her gaze swings back to mine. "I want our fans to know that I was the one who wronged you. And if you can't forgive me, then why should they?"

I raise my glass and down the rest of my Scotch. "Thank you, but you really don't have to do this—"

"I know I don't, but I will. I'm tired of hiding."

I chuckle dryly, remember just how much hiding I'd done right up until yesterday. "I'm with you."

"Then I'll tell Tam and Karen. And you'll forgive us?"

Slowly, I shake my head. "I don't think forgiveness is the kind of thing that's going to happen overnight. But I appreciate the efforts you're making, and I think we're headed in that direction."

She turns to Ethan, eyes shining, a diver on the edge of a sparkling seacliff. "Will you stay with me?"

"Yes." His smile spreads from his face to hers, and they both laugh a little, relieved and eager for their new chapter together. Warm joy and desire pulse between them, slowly drawing their faces together.

Seeing the two of them, the depth of their bond, feels like a knife in the gut. They get to have a future together. They get to *choose* each other.

I close my eyes against it, and instead I see a pair of wide, dark eyes and a naughty smile, the most perfect smile I've ever seen.

She deserves more than what I have to offer...

And she deserves to have her wishes fulfilled.

I clear my throat before they forget that I'm there. "I have another idea for how you two can make things up to me."

"Anything," they say together.

"I need your help." I pull out my phone and begin to search. "I have a promise to keep."

Chapter 26

Di

"Everything happens for a reason."

Sure, Mom, yeah. Darien and I were *destined* to meet. We were destined to fuck around and get busted so that I could answer my question about whether or not to stay here. Well, the city's been unambiguously clear: I need to go.

But my mom means everything happens for a reason for *her*.

"If you hadn't gone to Los Angeles, then I never would have met Arul."

I've just apologized to her about moving out here against her wishes, but instead of being disappointed that I wasted so much time and money, or happy that I'm moving back, she sounds like she's speaking from a different universe, one where it's just her and Arul, sitting in a tree.

"Mom, are you sure about him? How well do you really know him?"

She sucks her teeth. "I've been with bad men, I know them. Arul isn't a bad man."

For her sake, I hope so. Between the two of us, we've found enough rotten avocados to last a lifetime. And just when you think you've found a good one, it falls to the ground and rolls out of reach.

Well, I'm tired of avocados. They're nature's mayonnaise, and I fucking hate mayonnaise.

After making sure she knows what time to pick me up from the airport, I end the call with my mom, and for the fifth time that day, recount the zeroes and retrace the cursive of the written amount on the check: two-hundred thousand dollars and xx/100. Satisfied—but not satisfied at all—I drag my tongue across the envelope flap and press it closed, dropping it in my pocket to put in the outgoing mailbox later. My goodbye note to Darien.

Funny how I thought I needed him and his money. Yet my website's just about done and my line is nearly complete, and every cent of his money is accounted for, thanks to a gift from Mischa and our friends.

With or without Darien, I'm going to be okay.

But as much as I try to focus on the future, thoughts of him appear like worms after the rain. Lying across his chest and counting his smiles. The pads of his thumbs running along my jaw as he cupped my head to kiss me. The deftness of his eyebrows and all the silly faces he knew how to make. They come on like spasms, or stitches, right in the gut.

We only spent a month together, but even the shortest snippets of a song can snag on something inside you. And though I remind myself that his famous-guy problems are unique to him, the rest of him feels unique, too. Like a fabric that feels just so against my skin, the perfect weight and weave.

And yet, after their announcement, I haven't seen the paparazzi around anymore. I can say and do whatever I want, whenever I want. I have my life back.

Meanwhile, his life is splashed across every page, ready for me to read about, but I can't bring myself to see if he's enjoying his life without me, too. I block him everywhere, and I keep my eyes on the road when I drive around town.

Maybe that's why it feels like there's a hole in the back of my brain, like I'm forgetting something important every minute of every day.

But it won't help to dwell on what could've been.

Done loading my plants into her car, Mischa steps back into the apartment, bringing with her a warm rush of vanilla and sunshine. She's fostering my green babies, sewing table, and mannequin until I'm ready to send for them, or sell them. Everything else is already spoken for by an aspiring scriptwriter who's picking it all up tomorrow. May it bring them better luck than it brought the previous owner, or me.

Mischa leans against the wall in a studded black denim skirt, chunky pink designer boots, and a cream off-shoulder tee. "We're going for one last night on the town on Sunday, right?"

"Probably not. I'll still be packing."

"What? Then pack faster! Or don't leave."

I raise an eyebrow, and she gives me a cheeky grin. My flight back home is on Tuesday morning, the day after the Met Gala. Not that that's why. I just didn't want to pay for another month of rent, and it was the cheapest flight I could find on such short notice.

"You know I can't stay, and the only thing I like about this place is you."

"Um, hello? What about the rest of our friends? And are you forgetting all of the cheap, delicious tacos? Those awesome boutiques and store owners you met? Sugarfish? That Mediterranean place that we went to for your birthday—"

"You're mostly listing food."

"Yeah, well, the food in L.A. is amazing, isn't it?"

I toss a handful of old sauce packets into the trash. "I'm not a foodie like you, Misch. I only need a few good restaurants to be happy."

She takes the trash bag away from me and forces me to look up. "Fine. But Sunday night. Keep it open for me?"

"Monday night. I'll be staying with you on Monday anyway." And if we hang on Monday, then I'll have a reason to be out and about, not pointlessly wondering about the Met Gala. "Does that night work for you?"

"I think so." She clasps her hands behind her back and leans towards me. "And I think it'll work for the crew, too, if you want them to come."

Yeah. About that. After my last call with Darien, I'd crashed their cocktail hour later that day and angrily questioned them about the leak, until Alan pointed out that there were details in the article that none of us had known about, not even me. The leak hadn't come from any of us, and I owe them all an apology, and a drink. "I'd like that."

* * *

Sunday, I pack. Monday, we drink and party, and throughout the night, they're extra careful to avoid touching any of my ripped-out seams. Because we're not as young as we once were, we end the night with weed, non-dairy ice cream, and *Los Espookys* at Mischa's.

Even Attila lets me pet her without drawing blood, as if she wants to make amends before it's too late. But Attila's soft, quivery fur can't stanch the bleeding, and she soon hops off my lap to find Mischa's instead.

"Oh my god," says Alan from the couch.

"What?" asks Mischa, sitting up from the floor, Attila in hand.

Before they can answer, all of our phones buzz from our new group chat. We click on the link from Alan, each of us gasping like drowners at the headline.

ELIZA CHEATED WITH DARIEN'S BROTHER: "IT WAS ALL MY FAULT"

We frantically skim and gasp some more. Eliza went to the Met with Ethan, who, by the way, wore a plain gray suit. When the livestream hosts interrogated her about why Ethan was there instead of Darien, Eliza explained it all. Their split. Her disappointment in herself. Her apology, to both Darien and her fans. Her well wishes for Darien, and her gratitude to him for trying to protect her from public opinion. And most of all, her love for Ethan.

It's not the ideal way to start a relationship, but we're here, and we're happy, and no one can judge us for that. No one except Darien, and he's moved on. I'm truly grateful that we're still friends.

"Wow," says Mischa. "Wow. So she had it in her after all."

"When they asked her about the last-minute guest change," reads Donny. "Lana Winter responded, 'How dreadful. Both the affair and his suit. The man needs a tailor.' Damn, Lana."

"'Just yesterday, Darien was spotted shopping in D.T.L.A. with his brother,'" reads Opal. "'I'm shocked that he'd move on that quickly.'"

"Check their smiles. Do you think they're real or fake?" asks Donny. "Was it a stunt?"

There's a photo of Darien in the article, out shopping with his brother. Dressed in black.

Familiar black.

"Oh my god, he's become a total sadboi!" says Ella. "It suits him."

"Wait, Di," says Mischa, "aren't those *your* clothes? The old designs you were selling through that consignment shop?"

"Um...yup."

More gasps.

"That's so fucking cute!"

"He's *totally* into you!"

"Are you going to reach out?"

For one heart-hammering moment, I imagine the call. The apologies. Affirmations. Laughter. More.

But on the edges of that vision are all of the items I've sold, and the luggage I've packed for tomorrow. My booked flight. There are no refunds, and no turning back—

My phone buzzes again. Hana's sent me a link to an article.

Darien Lee has gone to the dark side and we are OB-SESSED

Darien Lee, 32, was spotted yesterday in Brentwood—or was it his evil doppelgänger? The Agents of Icarus *star wore a plain black tee and black tech joggers with buckles hanging from the two side pockets, paired with black and white low-top sneakers from Tom Ford. Who is this dark new Darien, and what has he done with Prince Charming?*

His transformation may be a result of his recent association with streetwear designer Di Ho. The two are rumored to be close, but no one knows how or when they first met...

It's the middle of the night where she is, but Hana keeps texting.

Hana: could you get back together already? i'd like to meet him in person

Di: we were never together!! go to bed!!!

I lock my phone and put it face down on my lap.

Two seconds later, it's back up again, and my fingers twitch open and closed, reaching out and drawing back from unblocking him, messaging him, thanking him, agreeing to meet, one last time. But as I give in and start to type out a message, an email notification pops up on my phone about baggage allowances on the flight.

I stare at that notification until it slips away.

With a gust-of-a-closing-door kind of sigh, I delete my message.

Hana sends me another post. It's a photo of Darien with celebrity chef and rapper Crypto Yoni, and they're all wearing my clothes. And Darien's hair isn't combed back in the usual way, but it's tall and messy and annoyingly cute, taunting my hands to mess it up even more.

He's not at the Met. Maybe he's around. Maybe if I send a text, he'll be here as fast as L.A. traffic will allow.

But Hana's not done.

Hana: je, you know I want you to be happy so I'm just going to say it

Hana: you always do this

Hana: you make up your mind, dig yourself into a hole, and refuse to get out until it's too late

Hana: you're like a cow who thinks it can only go up the stairs

Hana: cows actually CAN go down stairs. they just don't like doing it

Hana: i learned that in a presentation on pranks. Our principal really doesn't want any pranks from our senior class

Hana: pls don't be a cow. don't just keep going forward

Hana: you like living in LA and being near Mischa. you want to be a fashion designer

Hana: pls don't give up just bc of Darien

Di: i'm not doing anything bc of Darien. i have plenty of reasons to move back home

Di: and why would you compare me to a cow?? rude

Hana: I'm asking you NOT to be a cow!

I press the edge of my phone to my head, debating what to do.

The messages don't stop coming.

"Are you going to call him?" asks Ella. "Because if not, could I have his number, now that he's single—" Mischa lightly shoves Ella, who rolls off the couch and laughs on the floor. "I'm kidding! But seriously, you should call him."

Ella flashes me a teasing smile, her skin so flawless I honestly can't tell if she's wearing makeup or not. In her beautiful face, I see thousands of women just like her in this city, women who would be happy to do whatever it takes to date Darien, including join him in his gilded cage.

They watch as I turn off my phone and put it away. It's going to stay that way from now until tomorrow night, when I'm free, and safely on the other side.

The room settles back into quiet, and no one brings him up again.

* * *

I don't know what it is, a noise from the living room, or sleeping in a bed that's not lumpy. But I wake up in the middle of the night, and no matter how much I roll around, I can't seem to fall back asleep.

There. Another noise. A thump and a squeak.

I slip out of bed and tip toe over to the shadowy living room, where Attila sits in the dark, squatting at the edge of her pen.

"What's wrong?"

She hops and turns to face me. Stares at me, unblinking, as cute as can be with that giant bush of amber fur on her head. Her little lion's mane.

"Are you going to miss me?"

When there's no flippant reply, no hair tossing or Cocoa Puff droppings, I crouch and extend my hand. She turns her cheek into my thumb, fluttering with her breath, and my eyes begin to mist. I run the backs of my fingers along the top of her head.

"Is it okay if I pick you up?"

She wiggles her nose, but doesn't move.

Slowly, I pick her up and bring her to my face, waiting for Edward Scissorhands to emerge. But she closes her eyes and curls into a fluff ball, and suddenly I need to sit down.

I bring her to the couch and set her down on my lap like Mischa often does. "I'm sorry it took us so long to be friends," I whisper, rubbing her head from brow to back. "I promise that next time I see you, I'll—"

Freddie Kruger slashes me straight in my thigh, and she's off. The betrayal hurts more than the pain.

I lurch to standing and chase her as she hops towards the balcony door, which Mischa has left open barely a crack, probably to let out the weed smoke from earlier.

"Fuck," I hiss, scrambling to try to catch her, but she squeezes through the doors and I have no choice but to slide them open and follow.

She hops to the edge of the balcony and—

She stops.

I stop.

We stare.

The sky is beautiful, yes, midnight blue with a few twinkling stars and a waxing moon. The city shines quietly in the distance, strands of diamonds strewn across the dark plane. But it's the dozens of candles, the black rose petals, the pyramid of shrimp chips, chocolate and strawberry snacks, everything, that we stare at. The balcony next door is an explosion of candlelit black and pink.

And in the middle of it all, sprawled across a lounge chair, rests Darien in the most perfect outfit I've ever made, like a hero out of a fairy tale, but the kind that came before the brothers Grimm sanitized them for kids. His hair is a mess, like he's been running his fingers through it all night, and his jaw is tight, eyes shifting and jerking beneath his eyelids, trapped in a nightmare.

There's a prince next door, and he needs to be woken up.

"Hey."

He doesn't reply.

"Hey!"

His eyes snap open, and for a moment he looks like he realized that he forgot to cancel a free trial subscription. But when his eyes focus, his smile feels like moonbeams on dewy grass, sparkling with magic.

"Di. You came."

"I did? Was I supposed to know to come?"

He approaches, wreathed in moonlight, his eyes wide and drinking me in. I lean in to get a better look, too, starved for him. "I sent you a text. Several texts. And a letter."

"Oh. I left my apartment two days ago." *And I blocked you*, but that would be saying too much.

He grips the railing on his side like I do on mine. "Why?"

"I'm leaving L.A., for good."

His face and shoulders fall, like I've popped a small balloon inside of him. "I'm so sorry, Di. Please don't go."

"What are you sorry for?"

He runs a hand through his messy hair. Somehow, it feels right, like he should've had his hair this way all along. "For not keeping my promise to you, or standing by you. I let myself get caught up in things that don't matter, because it's what I'm used to. It's what I know. I convinced myself that you wouldn't want the kind of life I have to offer, but you were right, I don't want to live like this, either. But I'm not sure how to adjust my lifestyle so that we can both be happy, and it scares me to think that I might fall deeper in love with you, only to have you leave because of factors outside of our control." His eyes reach softly for mine. "But it didn't take me long to see the problem with my logic. I missed you too much."

Barely daring to breathe, I lean into the railing, let it dig into my side, and whisper, "I missed you, too."

He gives me another hopeful look, then takes a step back and pushes a button on what looks like a bluetooth speaker. "This song was playing most of the night. It was supposed to be playing when you came." He pushes the button again. "Oh wait, looks like the speaker's dead."

He pulls out his phone instead and plays it from there. From the first few seconds, I know it, and I have to blink away the sudden moisture. It's *Love Song* by The Cure.

"Why this song?" *How did you know?*

"I looked up goth bands and this was the only one I knew. It's a great song. And it's accurate. Whenever I'm alone with you...you make me feel everything again. You make me feel okay being me, because you're so unapologetically you."

But instead of taking it as a compliment, heat blooms from my neck to my cheeks. *Unapologetically me?* More like narrow-minded. "I'm sorry for being so stubborn."

"You have nothing to apologize for." He looks out across the distant, winking city before bringing his gaze back to mine. "During our last conversation, you said it felt like everyone else's opinion mattered more than yours. That hit me hard, because you're kind of right. Your opinion does matter to me. It's just, I've been afraid of letting other people down for so long that I lost sight of my own happiness, my own joy. But being with you, it made me selfish. Because of you, I want something for myself. There is no one who makes me feel more myself than you. And there's no one I'd rather talk to, and laugh with, and touch than you." He brings his gaze up to mine, and when he smiles, so raw and simple, it's the face of someone who's finally come home. "I love your sense of humor. I love the way your eyes curve whenever you have a dirty thought. I love your voice, your bad attitude, your gorgeous body—"

I yelp and almost lose my footing, but with a scary pivot, I grab the other banister and leap across the gap and into his arms, and then we're tumbling onto the lounge chairs. He catches me before I face-plant into the wood.

"Me, too," I pant, pinning him down and straightening to crouch over him. "I'll try harder to understand your lifestyle and to support your choices. I want to be there for you, the way you are for me." I wrap my arms around his neck, bringing my face to within inches of his own. "I love how you bring me food like some kind of bird performing courtship feeding. I love your smile, in all its forms, and I love your laughter even more. I love how fucking good you look in my clothes. Most of all, I love that you stayed out here all night instead of giving up on me and moving on."

Like I almost did, like an idiot. But I'm never giving up again.

Because his hands. *His hands.* So warm and heavy, so good at smoothing out my worry lines. I'd be fine without them, or without *him*, but why be fine when I could be won-derfully, stupidly happy, and not alone?

"I couldn't move on. The day the news broke, I was con-vinced that I did the right thing for both of us. But then I remembered that you made this incredible look for *me*. This is how you think of me. When I wear it, it makes me feel like my best self. *You* make me feel like my best self. And there's a lot of uncertainty in my life right now, but you're the one thing I'm certain about. You're the best thing that's hap-pened to me in a long time, and I'm not going to let you go. Not unless you ask me to."

The wind picks up, whipping my hair, and with the black rose petals on the ground, it feels like we're in some sort of gothic fever dream. Because he's here, beautifully dressed in clothes that I dreamed up, saying everything that's in my own heart under the light of the moon.

But the chair digs painfully into my knee, and I remem-ber the truth. "I still have to go, though."

"What do you mean?"

"Tomorrow morning, I have a flight to catch. I'm going to my sister's graduation, and I might not be back for a while. I postponed my launch because I was thinking of doing it from New York instead of L.A. I found a possible manufac-turing partner there."

"Oh. You're not quitting fashion design, or leaving be-cause of me?"

"No. That'd be ridiculous. I'm going to keep going, but at my own pace. And you're the one who reminded me that I can accept help sometimes, and it doesn't have to be all or nothing."

He laughs, and it's the sound of waves in the open sea. "Good. Then wherever you end up, we'll make it work. As long as they have good snacks there."

I lower my head to his neck and burrow in like a mole. "If not, you'll have to bring me some."

Before I can dig in too far, he turns and tips my chin up and kisses me like he's indulging in a frozen truffle pop, layer by luscious layer. "Then I'll bring myself. The ultimate snack."

I groan and pretend to pull away, though inside, I'm cackling. "Just for that, I'm leaving—"

"I'm kidding!"

"You're not."

"You're right, I'm not."

He covers my mouth with his, and we don't stop kissing and kissing until Attila digs her hedge trimmers into my feet and reminds me of her existence, and I have to bring her back inside.

Stupid, long-eared goblin rat.

I plant a kiss on her head and whisper my heart-felt thanks.

Chapter 27

Di

"I should've been living in a small town all along."

Next to me, Darien smiles and nods at a stranger whose eyes widen as we pass, but who doesn't stop on his way down the hall. It's been the usual response so far, except at Hana's graduation dinner, where Hana's friends mobbed him and asked for photos and autographs and strangely, also, career advice. When they see him, the youths get excited. Everyone else either doesn't care or doesn't know how to react, because his presence here makes as much sense as a goose in a grocery store.

I do mind it a little, but when enough is enough, he firmly but politely says no, with a smile. And when he looks up and gives me that secret special look, it doesn't bother me at all.

"In a place this small, if you lived here long enough, they'd probably get sick of you and stop bothering you." Hint hint.

"That's the dream." He swipes his key fob and ushers me into the large, bright suite of rooms he's rented for the past two weeks, his hand on my lower back, which soon disappears so that we can each unlace our shoes and kick them off. I love the softness of the deep blue carpet, if only because whenever I feel it against my toes, it means that we're finally, truly alone.

I sink down into the loveseat and smile up at Darien, immaculate in a pair of black pants and a simple gray tee. After the past month's events, he reevaluated his lifestyle and began to downsize, including canceling his sponsorships by various brands and wearing only comfortable clothes from companies known for their fair labor practices and sustainable materials.

So yeah, I'm pretty much wet whenever he's near.

He sits down next to me, his warm thigh pressing into mine, and takes my hand, returning my smile. "Why does it feel like prom night right now?"

"I wouldn't know. I didn't go to prom."

"I didn't either, except in the very first movie I did."

"*Shark Prom: Prom Bites Back*?"

He laughs. "You know about that?"

"Of course. I know about all your best movies."

He lies back against the couch and casually tosses an arm behind me. "God, that was a bad one. But at least it knew it was bad."

"Those are my favorite of your movies—the truly terrible ones." I lay back into the cradle of his arm, shifting so that my neck curves over his shoulder. "Should we watch it?"

"Is that really how you want to spend our night together?"

"What, it's only like an hour and a half, right?"

"Yeah, but...really?" He lifts his free hand and strokes my cheek with the backs of his fingers. "You'd rather watch a skinny twenty-year-old me get eaten by a CGI shark than make out?"

Ha. *Make out.* As if that's all we've ever done these past weeks, both days and nights. "Maybe, because then we could order room service. I didn't eat much at dinner."

For Hana's graduation, I'd rented out our favorite local Italian restaurant—Gimme Gimme Amore—for dinner and invited all of her friends. There was tons of food available, but I'd spent the night grilling Arul and his daughters, making sure that they passed muster, playing *FBOY Island, Family Edition*. They far surpassed my expectations, and I couldn't help but smile at my mother's girlish giggles whenever he made a joke. Glad I don't giggle like that.

Darien walks over to the phone. "What would you like?"

"Just something small. A salad, maybe. I'm not super hungry, just a bit."

He raises an eyebrow, as if he knows that I'm just trying to keep it light because after eating a huge meal is when I feel the least sexy. And then he scans the room service menu and places an order for mushroom gnocchi, a Caesar salad, and two slices of cake, one strawberry angel food cake and one Devil's food cake. "Thirty minutes."

"Perfect. Plenty of time to take a shower."

His eyebrows rise. "You sure? It might take you longer."

"I never take longer than...oh, I see."

He's stripped off his shirt. Even without all the dieting and working out, he still looks magnificent, possibly better. Less vacuum-sealed, that's for sure.

"Aren't you Mister Conserve Water?"

He unbuttons his pants. "Exactly why we should shower together."

"You know that doesn't really use less water, right?"

"Shhh. It can if we do it right. And anyway, individual consumers don't make as much of a difference as—"

"I know, I know."

We hop into the large waterfall-style shower together. He lathers my hair, I lather his, and we laugh and nudge the water temperature up and down until it's acceptable for the both of us. We clean ourselves, we scrub each other's backs, and by the end of it all, less than fifteen minutes, we smell the same.

When we're warm and dry and freshly abluted, he takes my hand and leads me to the bedroom, just in time to answer the door in a towel and make the room-service waiter's day with a smile and a huge tip. He leaves me to my meal at the dining table and leaps onto the bed, assuming a centerfold-worthy position, and when I've eaten enough, he beckons for me to join.

Rolling my eyes, I lower myself to the bed and scoot until I'm next to him, turning to soak up his fabulous jawline, his teasing eyes, that warm-white LED smile.

"I still don't understand how *this*," I gesture between the two of us, "ever happened."

He props his head up on one elbow and reaches out to trace my tattoos again. The dragon. The monkey. The snake. The rest. "The truth is, I'm a figment of your imagination. You conjured me."

"I mean, I kind of did. Remember? When I first met you, I'd just asked the Universe for a sign."

He shifts closer and rolls me onto my back, eyeing my skin like it's a menu. He inches closer, our noses practically touching, his gaze like lakeside starlight on mine. "And? Did I answer your question?" he asks softly.

"Yes. In a sense."

He waits for me to elaborate, patiently nuzzling my nose. His breath tickles my lips.

Slowly, eyes on his, I tilt my chin up until our lips connect.

He closes his eyes, accepting my answer, exploring it leisurely, teasing it apart bit by bit until both of us have forgotten the question.

It feels like the softest minor chord, sad and sweet at the same time. He plays it over and over, and I feel it, I listen, I drink him in, knowing that this is the last time for a little while.

He rolls on top of me, bracing himself with an arm. My hands rove his back while his hand finds my hip, my leg, his fingers dragging over me as if tracing my form in the darkness.

"You're right," he whispers. "I can't believe you're real, either."

"Do you need me to pinch you?"

"No." He smiles and lowers his face to my breast, taking a nipple into his mouth and rolling it with his tongue. I arch and whimper, massaging my fingers into his scalp. "I need you to lift your legs and let me fuck you."

Oh. Can do.

He lifts and spreads my legs, exposing me, his tongue darting out to wet his lips before he dives down and wets them on *me*, tasting me, each brush of his mouth and dip of his tongue sending small firecrackers up my spine. He takes his time with me, slow and pleasant as a lazy morning, not stopping until I'm gasping and writhing, dripping with need.

"Darien," I breathe. "Please."

He doesn't let up. His fingers barely touch me before I'm twitching, begging for more. "*Please.*"

With one last swipe of his tongue, he reaches over to the nightstand and rolls on a condom. "How do you want it? On your back? Standing?"

"Dealer's choice."

"On your knees, then."

I turn onto my hands and knees and wiggle my ass at him. He groans.

"Please tell me that you feel like being spanked."

"I do."

He gives me a hard slap on the ass that sends me forward with a gasp. "Good. Wider."

I spread my legs even wider, but when he pushes me forward, it's with his lips, his tongue even deeper than before. I close my eyes and moan as he presses a palm into my back, lowering my shoulders, guiding my ass against his face.

"Fuck!"

He spanks me again, and in an instant, he's inside me, filling me, pressing me forward. He waits there panting, letting me acclimate before he lines up our seams, pulls me taut, and turns me inside out.

He moves, slow at first, flowing in and out of me like the tide. I breathe and move in time with him, closing my eyes against the bedsheets and savoring every re-entry into the atmosphere, every reconnection between us.

His hands come to rest on my shoulders, the outer edges of his index fingers caressing the sides of my neck, asking.

"Do it," I whisper. "Tight. Fast."

From behind, his hands tighten around my neck. "This okay?"

"Yes."

He moves. Tight, fast, like I asked, grasping my neck just the way I like. Sweet, beautiful darkness comes, and I hold my breath and hold my hips to let him fuck me into oblivion.

Because holding my breath is holding the moment. I want to feel him, center him at the heart of me, for as long as I can.

Him. Darien.

Darien.

Darien...!

I gasp at the wash of stars, shuddering against him, the force of my spasms collapsing me into the bed. "Fuck! Let go!"

He removes his hands and helps me flip onto my back.

"I want to see you." He hovers over me, brushing my hair from my eyes. "I need to see you."

I nod, panting, working to catch my breath. But before I can, we're kissing again, kissing, and he's filling me, bending me, taking me down to new dizzying depths with his mouth, his hands, his body. He grasps my hips, hard, using me, and I'm gorged and glutted, already swirling back into another wash of white-hot pleasure. He holds me, I hold on, and when he lets go I'm right there with him, trembling against him, deliriously happy, laughing. He's laughing, too, and kissing me, and I keep my eyes closed so that he can't see the tears that've been collecting.

He kisses my cheeks, my neck, and I wrap my arms around him and pull him down, needing him against my skin. He nestles onto my breast, and I hold his head like it's the most precious thing in the whole wide world.

We calm. We breathe. And when we're quiet again, I kiss his forehead, reach to turn off the light, and hold him through one more night.

Relax, I tell myself, and loosen my choke hold on him. It's not goodbye, not really. He's just going back to help Claire, to sort out some career stuff, and to run a few errands to help me finish my launch. I'd delayed it by a few weeks, but support and demand has grown well beyond what I'd imagined, and after taking the time to give my business the attention it deserves, I'm actually, officially, ready.

With a little help from my friends, I made it happen. All I had to do was take myself seriously. Set my priorities. Go at my own pace. Be true to *me*. Because no matter what, I've got this. My hands are enough. I am enough.

Just you wait, Universe.

Epilogue

Di - One Year Later

I ring the doorbell at Mischa's house, shifting from foot to foot, desperate for relief after hours in traffic. No one answers, so I bang the doorbell with my finger eight times before yelling, "Mischa!" for good measure, even though you wouldn't be able to hear me from most parts of the house.

"Hold your damn horses," she says once the door is open, but I push past her.

"Can't. Horses are champing at the bit and about to explode."

"You mean *chomping* at the bit?"

"No, it's champing. Look it up."

She rolls her eyes. "Nerd. You remember where—"

"Of course I do." I turn to the door on the right and open it. Closet.

"It's two up, and—"

"I'm messing with you, I know where it is." I go two doors up on the left. The black porcelain throne glistens seductively.

I pull down my pants and sit on the seat, sighing as all the anguished spirits finally burst free.

Mischa's voice carries through the door. "Why are you dressed like that? Didn't we tell you to dress nicely?"

"This is nice enough for a *baby shower*. It's a cashmere blazer!"

"With your ripped jeans and boots?"

"It's nice, okay? Nice for me, anyway. And your unborn child isn't going to care how I'm dressed."

She mumbles something under her breath.

"What?"

Her footsteps disappear, and I'm left to do my business in peace. And after all I've been through recently, I deserve to kick back and take my damn time.

My first launch was kind of a disaster, but in the best possible way. The website broke from too much traffic, and I exceeded sales to the point of going over my supplier's inventory limits. But we figured it out. We asked people to wait, and they did. Especially because Tam—who found out that the leaker was one of the French cafe employees, who'd had an affair with one of Eliza's frenemies—apologized to me by putting me in touch with some major, like-minded celebrities to help promote my brand.

While customers waited for their orders, I launched a second line of clothing, this time for children. It did surprisingly well, but not as well as the adult line. Not as many goths having kids, I guess, which is understandable. Nothing's scarier than new life.

I also started selling patterns for clothes that didn't quite make it into my collection, and I started a YouTube series teaching people how to sew and mend their own clothes. Mischa pops in for some of the videos, but she's not as popular a guest star as my mom. Turns out, Mama Ho is a natural behind the camera. But when I asked her if she wanted to start her own channel, she said no. She'd rather spend her free time walking around with her boyfriend, or watching cheesy rom-coms together.

Attila is the biggest star. I make her little outfits and the internet goes wild over Attila the Goth Bunny. She still bites and scratches me every now and then, but it's probably to keep me on my toes and remind me of what I owe her.

Otherwise, that's it, and it's enough for now. The point of my kind of fashion was always to go slow, to love what you have, cherish it, keep it. That applies to more than just clothes.

When I open the door and wander out, my eyes drop to the floor, my heart leaps into my throat. There are black rose petals on the ground, starting from this very bathroom.

I follow the trail out to my favorite balcony, the one overlooking the silver and pale brown city, shimmering with noonday heat. But it's not as beautiful as the ornate black box on the table, delicately carved with swirling thorns.

I approach cautiously, my heart beating like I've had too many vodka-redbulls. I pick up the box and snap it open.

A key. A plain, silver key, with—

Everything goes black. Warm, familiar hands cover my eyes, and behind me, a warm, familiar body, with the light scent of soap.

"Guess who?" says a voice into my ear. Two little words, and already my oven starts to preheat.

"Um, Beyoncé."

"Close, but no."

"Uh huh. And how exactly do you qualify as 'close' to Beyoncé?"

"Well..." I arch my back as his hips grind against my ass, and we sway back and forth, reacquainting ourselves with one another after two weeks apart. "I met her at an event once and she was drinking the same cocktail as me. So we're *basically* the same person."

"So I've *basically* fucked Beyoncé?"

"Basically. But I'm pretty sure I'm better."

I laugh, but it's probably true, at least for me. He's been game for almost every suggestion I've had in bed, and a quick learner. The one act he's been uncomfortable with trying was pegging, but more than once, I've caught him reading about it on reddit. I think he'll come around soon.

"Right. Then who exactly are you, hmm, Mr. Better-Than-Beyoncé?"

"*I*...am the proud owner of the house next door."

We stop swaying. His hands slip down to my waist, and I turn in his arms. His gorgeous face has been seared behind my eyelids, and yet every time I look at it, I find some new detail to love, some brand new reason why it's my favorite face in all the world. "Really?"

"Yes."

"Is that what the key is for?"

"Yes."

"So now—"

"Yes. If you're cool with it, we'll have the house next door to Mischa and John."

"Oh my god!" I leap into his arms and nearly knock him over, but not quite. He knows to brace himself whenever I get excited. "Why didn't you tell me?"

"I wanted to surprise you. I mean, I knew you wanted it. You've been dropping hints every time we see them."

"But what about our Jersey house?"

"We'll let your mom and sister have it, as long as we can stay there whenever we need to."

"Oh my god, my mom will be thrilled. And we can finally fulfill our dream of connecting these two balconies!" He laughs as I kiss him, spinning, reveling in the fact that we're neighbors with my bestest friend. "By the way, what are you doing here? Aren't you supposed to be filming that weird climate horror movie?" It's a low-budget surrealist mockumentary that had Darien gushing for weeks after reading the script.

"We finished up yesterday. I flew back last night."

"No wonder Mischa was acting so weird. Did she know about this? Where is she?"

"She knew. She's probably getting ready."

"Ready for what?"

Overhead, there's whirring, and I look around for a rock to throw.

"Drones *again?* Why can't streamers monetize their lives elsewhere?"

Darien laughs. "Maybe because there's a nice view of the city from here."

"Ugh. Let's go inside." I start to push Darien into the house, but he stops me with an arm.

"You sure?" He do-si-dos me around until, frowning, I look up at the sky.

My vision blurs, but it takes only a second to see.

Up against the brilliant blue, there's a fluffy white question.

One that I knew the answer to a long time ago.

Afterword & Acknowledgments

It's been a long road with this book. I started writing this right after publishing *Take Me*, so I finished the first draft well before *Everything Everywhere All At Once* came out. It's truly the kind of movie that Darien was hoping to see more of. He would have been proud of the cast and movie, but also sad that he didn't get to play a part. But don't worry—he'll find a zany, epic, Oscar-worthy role someday.

I don't know any super famous people. I have no idea what their lives are like. But I think, "realistically," Darien and Eliza would've been busy throughout their four month moratorium with gala season. If anyone super famous reads this and wants to tell me all about their lives, I'm all ears (also, hi, thank you for reading!).

The balcony distance seemed to throw a lot of my beta-readers off. Mischa's house is loosely based on an Airbnb I stayed at in the Hollywood Hills for a friend's birthday party, a luxury villa with six bedrooms, eight baths, a pool and three decks, and an elevator, that went for almost $2,000 a night (trust me, I was just a guest). The balcony to the neighboring house was surprisingly close. Maybe not one hundred percent safe to jump to, but close enough to get my gears turning...

Many thanks to actors Jade Law and James Chen for their perspectives on acting and Asian American representation in Hollywood. All mistakes are my own. Also, thanks to Jade, Lan Nguyen, Katherine Grant[1], Fannie Watkinson,

---

1.   https://katherinegrantromance.com/

Mariana de Brito Barthelemy, and Sarah Flanagan for beta-reading this book. Those early drafts were rough!

Special thanks to Becca Mysoor, who gave me the starting idea[2]. Coming Clean isn't quite "Goth girl's garden + next door neighbor Hollywood's golden boy hiding out on a year long hiatus," but it's close! Also, Becca is a creative powerhouse and the ultimate writing cheerleader. If you need help with editing, plotting, or anything author-related, check her out[3]!

Finally, thank YOU, as always, for reading. If you liked this book, please spread the word and consider leaving a review!

---

2.   https://www.instagram.com/p/CH3ddNFgGtS/

3.   https://www.fairyplotmother.me/

XOXO,
Durian
Why is the "D" so big?
YOU KNOW WHY
Because you're a BIG DUMMY

Did you love *Coming Clean*? Then you should read *Crushing on You*[4] by Jen Trinh!

Finalist for Best First Book and Best Mid-length Contemporary Romance in the 2020 NJRW Golden Leaf Awards.

Anna Tang doesn't date Asian guys. Her own Chinese family is bad enough, and she's not looking to double the trouble. Besides, she's busy chasing her dream of becoming a music journalist, and she's going to march towards it single-mindedly—and *single*, if need be.

---

4. https://books2read.com/u/brPo97

5. https://books2read.com/u/brPo97

But when she meets a handsome stranger on a flight to a wedding, she's charmed. Intrigued. *Seduced.*

Too bad he's Asian, and not her type.

Ian Gao has a great tech job and rock-hard abs from years of climbing. His parents hope he'll settle down soon, but he's drawn to the fierce and lovely Anna, who doesn't plan on getting married. Ever.

But the more time they spend together, the more it feels like coming home. Does Ian have what it takes to make her to stay? Or are the walls around her heart too hard to climb?

Read more at https://www.jentrinhwrites.com/#comp-jac852ig.

Also by Jen Trinh

Burlfriends
Crushing on You
Falling for You
Take Me
The Burlfriends Collection

Standalone
Double Happiness
Coming Clean

Watch for more at https://www.jentrin-
hwrites.com/#comp-jac852ig.

About the Author

Jen writes funny, heartfelt, contemporary romances with diverse Asian American characters. Her debut novel, *Crushing on You*, was a finalist in two categories of the 2020 NJRW Golden Leaf contest, as well as a finalist for Best Romance in the 2023 Audie Awards.

She lives in a pile of blankets near a pretty nice Wawa, with her husband and multiple tropical plants. When she isn't writing, you can find her reading, climbing, drawing, or most likely, snacking.

Sign up for her newsletter to receive discounts, freebies, and updates!

Read more at https://www.jentrinhwrites.com/#comp-jac852ig.

www.ingramcontent.com/pod-product-compliance
Lightning Source LLC
Chambersburg PA
CBHW030756310726
48969CB00005B/1431